SUDDENLY, YOU

SUDDENLY, YOU

SHELLEY GALLOWAY

FIVE STAR

An imprint of Thomson Gale, a part of The Thomson Corporation

THOMSON

GALE

Detroit • New York • San Francisco • New Haven, Conn. • Waterville, Maine • London

THOMSON

GALE

LIBRARY OF CONGRESS CATALOGING-IN-PUBLICATION DATA

Galloway, Shelley.
    Suddenly, you / Shelley Galloway.—1st ed.
      p. cm.
    ISBN-13: 978-1-59414-571-1 (alk. paper)
    ISBN-10: 1-59414-571-7 (alk. paper)
    I. Title.
PS3607.A42S86 2007
813'.6—dc22   2006029975

First Edition. First Printing: February 2007.

Published in 2007 in conjunction with Tekno Books.

Printed in the United States of America on permanent paper
10 9 8 7 6 5 4 3 2 1

To Dad, for turning on *Gunfight at the OK Corral* all those years ago and watching it with me.
What a great night that was!

This book wouldn't be possible if my husband Tom hadn't believed in me, if my writing buddies hadn't read and edited every word, and if my agent, Mary Sue Seymour, hadn't tried so hard to sell it. Thanks.

CHAPTER 1

Cedar Springs, Colorado Territory 1872

Things were mighty quiet in Cedar Springs. Not quiet, calm-like . . . no, that would have been doable. This was a whole different kind of quiet. The kind of quiet that sets your teeth on edge when you bite into a piece of ice too fast.

Jarring and powerfully painful.

At least, that's what Jasmine Fairchild was thinking as she wandered along the dusty boardwalk. The air was thick, the wind seemed to have forgotten all about their town, and it was just about too hot to take.

It was as if the whole territory was just waiting for something to happen, for something to crank things back into motion.

To breathe some life into the wayward Colorado mining town.

"Whatcha doing, Jasmine?" George Lange called out from his position on the porch of the depot.

Jasmine glanced at her friend, one of the few good ones she had in town, before replying. "Oh, nothing, just taking a stroll, I guess. I've got a few hours before I'm due in to work."

"Things quiet over at the Dark Horse?"

"Quiet as a tomb," she replied, thinking that not even the town's most illustrious saloon was doing much business.

George spat out a fine stream of tobacco as he pondered her words. "Mercantile's slow, too." He motioned to the newfangled clock standing upright, right in front of the depot. "Good thing for us the stage is about to come in."

She followed his gaze. Yes, indeed. That clock was a thing of beauty. 'Course, it tick-tocked its way into the depths of her mind most nights, reminding her without a second glance that time was passing her by. She was approaching twenty-three and had nothing to show for it except a job and a decent place to sleep at night.

Of course, things had been worse. "Mind if I join you?"

"I'd be disappointed if you didn't."

With a laugh, Jasmine joined George on the steps of the depot, her faded calico's hem brushing against the dusty floorboards like a broom.

As she covered her knees and rocked forward, she asked, "How's Chrissy?" George had been courting Chrissy long before a clock—or the depot—had come to town.

"Fine. Working hard at the school."

"You ever going to propose?"

George stopped chewing long enough to give her a slow wink. "Now, ain't that a personal question?"

Embarrassed, she looked back down at her scuffed boots. It had been a personal question. And none of her business. "You don't have to answer."

"I'm fixin' to."

Enjoying their conversation, she prodded, "Nash Bond says you're just plumb afraid to get married. That you're all shook up about even the thought of saying 'I do.' "

A fine line of sweat appeared on his brow. "Nash needs to worry about his saloon and that wife of his."

Jasmine chuckled. She was a bar girl at the Dark Horse, and was right proud of the job. It was a giant step up for a gal who'd lived on the outskirts of town in a mining shanty, and who'd almost had to resort to a far different kind of service than just serving drinks.

Her boss, Nash Bond, thoroughly fascinated her, with his

dark good looks and his debonair ways. But it was his wife, Madeleine, who had always caught her attention. Madeleine was a true lady.

She had more elegance in her little finger than Jasmine could ever hope to have in a month of Sundays. And though she was more than a little uppity, she was real nice. Jasmine never noticed Madeleine try to avoid her or act at all haughty when she was around.

She couldn't say the same for some of the other women in town. When they walked by her, their noses turned up, as if she smelled of dirty sheets and rotten wood.

As if she smelled the way she used to, when her pa hadn't cared that she was sittin' all alone for hours at a time.

In short, those ladies couldn't look past her past.

Well, neither could she.

Oh sure, now she had a good life. She worked decent hours, few tried to paw her, and she had a nice room at Mrs. Midge's boarding house.

So why was she so restless? Inside, she felt as still and tense as the unseasonably warm air felt on her skin . . . as if she was just waiting for something, for *someone* to shake things up.

George spat another stream of tobacco, this time the orangey-brown liquid barely missing the hem of her skirt. "Yep. This place is deader than a chopped-up rattler."

Well, at least she wasn't alone in her feelings.

The clock chimed, signaling the top of the hour, jarring them both out of their lonesome reveries, and just loud enough to bring them both to their feet.

George cackled. "We're a regular greetin' party, huh?"

"I just need bells on to be all set," she quipped.

As the team of six came roaring to a stop, the driver touched his brim to them. "Ma'am. George."

George nodded in return as he called out to Butch. "What's going on?"

Butch grinned. "I've got a real live honest-to-goodness Texas Ranger in here."

George spat again, this time almost directly under the front wheel of the stage. "Yeah? What of it?"

Butch tilted back his hat. "The one in here's different. He's a captain, and on official business. Word is that he's been traveling for sometime, just to get to Cedar Springs.

Jasmine couldn't help but be surprised.

Cedar Springs had once been a fairly prosperous mining town, but now that things were drying up, on account of the railroads passing them by, it was more of a stop for folks on their way over the Rockies to California. Ranchers enjoyed coming to the place, and more than one couple liked to take a dip in the namesake's pools. But other than that, nobody much cared.

Which was why it was more than a little disconcerting to think that a real live ranger would make plans to visit.

"Woo-wee," George said.

Jasmine kept her mouth shut but eyed the door a little more closely. As it opened, five people slowly exited, each looking more put upon than the one before.

One couple eyed them both, then asked for directions for food and lodging. Another occupant was a rather worn-out-looking woman, her hair falling out of its neat knot. She stated that she was supposed to be met by one of the miners down the way.

Another woman alighted, this one, dressed to the hilt, managing to look fresh and crisp with a layer of dust. She was on her way west.

And finally, out came a real fine specimen of a man. All

muscle. At least six feet tall. His jaw was as square as an envelope's and his eyes as piercing a gray as a storm cloud. His shirt and denims were close fitted, and his holster looked well used.

So did his Colt.

Quietly, with a faint limp, he helped the other passengers gather their belongings, spoke a few words to Butch, then finally started walking their way. He seemed to be greatly favoring his right leg, but Jasmine couldn't be sure. The man didn't look as if much could get the better of him on any day.

"Lord have mercy," George breathed. "That, right there, is Quentin Smith."

"Smith?" The name sounded pretty ordinary to Jasmine.

"I doubt it's his real last name. Rumor has it he's changed it a dozen times," George whispered. "That man there is the toughest lawman this side of the Oklahoma Territory."

"What do you think he wants?"

"I aim to go find out."

And with that, George scampered right off the platform and trotted over to Quentin Smith. "Mr. Smith? Captain?"

"Yes?"

"Captain Smith, howdy. What you doin' in Cedar Springs?"

If the ranger was surprised that George knew his name, he didn't let on. "I've got some work here. Do you know Nash Bond?"

George's chest puffed up. "Know him? Why, he's my best friend. Jasmine here works for him."

For the first time, Quentin turned his gaze to Jasmine. She felt her cheeks heat as he looked his fill before turning back to George. "Could you—or the lady—take me to him?"

"Surely," George replied with an amiable smile. "Why, you are sure a sight for sore eyes. I'm telling you, this town could use some shakin' up. I'll help you with your bags and then get you on down to the Dark Horse. That's Nash's place, by the by."

"All right."

"George? George! You come here, now."

The call shot through the air like a bullet from a Winchester rifle. All the occupants of the stage house turned to the dusty road.

There stood Chrissy, her white apron smudged and an expression on her face that said George was in a heap of trouble.

George swallowed quickly. "I must have forgotten something. Jasmine, help the captain here."

And before Jasmine could say "Boy Howdy," George had scampered off to his almost-betrothed.

Now that they stood alone, Jasmine felt the other man's presence more than ever. "Um, if you'll follow me, sir, I'll take you to Mr. Bond."

He nodded. "Thank you."

Though he held a satchel in one hand, his other hand easily reached up to help her down the last two steps. The contact and the gesture took her by surprise. Had anyone ever helped her down a step before?

No. She'd remember such a thing. She was sure of it.

"It's just this way," she said, then did her best to lead him down the road, keeping to the left, where the wagon ruts weren't so deep.

Quentin said nothing, just walked slowly by her side, once again favoring his right leg. As they walked, his eyes seemed to take in every nail and board that made up the town. Every so often, he would nod to someone who'd stopped in their tracks to watch them.

A couple of men called out to him; obviously George had wasted no time in announcing who had just entered Cedar Springs.

Finally a dark-stained building came into view, its elaborate facade drawing the eye to it the way a moth found a flame. "That's the Dark Horse, sir. We're almost there."

"You work there?"

His voice had been even, not judgmental. "Yes. I'm a bar girl."

"Kind of a tough job for a little thing like you."

No one had called her "little" since she'd been too young to do much. Right about the time she'd turned fifteen, her body had decided it wanted to be a full-figured woman. "There's worse jobs, I reckon."

His footsteps slowed. He nodded. "I reckon so."

His easy acceptance made her falter and talk just a little too fast. "So . . . do you need a place to stay? Sometimes Mr. Bond rents out one of his rooms, or there's a boarding house down the way. Mrs. Midge's. It's that whitewashed one with the balcony."

He followed her gaze. "I'll keep that in mind."

Finally they were at the front steps. "I'll find Mr. Bond for you."

"Thank you . . . Miss Jasmine," he said as they entered the cool building.

"You're welcome, Mr. Smith."

A hint of a smile touched his lips. "It's been a long time since someone called me *mister*."

"I've never been called a *miss*, so I guess we're even," she said, then motioned to one of the tables near the back. "If you want to have a seat, I'll go find Mr. Bond."

And with that, she scampered up the stairwell, doing her best not to pay any attention that Quentin Smith was watching her progress.

Minutes later, Nash and the ranger were deep in conversation. Jasmine let herself out the back door and headed on outside.

A cool breeze caught her off guard as it blew her hair. "What in the world?" Slowly, she tilted her head up to the sky and smiled as another cool puff of air fanned her face.

Yes, a norther had come in, bringing the temperature down a good fifteen degrees in the last ten minutes.

Now where had that come from?

Walking down the side of the street, she actually had to hold onto the sides of her dress to keep it from belling out.

"Cool breeze blowin'," an old timer said from one of the front porches. "Winter's comin'."

Yep, something new and different had just blown into Cedar Springs. Jasmine had a feeling she was about to be looking for something to hold onto tight.

After months and months of waiting for something, for anything, to happen . . .

Change had come.

CHAPTER 2

Quentin eyed Nash Bond closely as he poured two fingers of whiskey into a couple of shot glasses. When he sat down with an air of satisfaction, Quentin couldn't help but think that the man had a way about him that seemed too good for such a godforsaken town.

His vest was brocaded. His jaw was freshly shaved. Blue eyes were as clear as the sky during a Rocky Mountain sunrise.

A contentment that couldn't be faked.

The idea was as foreign to Quentin as depending on another person.

Wordlessly, he raised his glass, nodded to the man across from him, then finally took a sip. Felt the swift burning, followed by the mellow warmth that came from good whiskey.

"Impressive," he said.

"I think so," Nash said with a satisfied gleam. "Pour you another?"

"One's enough."

"I've said that many a time myself. So, now that we've done our niceties, tell me why you're here."

Quentin couldn't help but notice that there was a calculated glint in Nash's gaze that contrasted with his easy smile. An alertness that a finely made vest and good boots couldn't hide. Didn't look as if much passed over Nash Bond. With a bit more respect, he drawled, "Not one to mince words, are you?"

"No reason to. I think we both know Quentin Smith doesn't

head into the mountains of Colorado without a good reason." Nash waited two beats. "What is it?"

There were more than a handful of men along the Rio Grande who would think twice before pressuring him about anything. Nash's pointed questions earned him Quentin's reluctant admiration.

Obviously, Nash Bond's persistence showed that he had nothing to hide and nothing to think twice about.

Quentin knew he needed an ally, and he knew that Nash's name had already been listed by more than one person as someone he could trust. "I've been hired by the Kansas Pacific," he said slowly. "A train was robbed outside of Cheyenne . . . good seven people dead. The lone witness overheard the robbers mention they were meeting up with their backer in Cedar Springs."

"A backer?" The other man looked visibly surprised. "Who would bankroll a train robbery? And, why in the world would they be meeting here?"

"Those are the things I'm hoping to find out. All I do know is that it might have something to do with the Carmichaels. One of the robbers was wheeling a pair of pearl-handled Colts. Boss Carmichael's known for those guns."

Nash nodded to a gent in the back before turning back to Quentin, his gaze penetrating. "I'm surprised they'd come here. Why wouldn't they head on up to the Indian territories?"

"They wouldn't stand a chance among the Indians, and they, the Indians, and I all know it." Quentin paused for a moment. Attempted to put into words everything he knew about the Carmichael Gang. "If it is the Carmichaels, Boss Carmichael is the leader. He's a banker's son, believe it or not. Likes to dress like a banker. Soft-spoken. Likes the women. And he's got a hankering for the good life. Cedar Springs has a reputation of being out of the way, an oasis of sorts. This witness thought they might be meeting someone respectable here. In short, someone in Cedar Springs might be interested in a whole lot more than just a visit to the hot springs."

Nash stared at him a good long minute, then went ahead and poured himself another shot. "I tell you, I hate to hear that."

"I realize that. These men are dangerous," Quentin stated, knowing that was a severe understatement. Truthfully, the men were killers and deserved far worse than a hanging from a tree limb. Nash folded his hands in front of him, his black onyx cufflinks catching the sun's light. "Why do we need to wait until they come to our town? Why can't you or another ranger just go hunt them down?"

Quentin steeled himself to tell the truth. Still, he was so used to commanding fear, it was damned hard to admit his faults. "I'm not with the rangers anymore. Retired."

Nash set his glass down.

Though Nash said nothing, Quentin felt a number of questions directed at him like bullets, each marking a place in his conscience. He was going to have to explain himself if he wanted assistance. Clearing his throat, Quentin said, "It was time. I, uh, lost my edge. Now I work for the railroad, and do things the way the folks at the Kansas Pacific want them to go."

"I must say that's surprising."

"Maybe. But this way does make more sense. Hunting for the gang in the foothills would take a lot of manpower, and yield too little to show for it. They're paying me to do things their way."

"I didn't think you were the type who cared about money."

"Even powerful reputations can't buy a ranch," he admitted. "And that's what I want. For just once, I want a job with a good amount of money at the end of it."

"You're looking to settle down?"

"I'd like to be able to go to sleep at night without worrying

I'll be home to a bullet hole by morning." Quentin swallowed hard and finally admitted what he'd been hoping not to think about again. "One day, I'd like what you have." He said no more, though his head had no problem adding more details.

He knew what he wanted. A real bed. A home. Someone to love. Maybe, one day, children.

Something flickered in Nash's eyes, whether surprise that Quentin knew so much about him or pity, he didn't know. "Settlin' down has its attributes," he agreed with a slow smile. "Guess your wife's ready for that, too."

The pain continued to be as sharp as ever. "I'm not married."

An eyebrow quirked. "I could have sworn I read otherwise."

Every instinct told Quentin to get up and leave. He had no patience—or experience—with explaining himself. But something was on the line that hadn't been before: his future.

He needed Nash Bond's trust.

"I had a wife. She's dead."

Blue eyes blinked. "I sure am sorry to hear that."

Quentin shrugged, pretended that it all didn't hurt as much as it did. Pretended that the breath-stealing pain didn't rear up every time he thought of Becky being killed because she was his wife. "That was some time ago. Five years."

Nash sipped on his whiskey, nodded to a few customers who were sitting around his bar, then turned back to Quentin. "There's not a person around here who will think you're anybody but Quentin Smith. Even dime novels make their way to Cedar Springs. Won't those robbers know you're on to them in a heartbeat?"

"I'm not trying to disguise who I am. I gave that up some time ago. But this Carmichael Gang is known to be stupid. Word's out that they think they're set. I'm going lie low. Nobody knows I'm working for the railroad right now. Plus, by all accounts, Boss thinks they're safe."

Quentin shifted positions, doing his best to stretch his right leg. The hard chair was causing his latest wound to throb. Not that he'd ever admit it. "I'm not about to advertise what I'm doing. I was hoping you could spread the word that I thought I'd rest here for a bit."

With little fanfare, he swallowed his pride a little more, unrolled his right sleeve, and showed Nash an angry gash, the skin around the three-inch cut swollen and red. "Got mixed up with a knife 'bout three days back," he said, thinking that the bar fight he'd been asked to break up had involved five men and more blades than grew in a field. "This, here, is the least of it. They got my leg good, too. It will make a good reason for a little rest and relaxation."

The man across from him was visibly paler. "I can see your need for stopping."

He'd counted on that. If the Carmichaels came in, Quentin hoped they'd hear that he was injured and weak.

It would serve his purposes just fine.

"I figure I'll listen a lot, sit tight, and find out what I need. If I can find the backer before Boss arrives, that would be good. If I have to wait until the men arrive . . . well, I'll be ready."

"What can I do?"

"Soon I'll be visiting with your sheriff. But in the meantime, I need a room, and I need you to get the word out that I'm only here for convalescence."

"Think people might believe that?"

Quentin shrugged. "At the moment, even *I* believe it. About a week before the bar fight, I got involved in a skirmish with some Indians. That left a gash about the size of Georgia in my left side. My leg hurts, my arm's screaming like a son of a gun, and I've slept on nothing but dirt and rocks for six weeks straight."

"There's some rooms upstairs. You're welcome to one. They'd be better than the boarding house, I'm thinking. More privacy, too." Nash paused. "Might be a good idea if you let word get out that you're hunting for a wife, too. People will be more apt to talk to you."

The sheriff's idea made sense. In Quentin's experience, his occupation guaranteed a lot of people would keep their distance. However, a courtin' man was always welcome. "Good enough."

"When do you expect to see these boys show up?"

Quentin almost grinned at the description. The Carmichaels were dirty, dishonest, and had the reputation of plundering anything in their path. "Any time. I reckon in about a month or so."

"Time enough to recuperate for real," Nash said with a small salute.

"Indeed."

Nash held out his hand and shook his own. "Well, I'm glad you're here."

Quentin nodded.

"I'm newly married myself. It's a crying shame to hear about your wife."

Not trusting his voice, Quentin nodded.

"Sooner or later, you'll be meeting my Madeleine. She's a sweetheart, though she's more than a little bit prissy."

Against his will, Quentin smiled. He'd always favored a woman who was completely feminine. "Those are the best kind."

Nash laughed. "Ain't that the truth? Hey, maybe you really will find yourself another wife while you're here."

"I don't think so."

He looked at Quentin hard. "Five years is a long time for a man to be alone."

Quentin nodded at that. He was lonely. But he wasn't ready

to go looking for a real wife. Becky still held a firm grip on his heart.

"Just an idea," Nash said, breaking the silence.

The conversation about females made him think of another woman, one who was as different as Nash's wife as night and day. "Gal named Jasmine walked me over."

"She works for me." Nash pulled out a cheroot and offered Quentin one as well. "Now, there's a story."

In spite of himself, Quentin found he was interested. He recalled too well the brown-haired woman with the exceptionally fine figure. "What's hers?"

"Her pa was a mean old son of a bitch. Dirt poor, always trying to find that lucky vein."

"Did he ever?"

"Hell, no. Her pa was a worthless piece of trash. The only good thing he had was Jasmine, not that he cared. He ignored her something awful." Nash puffed on his cheroot, remembering. "Anyway, the day he died, she gave his stuff away, burned what nobody wanted, and moseyed down here to ask for a job."

Quentin was surprised at both her audacity and Nash's actions. "You hired her?"

"Not readily. My wife was the one who saw through the gal's grime and backward language. Madeleine and I were just married, and I was willing to do whatever she wanted me to do if it would make her smile."

Quentin was impressed. Most wives didn't look kindly on their husbands being in the constant company of a woman who instantly brought forth feelings of lust. "Even hire a woman like Jasmine?"

"Even that," Nash said dryly. "Anyway, Madeleine helped her get a room at the boarding house, found her three new calicos, and asked a couple of women in town to give her a hand." Nash shook his head. "Turns out Jasmine's a real fine bar girl. Keeps to herself, never gets sick, isn't interested in a single cowboy, and spends her extra money on books."

Quentin couldn't help but be impressed by the fairy tale. "I've seen just about everybody, seen just about everything. I don't mind saying that her tale could have gone a whole other route."

"I'd be right there with you. Jasmine Fairchild is a mixed-up mass of contradictions."

"I'll keep that in mind."

With concise movements, Nash pulled out a timepiece from a pocket in his vest. "Let me have someone show you around. It's about time for me to head on up to supper."

"Thank you."

Standing up, Nash clasped his hand. "I'm glad you're here, Captain."

"Hope so," Quentin replied, thinking about just how bad it could all be when the Carmichaels came through.

He hoped everyone would still feel the same when he left.

CHAPTER 3

Quentin Smith was just a man.

Just a real fine, dashing, better-than-average, handsomer-than-sin man.

Nothing special.

Didn't need no special treatment.

Jasmine sighed. Oh, she hoped she'd remember that while she was at work. Last thing she needed was to make a fool of herself in front of the ranger and the whole crowd at the Dark Horse. Instinctively, she knew they'd never let her forget about it if she did. Most of the men treated her with a combination of brotherliness and flirtation.

They noticed the things she did.

Wrapping her shawl more closely around herself, she hopped over a rut in the scarred road, and just about ran into a trio of giggling girls standing right outside the schoolhouse.

Jasmine kept her head down. She knew who they were: pristine daughters who wore starched dresses to church. Clean in mind and spirit. They'd never had to work hard.

They'd never been the target of cross words or gossip.

They were as different from herself as chalk and cheese.

"Excuse me," one of them called out to her, stopping her right in her tracks.

Jasmine paused. Lifted her head and stared into the girl's clear blue eyes. Wondering what the girl could possibly have to say to her. "Yes?"

"I'm Caroline Harlow."

She knew that. Caroline was the banker's daughter. She had a dress for every day of the week, and had even been to Denver for finishing school. "Yeah?"

Caroline blushed prettily. "I heard you escorted Captain Quentin Smith to the Dark Horse."

"I did," Jasmine replied, feeling curiously disappointed. For a split second, she'd thought Caroline might have found something else for them to talk about.

Caroline leaned forward, with a secret smile to her girlfriends standing a safe three feet away. "So . . . what's he like?"

"I couldn't tell you," Jasmine said, speaking the truth. "We didn't say much."

"He's sooo handsome and debonair." Caroline glanced at her friends again and giggled. "How long is he going to be here? Did he say?"

"I don't rightly know, Miss Harlow. Like I said, I just showed him where Mr. Bond was."

"Oh!" Caroline glanced at the others. "That's what we should do. Talk to Mrs. Bond."

"That sounds like a fine idea," Jasmine said, belatedly realizing that they'd already turned away.

Unable to help herself, she watched them scamper down the road, their gingham skirts fluttering prettily in the wind, pinned curls bobbing next to their bows. She fought hard to swallow back a knot of envy.

It wasn't their fault they'd been born innocent, and had managed to stay that way for a good twenty-three years.

Stifling a whole slew of feelings that would do her no good, she walked on. Closed her eyes when yet another burst of wind came out of nowhere and tried to knock her down.

"This wind's so danged irksome, I'm thinking I'm gonna fly a kite," George called out from the mercantile. "What do you think about that, Jasmine?"

"I don't know when I last heard of a kite that wasn't in a book," she replied, thinking she was glad at least the men in the town knew her name. "What does yours look like?"

He held up a contraption that looked to be about as big as a good-sized goat. "Think the wind will keep it up?"

Jasmine tilted her head up. Felt the fierce breeze press against her cheeks. "Reckon so."

"Want to come see it?"

Yes! her heart called out. Wouldn't it be something to spend a whole afternoon doing nothing? To be able to enjoy the wind, not wish it away. Maybe even run in one of the fields surrounding Cedar Springs?

When was the last time she'd run in a field, anyway?

In the distance, the stage's newfangled clock chimed, reminding her of duty. Disappointment settled in her bones. "I . . . can't. I've got to get on to work."

George shrugged. "See you later, then."

She knew he'd be in around nine to have a drink with Mr. Bond. They always had a glass of whiskey together before Mr. Bond went up to be with his wife. "See you," she called out, then hurried down the street to the back entrance of the saloon.

She had a good fifteen minutes to put on an apron and check in with Misty, the cook. Someone had mentioned that Misty might be having some leftover fried chicken from dinner.

She'd love a piece of that.

Quickly, she smoothed her hair, slipped on her apron, and hustled to the back where, sure enough, Misty was cleaning up the last bits of the Bonds' dinner.

"Hey, Jasmine. I just was putting together a plate for you," she said in greeting. "A chicken leg and a hot piece of corn-bread."

"Thank you." She dug in quickly. It was Friday night, which

meant cowboys from the neighboring ranches would be in. More than a few miners with their week's paychecks, too. If she smiled a lot, maybe she'd bring home a good-sized tip.

"Whoa. You're going to choke, eating so fast, don't you think?"

Jasmine glanced up at the man who gave the warning and just about really did choke.

Quentin Smith was watching her stuff a piece of cornbread into her mouth quicker than a gal could say "sakes alive."

Without even being invited, he sat down next to her, shaking his head when Misty offered him another plate.

Jasmine swallowed hard. Wished she had a glass of anything to wash it down.

As if he read her mind, Quentin turned to Misty. "Got any buttermilk?"

She poured a small glass and handed it to Quentin. He, in turn, slid it to Jasmine. "Drink."

Jasmine drank. The cool, slightly sour liquid slid down her throat. "Thank you."

He nodded.

"I don't believe I recall the last time I had buttermilk," she said.

His gray eyes sparkled. "I can't say I've had it lately, either."

Misty shuffled in the background, clanging pots and pans. Jasmine looked at her plate and knew she couldn't eat another bite.

"I just wanted to say thank you for escorting me here earlier."

Escorting. There was that word again. Like she'd done something special. "You're welcome, Captain."

"Quentin."

"Quentin," she dutifully replied.

"So, you're working tonight?"

"Yes. I'm on with Constance."

"She the gal with the red hair?"

"She is."

"I'll probably be seein' you. I'm going to be rooming here for a while. Might even stay in Cedar Springs for a few weeks."

She recalled his limp. "You hoping to heal?"

"You could say that." He chuckled. The noise that surfaced sounded rusty and foreign, as if the man wasn't used to the action any more than she was used to hearing him laugh. "You could definitely say that." He cast her a sideways glance. "So. You ever been to the hot spring?"

"Once."

"Just once?"

She nodded. Once had been enough. She'd come home late after forgetting about the time and been whupped good. Hadn't really had time for such things since she started working.

"Was it worth it?"

What could she say? "I don't know."

The echo of Jeremy playing the piano filtered on through. Jeremy played whenever the customers came in, which meant that Constance was currently earning all the tips. "I've got to go," she said. "I'm going to be late." Her chair scraped the floor as she stood up abruptly.

He stood up as well. Almost too smoothly for someone who'd limped so badly when he'd arrived. "Bye, Jasmine."

She nodded, quickly gave her plate to Misty, then hightailed it into the bar. Plastered a smile to her face, and batted her lashes at a couple of fresh-faced cowboys. "Hey, y'all. What can I get you?"

"You, sugar."

She laughed, slipping into their flirtatious routine with ease. She was good at her job. She had to be. "How about a bottle instead?"

"If I can't have you, I'll take the bottle," Emmitt McKade,

one of her steady customers, called out.

"Then I'll go get it," she quipped, and almost faltered again as she noticed Quentin Smith standing in the shadows. Watching the crowd. Watching her.

Something flashed in his eyes. Anger? Disgust? Pity?

He stepped forward when another regular, Jared Bailey, squeezed her waist.

She ignored the ranger's look of distaste. Disregarded the sparks of interest she felt about him. Quentin Smith would be gone soon enough . . . and would be watching someone else, more likely than not. It was best not to forget that.

The men might be more forward with her than with a lady they'd meet in church, but they'd always been respectful. Few had ever pressured her for more than a drink.

One or two had even come to her aid when a randy stranger wandered in.

The captain just didn't understand. She was not the sweet young thing a man met at a Sunday social. Providence had made her a poor miner's daughter. She'd done all right. She was strong and she had a right fair amount of common sense. Over the years, she'd begged books and asked for help from Chrissy with the words she didn't understand. George over at the mercantile had helped her with figurin' money some time back.

Yep, she'd done just fine.

And, most importantly, she'd learned years ago that wishes weren't worth much more than the number of pennies in a wishing well.

"Get me some peanuts or something, too, sweetheart," Jared said. "I'm just about dying of hunger."

"Why, we can't have that!" she teased, knowing Jared's two-hundred-pound girth would prevent him from starving any time soon.

He patted her hand. "You're an angel."

"I'm a barmaid, honey," she replied with a saucy tilt to her head. She'd known Jared forever. His touch meant nothing. His words meant less.

But, why, all of a sudden, was she aware of it at all? Men had been touching her and flirting scandalously as long as she'd worked at the Dark Horse. A part of her had liked being around all the men. She liked their humor; she loved their stories. While she was working, she was accepted. She knew her place.

So, why, all of a sudden, did she wish she was as pure and innocent as Caroline Harlow?

Of course, she knew the answer.

And he was standing just six feet away.

Jasmine sidled up to the bar and asked Nash for two bottles and several shot glasses. He pulled out two bottles of beer for her as well.

Quickly, she delivered the libations, pocketing a couple of pennies for her troubles. Just as she was about to make another round, Quentin's gaze held her.

"Ma'am," he said, nodding.

She stepped forward. "May I get you a bottle of something, Captain?"

"Not right now."

"All right, then," she said, and went back to work. Tried not to wish he wasn't watching her. Tried to recall that he was probably just watching everyone.

Even so, she wished he'd stop. Stop or come closer.

Jasmine was still thinking about Quentin Smith when a gloved hand rapped on her boarding-house door at precisely ten the next morning.

"Yes?" she called out, putting her mending away. She'd been

31

up for only an hour and wondered who could be coming to visit.

"It's Madeleine Bond, Jasmine. May I come in?" she asked through the thin wooden door.

Jasmine straightened her skirts and said a prayer of thanksgiving that she'd made her bed earlier. "Mrs. Bond, how nice to see you."

Madeleine smiled brightly. "I could say the same for you. My, I do like that color on you."

The rose calico was old, and a former dress of George's Chrissy. But still, feminine wiles kicked in. "Thank you." Jasmine motioned to her lone chair. "Please, have a seat."

"Thank you." Madeleine seated herself, her fussy gown not showing a single smudge or wrinkle. As she perched on the edge of the chair, she said, "I've come to ask a favor of you."

Jasmine had no idea what Madeleine would want from her that she couldn't get more easily from the other thousand women in Cedar Springs. "Yes?"

"Winter's coming. Have you noticed?"

Thinking of the wind that had brought in Captain Smith, Jasmine nodded.

"The wind is something fierce. More than one person has commented that it's bringing in winter at lightning speed." Madeleine pursed her lips. "And that got me to thinking."

As the lady paused, Jasmine did her best to keep her lips relaxed and even. It wouldn't do for her employer's wife to think she was being laughed at. But, boy howdy, Mrs. Bond was known for scapegrace ideas and even more harebrained ways of expressing them.

"I decided our restless women need a project," Madeleine said. "A quilting project."

Jasmine had never heard of such a thing. "A what?"

"Have you noticed the number of poor children there are,

32

just on the outskirts of our town?"

Since Jasmine had been a poor child herself, she could only nod.

Madeleine looked pleased. "Aren't you concerned about their welfare? I know I am," she said without waiting for a reply. "These poor children are going to be cold this winter unless we women take it upon ourselves to do something."

Did Jasmine dare say that new blankets and quilts were the least of their worries?

"And all I've heard lately is how everyone has been restless," Madeleine added. "On edge. I think this wind was just what we needed. It's going to spur us into action. We're going to form a committee."

Jasmine didn't know a thing about committees, ladies' societies, or being a "restless woman." She wasn't sure she was cut out for any of that, either. Life was hard enough without worrying about fitting in with women with whom she had nothing in common.

Cutting to the chase, she said, "Mrs. Bond, what would you like me to do?" Maybe she could work on a quilt or two in the mornings before she went off to work.

"I think it would be grand if you joined our sewing circle. We meet every Tuesday."

Oh, Lord, it was worse than she'd thought. "Mrs. Bond—"

"For our charity project, we're going to meet in the saloon at nine in the morning!"

"I don't think—"

"I don't think it's going to be busy, either. I told Nash that the men in the town are just going to have to hold off a little bit on Tuesdays." She looked pleased. "Don't you agree?"

Jasmine was pretty sure she would still be sleeping at nine on Tuesdays. But how did she tell her boss's wife that?

"Actually—"

"I was thinking we could make crazy quilts out of our rag bags," Madeleine added, clapping her hands. "So bring yours, all right, dear? I'm so glad you'll be attending. Oh! I must go. Nash has a list of errands for me to run."

And off she went, without so much as a backward glance. Jasmine tried to figure out why she hadn't been allowed to get two words in edgewise.

And what in the world she was going to do, sitting in a sewing circle with a bunch of ladies? Discuss what their husbands had done at the saloon the night before?

Oh, what a pickle!

Perhaps she could ask Mr. Bond to explain to his wife that such things just weren't done? It would be a difficult conversation, but possible.

Yes. She'd go ask him to take care of that.

Or she'd tell Madeleine that she just didn't have time for such meetings, but she would make a quilt in her spare time.

Just as Jasmine was about to take her laundry to Mr. Chin, someone rapped on her door again. Hurriedly this time. Hastily.

She pulled the door open in a hurry. "Jasmine, thank goodness you answered," Mrs. Midge, her landlady, said.

"What's wrong?"

"It's Miss Madeleine. She tripped going down the front stairs. I do believe she twisted her ankle . . . or worse! She's lying prostrate on the street." Lowering her voice, Mrs. Midge said, "She's asking for you to help her."

Jasmine threw on her shawl and rushed out to see Madeleine. Sure enough, there she was lying on the ground, obviously in pain. "Mrs. Bond!"

"I'm all right, Jasmine. My pride's more hurt than anything. But I think I will need your help getting up."

"How about I send someone over for your husband?"

"Let's not bother him. If you could just help me, I'd be much obliged."

Jasmine did her best to help Madeleine up, then walked slowly with her, back to the saloon. More than a few people asked about Mrs. Bond. Jasmine didn't say a word, though. She could tell that Mrs. Bond was in terrible pain. She was clearly favoring one foot, and her right arm was curved protectively around her midsection.

As soon as they got to the saloon, they were met by none other than Quentin Smith. As soon as Jasmine told him what had happened to Madeleine, he scooped her up into his arms and carried her to her private quarters, calling for Nash as he did so.

Just as she was about to walk right back out, he called down to her. "Wait a minute, would you? Have a seat."

And Jasmine, because she was who she was, sat right down.

When he appeared again, she stood up. "How is she?"

"I'm not completely sure. Nash sent for the doctor."

Out of habit, Jasmine supplied the name. "Doc Neely." That seemed a little extreme. "Over an ankle?"

"Not just because of an ankle." He looked away. "Mrs. Bond is in a family way."

"Oh, my!" Now it made perfect sense why Madeleine had been holding her stomach. "I hope she's going to be all right."

"She seems to be. She sent a message for you."

"Yes?"

His eyes twinkled. "You're now in charge of the Ladies' Auxiliary Quilt Guild."

"Oh my goodness," Jasmine said again. But this time, it came out more like a moan.

As she double-checked Captain Smith's reaction, she could have sworn the corners of his lips twitched.

Jasmine stared at him in shock. Quentin Smith was almost

smiling, Madeleine Bond was in a family way, and she had just been asked to head up a ladies' club.

Sakes alive. Strange things were happening in Cedar Springs; and that was a fact.

CHAPTER 4

"Chrissy's not going to wait forever, George."

"I know that." George grimaced as yet another good-for-nothing, nosy customer gave him another piece of pitiful advice. "You want to pay cash for that feed or put it on your account?"

"Account, please," Mrs. Brady said. "If I were you, I'd order a ring real soon. New men come into Cedar Springs most every day. If you don't stake your claim, Chrissy will be up and gone."

George didn't care for the land-grabbing comparison. "Duly noted. I charged your account. Good afternoon, Mrs. Brady."

Mrs. Brady looked like she would love to tell him a few more unsolicited pieces of information, but George hightailed it to the front door and held it open for her. With a sniff, she sauntered out.

Leaving George to ponder why in the world it was taking him so long to do the right thing.

Was it because he was afraid Chrissy would say no?

No, far from it, George reflected as a pair of sodbusters came in, hunger and need evident in every part of their being. Their clothes were worn and shabby, their faces creased like leather from long, hard hours in the blazing sun.

"Help you?" he asked.

"In *einingen Minuten,*" one said in German, which George was learning meant "in a minute or two."

Leaning back on his heels, George watched the poor man stare at his wife and try not to care that she was fingering the new fabric as if it was her birthday.

George knew that look real well. It was exactly how he felt inside whenever he thought about being married. Wanting something so bad, but being afraid to give up enough to make her happy.

It was why he was afraid to ask Chrissy. What if she said yes . . . and the time came when he couldn't make her happy?

What happened to dreams and vows then?

Clearing his throat, George lied through his teeth. "You came in on just the right day. It just went on special. On *Verkauf!*"

"It's going on midnight, Al," Mitch Dixon growled behind his hand of cards. "Put up or shut up."

Quentin leaned back in his seat at his table near the stairs, and wondered what the banker was going to do. He'd heard the man was notoriously stingy with his bets . . . but all night Al Harlow had been playing fast and loose with his bills. More than one player had commented on it, and the banker hadn't done more than shrug.

Quentin couldn't help but wonder if Harlow was the Carmichael Gang's mysterious backer. The man had the means and the ability, but it sure would be a crying shame. From what he could tell, Al Harlow was well respected in business, if not in poker playing.

As Quentin stifled a yawn, he grimaced at his own weakness. A week of sleeping in a bed had made him plumb lazy. Every night he'd had almost seven hours of sleep—a good double what he usually got on the trail. Now, at just midnight, his head was crying for the comfort of soft sheets and a warm blanket, numbing his mind to almost everything else.

It was disturbing. Without a doubt, he needed to forget about living the easy life and concentrate on finding who the devil was working with the Carmichaels.

Angry voices pulled him out of his reverie.

"I'm out," Vince, the fourth man at the table, said.

Mitch scowled. "You're always out early."

"It's midnight," Vince whined. "Rosalie's going to have my hair if I don't go on home."

"You got no hair to speak of," Dixon said. "Shouldn't hurt too bad."

Laughter broke out among the men at the table, and more than a few of them shot off ribald comments to go along with Dixon's remark.

Quentin chuckled, as well, but was more keen on the time. Now that midnight had come and gone, Nash would be announcing last call. And with the hope that a down pillow was just around the corner, a far more burdensome bit of knowledge had come around, too.

Another day had passed and he was no closer to finding out who'd financed the robbery than he'd been the day before. He had to find out what was going on, and fast. If not, the Carmichael Gang would attack again, and more bloodshed would result. He'd be wracked by guilt, knowing he could have prevented such a thing.

He'd be fired by the Kansas Pacific. And he'd be forced to go back on the trail, the reality of owning his own piece of land a distant, unfulfilled memory.

Since it looked as if the banker was heading home, he was tired, and nothing else was about to happen at the moment, Quentin stood up.

His action didn't go unnoticed. Twenty pairs of eyes flashed in his direction. He felt their gazes pierce him as sure as he'd felt the Sioux's arrow last year.

"You in, Smith?" Dixon called out.

"Naw. I'm heading out."

Al Harlow smirked. "Why's that? You got no woman waiting for you."

No, he didn't. "Don't need a reason," he said sensibly, but with just enough resolve to make the other man think twice about questioning his actions. Then, because everyone needed to be reminded about his convalescing, he winced as he rolled up his sleeve, showing the jagged scar off like a diamond ring.

He certainly hoped Ben, his former corporal, never heard about such sissy behavior.

It seemed to work. Harlow looked away. Dixon backed down. Then, as Quentin turned the corner to take the stairs, he spied Jasmine putting on her shawl.

Though he'd never been called a gentleman, something propelled him to her, just to take another look at her face.

She paused as he approached. "Captain Smith."

"Quentin," he corrected, not able to help from teasing her.

Warmth settled in her gaze. "Quentin."

He dared to crack a smile. "When are you going to say my name without prodding?"

"I don't know."

"Why? You're not in the habit of talking to lawmen?" In all of his hours of watching her, Quentin noticed that she called most customers by their names . . . except himself and the sheriff.

She shrugged. "Maybe."

"You heading home?"

"I am. Constance is working until close tonight. I swear, I'm tired enough to sleep standing up. We had a thirsty group."

He hadn't really noticed; most of his attention had been on the banker's table. "You look worn out."

A faint band of red tinged her cheeks, as if she was embarrassed.

Now he was embarrassed, too. What had he been thinking, saying such a thing? When had he forgotten how to talk to a beautiful woman?

"Oh. Well, I'll be all right," she said, a flush of color staining her cheeks. Tightening her shawl around her, she murmured, "Well. Good night, Quentin."

He did love his name on her lips. A small wave of protectiveness filtered through him. "Anybody walking you home?"

Her chin jutted up. "No."

"How about if I do it?"

"I think it might be raining. You shouldn't risk it with your leg."

It was embarrassing to think that a woman was worrying about his body instead of her own safety. Ironically, he cursed his weakness and the way he was having to play into it. "You need an escort. It's not safe to walk the streets at night."

Her eyes widened. "Oh, my goodness! Someone should have told me that before I started working here."

She wouldn't give him a single solitary inch. It made him aggravated, irritated, and just a little bit amused. "Hold on. Let me get my jacket."

Warily Jasmine glanced across the room. Already more than one cowboy was watching their exchange with interest. She took a good step back. "Thank you, but no."

The gal could try the patience of a saint. "Jasmine—"

"My reputation is about as flimsy as a woman's can get," she whispered. "The only thing that saves me is that it's common knowledge I sleep alone at night. If you walk me out, people will think I've crossed that line. Tomorrow I'll get offers for more than just drinks."

Good Lord. Now he not only had to pretend to be injured, but also to give a damn what townspeople thought of him? He wondered how long he was going to be able to maintain that act. "Listen, honey, I just want to walk you home. I certainly don't want to bed you." His irritation caused the words to slip out louder than he'd intended. Two men in the back raised their eyebrows.

Jasmine's cheeks flushed again, this time from embarrassment or anger, he didn't know. "No, thank you. I'll be leavin' alone."

"So you're saying your reputation is worth more than your body?" he asked. He'd seen more than a handful of women after the war wearing the effects of late-night manhandling. None of it was for the fainthearted. "What if someone attacks you? There's more drunk cowboys around here than you can shake a stick at."

"No drunk accosts me because no drunk ever has. Once someone thinks I'm available, I'll have nothing but trouble."

"That makes no sense."

"That's because people fear you." She swallowed hard.

"People don't fear me. I'm barely a half step above poor miner trash. I know, because it's taken me every one of my twenty-three years to get that far. No way am I going to let you take it from me."

"I'm not trying to take a thing from you. I'm just trying to do you a favor."

"If you really are, turn away and walk upstairs right now."

Quentin didn't know if he was more annoyed with Jasmine, for refusing him, or with himself, for caring so much. "I'm not accustomed to taking orders," he warned.

Her chin lifted. "Neither am I."

Because he knew she was right, and because he had no desire to create even more of a scene, he did as she bid.

From across the room, jokes were shot out like buckshot, ribbing his efforts to get Jasmine between the sheets and her refusal.

"You tell 'em, girl," an old cowboy called from the bar. "You tell 'em you're not for sale. Not yet, anyway," he added with a wolfish grin.

Quentin dared to sneak a peek at Jasmine. Her face was pinched, and for the first time all night, she didn't even attempt to act flirty with the customers. Instead, she just pivoted and walked out the door.

Quentin shuffled up the steps, his clumsy maneuvering and hard glance effectively silencing anyone who thought to give him grief. Just the way he'd intended.

Still, he couldn't help but think that Jasmine was completely right. The men weren't concerned about her having loose morals. No. In their minds, if she worked at the Dark Horse, she already did. It was only a matter of time before she became a scarlet lady.

Men didn't expect her to do a thing without getting paid for it. The thought made him both disgusted with the men and with himself. He was three times a fool. What had he been thinking, attempting to walk her out the door?

With a touch of humor, Quentin realized his nether regions knew exactly what he'd been thinking. She had the kind of aura of innocence and sin that kept a man up at night. The lush figure, the hint of creamy pale breasts when she'd leaned forward, the throaty way she'd giggled.

He wanted her, plain and simple.

Oh, he wouldn't act on it. He was too much of a gentleman to do that. He knew that no matter how much he wanted a woman, she was off limits. He was on a job. The last thing he needed to be thinking about was her pretty smile.

The way her presence calmed him.

The way she walked through the saloon, her hips gently swaying, stirred his body and pulled his mind to imagining her, bare, beneath him.

He limped down the hall, his sore leg truly throbbing with the effort. Just as he was about to curse his weakness again, Mrs. Bond came out, dressed in a loose, violet dressing gown that still managed to show off her figure and complement her eyes. "Oh! Captain Smith. Good evening."

He nodded. "Mrs. Bond."

"I was just peeking downstairs to see if my Nash was on his way up. Have you seen him?"

He hadn't seen Nash since he'd left the bartending to Constance and disappeared into the storage room. "I'm sorry, no, ma'am."

"Oh." She sighed. "He told me he had to work late, that after the crowd started thinning, he was going to be doing some work on the books. I guess that's where he is."

The way she walked, the hesitancy in her face, made him try yet again to be chivalrous. "Did you need something, ma'am?" He hadn't forgotten she was in a family way. "I'll be happy to go find him for you."

"Oh. Oh, my, no." A faint flush filled her perfectly milky complexion. "It's just that . . . Well, you were married, right?"

"Yes. Yes I was."

"Then you'll understand." She bit her lip. "I can't bear to sleep without my husband by my side." She lifted her gaze to his. "I'm sure you think I'm foolish."

Images, passing as quickly as pages in a book flipping, darted through his mind. Images of Becky in a white linen nightgown, dark hair flowing down her back, her bare toes peeking out. Her chin tilting toward his. Arms outstretched. Loving him.

No. Mrs. Bond wasn't being foolish. With extreme forbearance, he kept his expression impassive. "Not at all, ma'am. Are you sure you wouldn't like me to go find your husband for you?"

A wistful expression crossed her face before she tamped it down firmly. "Oh, goodness, no. I'll be all right."

"It's no trouble."

"You are a dear. But, I'll be all right. Nash knows how I feel," she added with a smile. "I expect he'll be here shortly." She turned, but glanced at him over her shoulder one more time. "But I thank you kindly, Quentin. And good night."

"Good night, ma'am." He stood to attention as she made her way back to her suite of rooms, then, when she was safely inside, he ventured into his own room.

It was cold and dark. Quickly he lit a fire, held his hands up in front of it before taking off his clothes.

His actions discomfited him.

He was getting soft. Acting like the comforts of home were all he needed. Wanting to be warm. Needing a bed. Soon, he'd be looking forward to cooked breakfasts and clean laundry. Wishing for a woman . . . a wife in a linen nightgown yearning to sleep beside him.

It was enough to completely disgrace him.

But, just as he laid his head on the soft pillow, Quentin knew one thing. If he ever again had a home and a wife she would never have to go looking for him at midnight.

No, he'd never take that for granted again.

CHAPTER 5

The day was rip-roarin' cold; there was no other way to describe it. All traces of the heat that had underlined the wind had disappeared, leaving the inhabitants of Cedar Springs itching for new mittens and hot apple cider.

The residents walked quick-like, heads bent toward their feet, eyes watering all the while. Doors and windows were firmly shut, cotton batting stuffed in any visible crack.

Yes, a hush had sprung up around the town that was only broken at dusk, when the more enterprising members of the population congregated in the saloons and dance halls for libations and genial company.

All Jasmine could think of as she made her way into the mercantile was that she wished someone was planning on making *her* a new quilt to fight off the biting wind. She was cold, her wool coat had seen better days during the war, and she had no hope at all of having the time—or the money—to piece together something better. Though she'd done her best to sew garments in the past, her efforts were pitiful, even in the dim light of boarding house's parlor.

Yep, the Ladies Auxiliary Quilt Project smacked of irony, to her way of thinking. Who in their right mind had decided that Jasmine Fairchild was just the person to stitch together a blanket?

'Course, she knew the answer to that one right away: Madeleine Bond. Only a woman like her could piece together such a foolish notion and have people listen to her.

Jasmine grumbled as she fought to open the door against the determined wind, finally pulling it so hard she almost lost her balance in the process.

"Jasmine? That you?" George called out from behind the counter, his arms laden with bolts of calico.

"It's me," she affirmed, struggling with the door before finally slamming it hard enough to meet its maker. "Whew."

"Wind's something fierce," he said, stating the obvious.

"It is," she agreed, then almost beat a sharp path right back out when she saw what was lying in wait for her: three brand new bolts of fabric.

Madeleine had sent word, asking for her to inspect the cloth, then asked that she take it on back to her place so it would be ready when the sewing circle was ready to cut it up.

Jasmine eyed the bolts with more than a little misgiving. That much material was heavy, and her place was cramped. It was going to take every bit of strength she had to carry the bolts back home in the bitter wind. Yep, there was no good reason for her to be heading up a quilt project.

But the fabric sure was pretty. Almost against her will, she patted the material on the counter. All the ladies had chipped in for it. All she had to do was get the bolts out of the mercantile and then divide the fabric up evenly for their first official meeting at the Dark Horse next Tuesday.

Which was a whole other thing.

Now who in their right mind had ever heard of a saloon sewing circle? Even *she* knew such things weren't done. Ladies who could afford to be other places didn't have any business even knowing what the inside of a saloon looked like.

It just wasn't seemly.

George watched her from his position on the other side of the counter, a half smirk lighting his face. "Jasmine, I just think it's a right good thing you're doing, taking up the blanket brigade like you are."

Quilt. It was a *quilt* brigade. "George, you know it's only temporary, and I'm only doing it as a favor to Mrs. Bond."

"All I know is that Mrs. Bond needs your help. I heard she's acting plumb lazy around her place, and Mr. Bond likes that just fine."

"I've never known Mrs. Bond to be lazy."

"It's happening. I heard that for a fact. I heard Mrs. Madeleine Bond is sleeping late, eating apple pie like nobody's business, and even cried when Nash wanted to take her out for a walk the other night."

Did she dare mention that any woman in her right mind would be crying at the thought of walking in the cold night air? Especially one in Mrs. Bond's delicate condition?

But, still, the things George were saying didn't make a lot of sense. The Madeleine Bond Jasmine knew was the exact opposite of the woman George had described. "Really?"

"Really." George puffed up his chest. "Mrs. Bond is in a delicate way," he whispered knowledgeably. "Women like that are filled with child-bearing feelings, if you know what I mean."

Jasmine didn't. And she was pretty sure George didn't know a thing about child-bearing feelings either. "Well, I hope she feels better soon. Stitching crazy quilts for the needy has never been my calling."

"Could have fooled me."

Voicing her concerns, Jasmine said, "Honestly, George, I need to get out of this project, fast."

"You're talkin' to the wrong person."

"I don't know who else to talk to. Something's gotta change. Maybe the women will decide they don't want to be around me?" She lowered her voice. "Surely they'll see my hands and realize I'm not fit for good company."

Then, of course, things turned difficult.

"Oh, Jasmine!" Anna Harlow, the banker's wife, called out as the mercantile's door opened, bringing with it a bevy of ladies, all making a beeline toward her.

Stunned, Jasmine looked to George for help. Good old George, who always had talked to her, even when most people didn't. Who'd smiled nice to her even when her pa had owed him a heap of money. "Help!"

"Can't do a thang," he whispered as he sidestepped away. "This here is women's talk."

And the women descended upon her like a dust storm in the desert.

"Jasmine," Mrs. Armstrong bellowed. "Just the person we need to see."

Jasmine felt the strong hands of fate grab her by the arms and hold on tight. "Ma'am?"

"When are you going to start organizing our sewing circle? Time's a tickin'."

"We need fabric," Mrs. Harlow added.

Mrs. Armstrong lifted a shaggy brow. "Yes we do, indeed. Do you feel you're up to the task of heading up our group?"

"Our group of gentlewomen," Anna Harlow interjected.

Yes. They were gentlewomen. Trying not to let the sting of their reminder bother her, Jasmine tilted up her chin. "I was thinking that perhaps you, or one of the other ladies here, might be more suited to managing the project."

"Mrs. Bond chose you," Mrs. Armstrong pointed out.

Jasmine still had no earthly idea why. "I am awfully busy."

"The poor are always cold," Mrs. Armstrong chided. "Especially with our recent weather developments, dear. I have a feeling those shanties aren't providing much in the way of shelter. Have you ever thought about that?"

She didn't have to conjure up images of being cold in a

shanty; her memory was just fine, thank you.

But as she glanced at the woman who'd just spoken, Miss Allison or whatever her real name was, Jasmine was reluctant to speak the God's honest truth.

Miss Allison was at least a hundred years old, and talked high-pitched enough to make dogs howl. "I realize that. But . . . well, I think Mrs. Bond was a little preemptive when she nominated me as the leader."

"Don't you think it's time to step up to the nomination?"

"Well, I—"

"Or, do you mean to tell us that you now have no interest in the poor, now that you are a working woman and all?" Mrs. Armstrong chided.

Working woman? She was a bar girl. She lived in a tiny room on the top floor of a boarding house. She owned three dresses, two of which were old ones from other women in Cedar Springs.

"No, ma'am. I was just thinking that perhaps someone else would be better qualified—"

"No one is better qualified than you," Mrs. Harlow said sweetly. "I know! I'll even bring along Caroline. She's just about your age."

Jasmine could barely swallow. Recalling their conversation about Quentin Smith, Jasmine knew that although they were near in age, there might as well be twenty years separating the two of them. Caroline was the owner of delicate sensibilities, blond hair, sweet blue eyes, and a full year's worth of finishing school. Caroline and Jasmine were not—and were never going to be—more than distant acquaintances.

Mrs. Harlow continued. "This is going to be such fun. So we'll see you Tuesday at ten a.m., sharp." Her very fine brown eyes lit up. "I know! I'll bring muffins."

"Yes, ma'am."

They chatted for a little longer, graciously including her in

their conversation about new fashions, difficult toddlers, the church sermon on the Sunday past, and the benefits of gardening.

Jasmine felt as if a whirlwind was surrounding her and she had no hope of finding a way out. She had little experience with much of what they were speaking of. And, although she did have some thoughts about the sermon, she wasn't sure how her thoughts would add much to the conversations.

And then, of course, the talk flew to the most interesting man in Cedar Springs, Quentin Smith.

"What is he really like, Jasmine? Is he really looking for a wife? Do you think he might like my Caroline?" Mrs. Harlow whispered. "I've heard you know him quite well."

Know him quite well? Had they heard how he'd tried to walk her home and finished the story on their own?

The scrutiny was unbearable. So was the thought of Quentin Smith with her perfect counterpart. "I wouldn't say I know him well. Actually, ma'am, I don't believe I know him well at all."

"Well, you must admit that you have the advantage over us, being in the saloon 'most all the time. Tell me, what does he like?"

She'd never heard her situation put quite like that before. "I couldn't say."

Mrs. Armstrong pressed. "Come now, you can tell us. What does he do there? What does Captain Smith do all day and night in that saloon?"

Jasmine glanced toward George for help, but he only smirked and winked from across the way.

"Well?" Mrs. Armstrong asked.

There was only one answer. "Drink."

The ladies' eyes widened like she'd just divulged a mighty secret. "Really?"

Jasmine winced. Oh, for heaven's sakes. What should she say?

"It is a drinking establishment."

Questions started firing her way like she was the grand prize in a turkey shoot.

"Does he play cards?"

"No."

"Does he sleep in?"

"I don't—"

"What about his eggs?"

Jasmine could hardly keep up. "Eggs?"

"Yes," Miss Allison screeched. "How does he eat them?"

"I couldn't say—"

"We had better get on our way, now, ladies," Mrs. Armstrong said. "We'll see how Mr. Smith does things soon enough."

"I imagine so," Mrs. Harlow replied, before playfully fanning herself. "I must confess, he is so handsome."

Yes, he was.

Quentin Smith was very handsome. And good. And his gray eyes had a way of capturing a woman's soul and making her feel as if she could be happy, if she had half a chance. His strong arms felt as if they could hold the world. His quiet demeanor made her wonder what he'd feel like, if they ever got up close and personal.

Would his bare skin feel as worn as his hands looked? Would his skin feel supple and oh-so-masculine underneath her fingertips? His chest a study of hard planes and intriguing angles?

Did he enjoy kissing? Kissing like there was no tomorrow, just like in her favorite novels that were so full of action and adventure?

There was no doubt about it; Quentin Smith would capture some woman's soul. After all, he was in town to relax, heal, and, rumor had it, meet a prospective bride.

A Bride. Someone chaste and sweet and good.

Swallowing hard, she turned to George, eager to place some distance between herself and the women. "I think I'll go ahead and take these bolts now."

George shook his head. "Don't you worry, Jasmine. I'll walk them on down to the Dark Horse and ask Nash to put them in a spare closet for you. I'll be down that way anyhow. I'm paying Chrissy a visit this afternoon."

Feminine laughter rose to the rafters as the women good-naturedly started teasing him about his hesitancy to pop a certain question.

Jasmine used the change of topic to scamper out of the establishment and back into the cool air. Yet once she was on the road, she had no idea of what to do. The day was too young to go to work, and her room sounded terribly confining.

Pulling her coat more closely around her, she walked toward the river, past the saloons, past the depot, past the copse of trees lining the banks. Within the hour, she was sitting against a pine tree, her skirts wrapped around her. If she leaned against the trunk just right, the wind was blocked, cutting the frigid temperature in half. Making it almost comfortable. Enough to enjoy the blessed silence.

When she was younger, she'd sat in that very spot all the time. Her pa was always in the mine, or spending his hard-earned cash the old-fashioned way—on drink and loose women. He'd had no call to keep her company, which had been just fine with Jasmine. She'd never had much of a desire to be in her pa's company.

Later, after she started working at the saloon, she went to the shores of the river just to count her blessings and enjoy the novelty of being surrounded by peace and quiet.

The wind blew yet another gust her way. She hunkered down low to escape the onslaught. But then the crunch of twigs behind her made her lift up her head in confusion.

"Captain Smith. Hello."

"Jasmine. It's cold as hell. What are you doing out here?"

"I could ask the same of you," she said as his boots crunched over the spray of pine needles along the banks. "Shouldn't you be resting your leg?"

"Yes," he answered simply. "Shouldn't you go on inside before your fingers get frostbitten?"

She couldn't help but smile. "Probably, but I couldn't help myself. Sometimes I just yearn to be where it's peaceful. The spring over yonder sounds soothing." Realizing she'd probably just told him far more than he wanted to know, she said, "Why are you out here?"

"Same reason as you, I guess. Fresh air. Peace."

"I guess we have something in common, then."

He treated her to a hint of a smile, laced with flirtation. "Mind if I join you?"

"No." She didn't mind if he sat next to her, though she did mind a lot of things about Captain Smith. She minded how good he smelled. About how she glanced at his lips too often. About how she worried about his injuries and if he was getting enough sleep.

He nodded thanks, then carefully lowered himself to the ground. Jasmine felt bad for him; she hadn't even thought how difficult it might be for him to sit on the ground.

They sat together for a few moments in silence, Jasmine watching the gentle movement of the water. "What's the Rio Grande like, Captain?"

"A whole lot bigger than this little river." Narrowing his eyes, he added. "It's still. Murky. It's dotted with brush and shrubs. I was always on the lookout for water moccasins hanging over the edges, sunning themselves."

The image made her smile. "You've been everywhere, I suppose."

"No, just everywhere that matters."

"Like Texas?"

His lips twitched. "Like Texas." He looked around, shrugged. "And Colorado."

"And just about everywhere in between."

"That's a fact."

A fresh burst of wind struck them, making Jasmine press more closely to the tree for shelter. The river water wasn't so lucky; whitecaps appeared as the waves splashed against the shores. Somehow, Quentin positioned himself closer, warming her with his proximity. The muscles in her back relaxed.

Because Quentin wasn't going anywhere, and she was in no hurry either, she gave in to her curiosity. "I guess you've seen more than one Injun out on the plains."

"Yep."

"And bank robbers, too."

His eyes narrowed. "One or two."

"Ever seen Billy the Kid?"

Imperceptibly, his posture relaxed. "No." Now their shoulders touched. So innocent, yet a wave of desire rushed forward, startling her with its sneak-thievery.

"Oh."

"Tell me about you," he said instead, his voice low and husky, sending a spark of joy bubbling through her. It was as if he really cared. As if she really mattered to him.

The idea made her feel special.

And nervous. No one besides Emmitt had ever shown her any interest . . . and a sixth sense told her Quentin wasn't eyeing her figure with marriage in mind.

Not that Emmitt McKade had said anything about marriage, either.

Her reply stumbled out. "There's not much to tell."

"I heard you know how to read."

"I do. I've read the Bible, and more novels than I can recall." She sighed. "One day, I'm going to have me a table just for my books."

"One day?" He smiled slightly.

"One day if I'm lucky," she finished, knowing she was sharing pipe dreams, nothing more. "That's what keeps me going."

"I know the feeling. One day, I'm going to have a home." Forgetting that he was a whole lot closer to that than she ever would be, she sighed. "Now, wouldn't that be something? A real place. Land. You could plant flowers."

His lips turned up for a second. "Not me. I'd have my wife do that."

"Of course."

"But you could plant your flowers, couldn't you? I mean, your man would be busy providing for you."

"My man?" The wording made her smile. "Oh . . . my husband?"

"Of course."

"I . . ." What could she say? The only man she was likely to have would be one who'd pay for her by the hour. But, because they were alone, and the air was finally still, bathing them both in a blessed silence, she spoke her heart. "I'm not the kind of woman men dream of marrying, Captain."

"Is that right?" Very slowly, his eyes traipsed over her body. Jasmine's pulse quickened, enjoying the interest in his eyes more than she should.

Quietly, Quentin asked, "What do men think about in the middle of the night? It's been so long since I've dreamed of the future. Of anything but my past. What do you think most men dream of, sugar?"

The endearment made her falter, and her heart skip yet another beat. "Innocence," she said without thinking. "Goodness."

"And you? Do you dream of those things?"

"No. I haven't dreamed of those things for a coon's age."

As soon as she made her admission, Jasmine wished she could take each word back. Captain Smith was not her beau, was not her friend. They were acquaintances, thrown together by chance.

He knew very few people.

She got along with few.

Soon, by the time the winter settled in, he would be gone, carrying with him mere memories of Cedar Springs and the people in it. "I mean—"

He leaned forward, worry in his gaze. "Is that not you? Are you not innocent?"

She blinked. Felt hot waves of embarrassment float through her. "I am. I mean, my body is," she clarified. "But . . . but my mind's seen too much for too long to ever be its match." Her heart felt as if it stopped. As if she'd just run through the whole town; she drew a deep breath. Wished she sounded more self-assured.

Wished she felt as comfortable as her body seemed to be. Trying again, she said, "I don't think I'm making a lick of sense."

"I think you probably are."

Against her will, she wrapped her arms around her knees, then leaned into him, hoping to shield the majority of her body from the wind. While she reaped the benefit, she avoided his gaze.

For the first time in a long while, she viewed herself as if from afar. Before, she'd never dared to think about how it would seem to other people, to be the gal who held firm to her virginity but made money by flirting in a saloon. Who walked home by herself at night, but had dreams of being courted by a man who wanted to escort her.

Suddenly, she felt dirty and used, and not much better than most people thought her to be.

She should just stand up, right that minute, and walk away. Walk away from Quentin and all the mixed-up feelings brewing inside of her.

The temptation to be more than she was hit her hard. She wanted to live, not to guard her reputation, not to attempt to be accepted by women like Anna Harlow.

She wanted to be wanted. For herself. For her attributes, both inside and out.

Carefully, Jasmine glanced his way again. Quentin was staring at the water as if it held a thousand ships. Oh, for heaven's sakes. Captain Smith hadn't come over here to listen to her life's story. He was just trying to make a friend. Even world-famous rangers needed friends, right?

Quentin moved closer, ever so slightly. His scent drifted toward her, so masculine and attractive. Bay rum and horses. Leather and worn denim. Man.

"Have you ever been kissed, Jasmine?"

No. No, she hadn't. Daring to clarify, she whispered, "On the mouth?"

Silver eyes darted across hers. "On the lips."

She glanced at his. His lips looked as firm and chapped as a man's could be. No different from anyone else's.

So why was she now thinking about getting to know them a whole lot better?

"Are you going to tell me?"

There was no reason not to. It was nothing to be ashamed of.

No, she'd never been kissed. She'd been pawed, hugged too tightly, and rubbed too familiarly. Her rear had been pinched, her arm had been squeezed, and one time a drunken cowboy with a very silky voice had reached out and grabbed her left breast.

She'd slapped him good.

But she'd never had a man's lips touch her own. Not ever.

"I . . ." She closed her mouth, and tried again, cursing herself for being so childish. For some reason, her body had decided to completely leave her no air whatsoever in her lungs.

Which was really kind of ironic, if you wanted to know the truth, since they were sitting outside where the air was fresh and sweet.

Finally, she just settled for shaking her head no.

There. Question answered. Now it was really and truly time to leave. Save herself a whole heap of trouble and embarrassment. Rolling her hips to one side, she placed a hand on the hard ground and pushed up—

Just as he covered her hand with his own.

"Wait," he murmured. Then, he kissed her. Kissed her! Jasmine!

Firm lips covered hers, more gently than she'd ever imagined a man of Quentin Smith's character could do a single thing. His hand—his very callused, very large hand—moved from her hand to brush her cheek, then to her jaw. As slow as molasses, he positioned her head just a little bit more to one side, then deepened the kiss.

Before she knew it, his tongue was making friends with hers in ways that would have been shocking if it didn't feel so good.

So slow.

So methodical. Like she was worth his . . . time.

A warm trickle slid through her, making her feel languid and tingly, all at once.

Jasmine was sorely afraid her lips were still parted when he pulled away.

Quentin stood up. "I think it would be best if I was going," he said, grimacing slightly when he balanced himself. "Being here, doing this—it isn't good for either of us."

As if she was a spy in one of the adventure novels she loved, Jasmine pictured just how she and Quentin must have looked, all tangled up together on the banks of the river.

Saw how she must look right now, her lips swollen from their first attentions in a lifetime, her cheeks flushed from the knowledge that she wanted more.

With cold comfort, she realized that no words offering a blissful future had been mentioned. Of course not. She was Jasmine Fairchild. He was Quentin Smith, famous former Texas Ranger. They did not have a future together. Their paths should never have collided as they had.

Memories of her father belittling her, telling her she was no good and would only amount to one thing, hit her hard. And, although she knew that Quentin had not been trying to compromise her, Jasmine knew that she had almost compromised herself.

And that wasn't an option. She'd come too far to allow herself to fulfill her father's dire predictions.

So, saving herself and her dreams, she asked, "Have you, by any chance, met Caroline Harlow? She's a real nice girl."

"Hmm?"

She stood up, as well. "Caroline Harlow is the banker's daughter," she said, and then, almost believing that she meant it, "She's very sweet. Beautiful."

Finally he stared at her. His eyes narrowed. "Did you say Harlow?"

It took all her pride to spell it out to him. "Yes. Caroline Harlow. She's just the type of woman to take courting, the perfect kind of lady to make a real fine wife. She'd keep a real fine home, Captain."

And before he could ask any more questions, she ran off, back to the boarding house. Back to . . . home.

CHAPTER 6

The cry resonated through the empty streets. Quentin sprang to attention. He was already reaching for his Colt when the high-pitched call echoed through Cedar Creek again.

Slowly, its origin registered. It was no cry from a woman. Just a howl. From a coyote.

As the knowledge sank in, Quentin leaned back slowly, his eyes adjusting to the dim light as he did so.

Damn.

It was before dawn. Again. Fumbling on the nightstand, he found his pocket watch and grimaced. Four a.m. Shoot, he'd woken up before the sun had even begun to think about gracing the sky with its brightness. The coyote howled again, as if crying out in sympathy with his predicament.

As his heartbeat slowed, Quentin took stock. He was in Cedar Springs. At the Dark Horse. In a bed. With another curse, he shifted. The sheets were damp and close to freezing in the chilly room. Sometime during the night, he'd had another nightmare about Becky. And, as usual, the harsh memories pushed his body into a cold sweat.

He closed his eyes as the disturbing visions came back in a flash. Becky dying before his eyes; her blood pouring out from her body and he, foolishly, attempting to staunch the flow with his fingers.

Becky smiling at him sweetly, whispering that she loved him, that she'd been glad they'd married.

Glad.

Fresh waves of raw emotion tore through him once more. The familiar cloak of ideas . . . the hoping against hope that Becky hadn't been shot because of him. That it was just some strange occurrence. But it was all for naught. Plain and simple, Becky had been shot because he'd done his job. Because he'd hunted down a cold-hearted killer and brought him to justice, out in the open. And the killer's brother wanted a taste of revenge.

He'd left his house mere hours after burying Becky. He'd saddled Pack, his palomino, and went on the trail.

He'd been numb for the first two weeks. And, sorry to say, hadn't even felt much beyond a sense of accomplishment when he'd found Kit Warren and strung him up, without benefit of the law.

Oh, no one had faulted him much. The bastard had raped and killed more than one woman. Justice was still in a man's hands when it came to protecting his own.

And he was Captain Quentin Smith, Confederate war hero and storied Texas Ranger.

After he'd found Warren, Quentin went back to work with a vengeance, tracking and capturing whoever he could. Ignoring the hush that followed him in saloons and towns.

Years passed.

Sometimes, he even smiled.

But sometimes, in the still of the night, when he wasn't plumb exhausted and sore from riding, if he hadn't lain with a woman in months and certain parts of him ached with the reminder, he'd dream of Becky. Of making love to her all night.

Of how she'd look at him and smile. Of how she looked at him as she died. A part of him had died along with her.

The part that had strung up Warren without benefit of a trial. The part that realized that Becky was never coming back.

No, all that really mattered, in the end, was that Becky had died and he was left alone.

Padding to the pitcher and bowl on the dresser, Quentin hastily rinsed his face and hands, then quickly donned a pair of trousers and lit a fire. Damn, but it was cold. Briefly he contemplated going back to sleep. Shoot, if he got lucky, he'd sleep another two hours. Maybe even enough to erase some of the smudges around his eyes.

But he knew it wouldn't happen. He was now awake, and though his skin cursed the frigid temperatures, his brain felt invigorated. Images of the past week clicked across his memory, like picture postcards, bringing to mind Jasmine.

Jasmine, in his arms. She'd felt supple and womanly. The generous curve of her breasts had brushed his side when they'd kissed.

And yet, she'd been so cautious and shy. Her hesitancy had brought out the best in him, making him want to keep the moment between them as sweet as possible.

Kissing her had been exceptional, by his estimation. She'd been the perfect combination of innocence and passion that made him yearn to take her in his arms and teach her everything he knew. The feel of her lips had stirred up desires he'd tamped down for too long. The way she'd gazed at him, her brown eyes filled with yearning, had warmed him in a way no fire ever could.

For a brief moment, he'd been sure he was going to be all right. Maybe he'd learn to sleep through the night. Maybe he really could find a home and some land.

A wife.

And then she'd gone and said some such foolishness about Caroline Harlow.

Harlow. Oh, he knew who her father was. Cedar Springs' banker. A well-fed man who spent too many hours playing poker when he had a wife and daughter at home. There was also a hint of desperation in the man that couldn't be ignored.

Al Harlow had already positioned himself to be one of Quentin's main suspects as backer for the Carmichael Gang. For that alone, Quentin knew he had no choice but to pursue the girl. After Jasmine ran off, Quentin took a stroll about town and found Caroline.

What he saw was much like Jasmine's description. After that, he asked Nash about her, and got an earful. Caroline was a true lady, gently bred, younger than most, more pampered than many.

Caroline wore starched dresses and dainty kid boots and gloves. Very attractive.

To Quentin's way of thinking, she seemed like a like a wildflower in Texas. Pretty to look at, but too delicate to live long. There was no future for a gal like her and a man like him. He'd lived too much, been coddled too little.

She would need a better kind of man.

If he did stake a claim on a piece of land, Quentin knew he'd still have to do his job; which meant Caroline would be alone for long periods of time. That would never do. Never again would he lay claim to a woman who couldn't handle being alone. Who couldn't handle everything his job entailed.

But no matter what the future held, Quentin knew he was in Cedar Springs for one reason: to find the backer and stop the Carmichael Gang. Because of that, he had no choice but to go courting.

With a sigh, Quentin slipped on his boots and hoped Caroline wouldn't expect too many pretty words from him. He also hoped she talked a lot about her pa. Then, at least, he'd be able to justify courting her when his mind couldn't keep from thinking about someone else.

★ ★ ★ ★ ★

Some things Chrissy Sinclair knew to be true. Bicarbonate of soda relieved toothaches. A bit of ox gall set colors just fine. Dry cornhusks worked better than straw when no feathers were available for bedding.

Pine trees were never good shelter choices during thunderstorms.

And George Lange would always be her true love.

Not that her steadfast devotion was getting her anywhere. His pussyfooting around was making her hair stand on end and giving her a fierce stomachache, never mind everything else that was happening to her.

Sweaty palms. Aches in places she had no business thinking about when he kissed her. An inconvenient habit of waking up at four in the morning, mooning over him.

Damn that stage clock, anyway. Did it really need to chime at all hours of the night?

Oh, George.

Most women would have given up on him.

Her mother was convinced she should've moved on to one of the fancy men that came to Cedar Springs when they were passing through.

But ever since Chrissy had moved to Colorado and spied George's twinkling brown eyes, she'd been in love.

She just needed to prod George a little bit and show some action.

"Captain Smith," Mrs. Harlow said when Quentin arrived at their doorstep, hat in hand. "What brings you here?"

"I'd like to pay a call on Caroline, if I may."

Anna Harlow stared at him for a full second before remembering her manners. "Well, my goodness. Of course! Come on in."

From the moment she closed the door behind him, the confines of the house made him feel choked. The scent of dried rose petals permeated the air.

Every space was filled with useless items. There were enough gewgaws to capture a man and hold him hostage. He was afraid to move and knock something over. Even Mrs. Harlow's effusive smile felt confining.

He held his hat and shifted his weight.

She rushed over to the stairs. "I'll go tell Caroline you're here," she said, clasping the banister. "She's going to be so surprised. And pleased!"

Quentin stepped farther into the room, and hoped his boots wouldn't sully their fine rug too much. He swallowed hard.

So surprised.

Yes, weren't they all surprised he was there? He knew he was on a fool's errand, but what could he do? He needed information, and only Caroline or her family could give it to him.

Almost too quickly, Mrs. Harlow appeared again. "Caroline's on her way. Please do come in, Mr. Smith."

He nodded. "Ma'am." Following her petite steps, Quentin did his best to avoid knocking into a kerosene lamp perched on some kind of plant stand. His hands tightened into fists as he entered the parlor, noticing the fine furniture and the real lace curtains. The room was also warm as toast. The marble fireplace housed a blazing fire, giving the room a welcoming glow.

"Please sit down, Mr. Smith. I'll have Olive get you coffee." Just as she turned to waltz out of the room, she faced him again, her mouth tightening with nervousness. "My goodness. You do drink coffee, don't you, sir?"

"Thank you. I do. I'd appreciate it."

She smiled and walked on.

Alone again, he crossed the room and took stock of the tintypes decorating a table, as well as an oil painting of Caroline as a young girl. The Harlows were society, or as much of society people as a family could be in Cedar Springs, Colorado.

Far different from the burnished red walls of the Dark Horse. From his plain clapboard house in the hills of Texas.

From what, he imagined, Jasmine lived in.

Olive, their servant, brought in a tray with a coffee pot, a delicate china cup and saucer, and a plate of sandwiches and cookies.

He took one and chomped down, smiling in appreciation of the baked good.

He stood up as dainty footsteps greeted him. "Mr. Smith," Miss Harlow said.

He stood up. "Miss Harlow. Thank you for seeing me."

"It's my pleasure. Thank you for calling." A dimple appeared. It complemented her pink dress with its lace collar very nicely. Her blond hair fell across her shoulders, fastened in parts with some kind of silver combs. Quentin imagined more than one man had stared at her hair and wondered how it would feel falling across his fingers.

"I see you have coffee?"

"Yes. Thank you."

Carefully she seated herself. As if by magic, her skirts billowed out and then fell in perfect folds around her on the chair. She looked as if she were sitting for one of the photographs decorating the room. Then, realizing she was waiting for him to give some sort of reason for his presence besides staring at her, he racked his brain to think of something to say.

But she began to talk as if she was used to grown men acting foolish and tongue-tied around her.

"My, isn't the weather something terrible? I just don't know quite what to think of it. Of course, you, I'm sure, have a wide array of knowledge about the weather. What is some of the most peculiar you've seen?"

Peculiar weather? He thought quickly. Tried to think of an amusing anecdote, the kind he'd heard more than one gentleman spout in polite company. Not much came to mind.

Caroline's lashes fluttered.

He set his cup down. "Well. Once, it snowed in Abilene in June."

"Snow in June! In Texas! Well, my goodness," she said, sounding just like her mother. One beautiful pale hand pressed against a high-perched breast. He wouldn't have been a man if he didn't take that moment to imagine his own palm there.

She continued. "Once we had snow here in June. I tell you, I quite didn't know what to do with myself." She leaned forward, her face all perfect innocence. "May I pour you some more coffee, Captain?"

More? He glanced at his cup. It was empty. "Thank you, miss."

She leapt up to do as he bid. "Now, isn't this something? When I first saw you come to town, I said to myself, 'Now there's a man who would never care to sit and drink coffee in our parlor.' But here you are." She smiled sweetly. "I guess appearances can be deceiving."

Just as he tried once again to think of something to say, she went on. "Take this dress, for example. Now, most people here in Cedar Springs would say a pink gown like this has no place in such a rough and rowdy area. But here I am, dressed in it and having coffee with you, Mr. Smith. A real, live Texas Ranger."

He knew enough to give the expected reply. "You do look lovely, Miss Harlow."

Her eyes sparkled. "Thank you. I'm so glad you stopped by. My pa has been in such a mood lately. Our house has been positively death-like. You're just the person to brighten our spirits."

No one had ever accused him of brightening anything. "I—"

"I hope my father's mood improves soon," she hurried on. "Why, you'd think banking was just the most difficult job in the world."

His hand stilled. "Perhaps he has problems you don't know about?"

"Oh, I'm sure he does," she replied innocently. "Why, just the other day, he informed me that there were certain things in his world that I must never question."

The man was either hiding criminal activities or a woman. Quentin wondered which it was. "I see," he murmured, trying to recall what he'd seen Al Harlow do during his last visit to the Dark Horse. Had the man been making crazy bets? Commented about a woman? He couldn't recall anything in detail.

But Caroline took his word to be the Gospel. "Do you, Captain? Do you see? Do you know what all that means?" She tilted her head in a studied way, waves of curls falling across her left shoulder.

She was lovely. Extremely so. Any man in the territory would thank his lucky stars to be her escort. Women were few and far between in Colorado. A woman like Caroline was truly a prize.

If Quentin were Al Harlow, he'd hardly let Caroline out of the house.

But he wasn't.

Man enough to appreciate her looks, and curious enough to want to investigate what else she might spout about, he drawled, "Miss Harlow, would you care to go out walking with me one evening? I won't take you far. Just perhaps to the banks of the creek." Even as he said the words, he winced. *Out walking in the dark?*

She looked at him like he was plumb crazy. Matter of fact, he probably was. It was cold as hell outside; it was no place for a gently bred girl. And her parents would think he had only one reason for taking her out into the cold air. To hold her close and press his attentions.

But Caroline Harlow was no fool. They both knew an unmarried girl did whatever it took to catch a man . . . even go out walking in frigid temperatures.

She smiled, the dimple appearing and catching his attention. "Why, I'd be delighted."

Her words sounded stilted and fake even to his inexpert ear. He felt like a fool, and like a snake, knowing that he had no real interest in her. He'd feel like her father if he were courting her for real. Yet he had no choice. Standing up, he said, "Tomorrow? At seven?"

"I'll look forward to it all day and night."

He had to leave. Immediately. "Please tell your mama thank you for the hospitality."

"Don't you want to stay for a few minutes longer? I'm sure my daddy would love to see you." She gestured toward the plate of sandwiches. "You could have another."

He stood up. "I'm sorry. I just recalled I have an appointment with Mr. Bond."

"The saloon keeper?"

"For business, not pleasure."

She blinked, obviously not understanding a word he meant. That was fine; he was well aware he was talking nonsense. "Good evening."

He practically ran outside, pulling his coat close to him as he was blindsided by a great gust of wind. He closed his eyes as red dust flew up and scratched against his face, taking refuge in every pore. Damn, but the weather was peculiar.

Just as he was wiping off his eyes with an old bandana, he practically ran into Nash Bond. "Watch out, Smith."

"Sorry. This wind—"

"Is threatening to take the shirt off your back, I know it. I've been blindsided a time or two myself," Nash commented.

Half certain the entire Harlow clan was watching from their front window, Quentin said quickly, "Mind if I have a moment of your time? I learned something that might be of interest."

"Sounds interesting. Come on down to the Dark Horse, why don't you? We'll chat."

CHAPTER 7

Jasmine wiped the bar a little more forcefully, all too aware that her employer and Quentin Smith were sitting in the far back corner of the room. They'd entered the Dark Horse together, their expressions grim. Mr. Bond had asked her to fetch two cigars from his office desk and a bottle of whiskey.

When she'd delivered those things, they'd been talking about something terribly serious. Mr. Bond hardly looked up when she set the glasses on the table. Quentin had hardly glanced her way at all.

She wished he had. She couldn't think about anything else but the way it had felt to kiss him. And that he'd just come from Caroline Harlow's house.

Moving to an empty table, she quickly picked up two shot glasses and wiped down the wood. And peeked at Quentin again.

As he caught her eye, she pivoted. It wouldn't do for either of them to catch her staring. On the other hand, who was she trying to fool? She'd been staring at Quentin Smith from the moment he'd entered the bar, just as her mind had skipped over to how good it had felt when her body had brushed against his.

You have no business even thinking about that man in the ways you're thinking, she chastised herself. *He paid a call to Miss Caroline Harlow. Not you.*

Most definitely not her.

George had stopped in a few moments earlier, saw that Nash was busy, and talked to her instead. He'd been full of talk about

Quentin's visit to Caroline. If his sources were correct, then it seemed that the ranger had stayed at the Harlow house a full thirty minutes. Had coffee, and made plans to go back.

Not that it was any of her business.

Plus, his courting was her idea, Jasmine reminded herself. She'd practically presented the girl to Quentin on a silver platter. Caroline Harlow would surely make a man a real fine wife, especially a man of Quentin's stature. A famous man like that would attract attention from miles around. Garner looks from everyone and his sister. He needed a lady worthy of him by his side.

Not too many men were actually as true as the talk was about them.

Quentin Smith was the exception, and that was a fact.

But, oh, it was hard to forget how it had felt to be in his arms. She'd felt safe and secure and special. His lips had felt so right against hers, and his hands, when they'd brushed her cheek, had felt like her every dream come true.

For a brief moment, she'd felt as if dreams could come true, and that there was more to her than a dismal past and an unpromising future.

Across the room, Mr. Bond offered Quentin a cigar. Both men were puffing with expressions of satisfaction.

"Jasmine? You dreaming or working, darlin'?"

"Huh?" Quickly she glanced at Lucas Brown. At the moment, he was leaning back in his chair, a half smile playing across his lips.

"I've been calling your name," he said in that slow-as-molasses drawl he had . . . all the way from Mississippi. "What you doing?"

Nothing she should be. Resolutely, she turned her back on the far table and stepped to Lucas's side. "Sorry. What can I get you?"

"How about a little company?" Lucas patted the chair next to him.

Well, now, that was a first. Through narrowed eyes, Jasmine examined the cowboy a little more closely. Though he wasn't drunk, his state of mind didn't look too good either. Lucas had been a regular customer of the Dark Horse for nigh on seven months, ever since his wife up and left him for a cowboy from Texas.

No one had been able to figure out why a gal would leave a man like him. Lucas Brown was a tantalizing combination of southern charm and lanky good looks . . . and, lately, violence?

Jasmine felt right sorry for him. Her first instinct was to go ahead and sit with him a while, but there was something she didn't quite trust lurking in the shadows of his eyes. He was wearing a look she'd felt during the last months of her father's life: desperation.

She'd been tired of her situation, tired of her father's abusive behavior. Tired enough to do just about anything to change her circumstances. She was really lucky her pa had up and died before she'd done something she'd regret.

"Come here, sugar." Lucas patted the chair next to him, his voice like thick syrup, his eyes calculating as a cat's.

Jasmine knew there was only one reason he'd be heaping on the charm for her. He was hard up and looking for her to ease his pains.

"I better not," she said, deliberately making her voice light and flirty. No reason for him to know just how uneasy he was making her.

" 'Course you should," he retorted, circling her wrist with his fingers. "I need some company. I'm lonely as hell."

The stark taste of panic settled in. Why was he acting like this? Had someone seen her and Quentin by the springs? Did she have a couple rumors of her own circulating around town?

Pulling her wrist out of his grasp, she said firmly, "I'm sorry, Lucas, but I just don't have time." Seeking to come up with an excuse he would understand, she added, "Besides, the boss is here."

She glanced again in Quentin's direction. He was staring straight at her, his cool silver eyes fastened on her wrist.

Lucas's eyes hardened. "Nash won't give a damn. You shouldn't, either. There's hardly anybody here except Bond, me, and that ranger." Lazily, he leaned forward. One long arm grasped her again and tugged her closer.

The cowboy was strong.

"Lucas—"

"You got a room upstairs?" he murmured. "We could go put it to good use." Winking, he added, "I've got money."

The words hurt more than his tight grip. "You know I don't do that."

He had the gall to laugh. "Actually, I'm thinking you just might, Jasmine."

"Oh!" she cried as he pulled her onto his lap. Pressing her palms against his shirt, she tried to release herself. "Lucas! Stop—"

"No, no honey. You stop."

Suddenly, strong arms grabbed her by the waist and pulled her out of the randy cowboy's grasp. Lucas swore. She winced as his fingers gripped her hard before finally releasing her. Finally, Lucas fell to the ground, just after Nash Bond hit him good and hard with his right fist.

Jasmine exhaled deeply, then, realizing her legs wouldn't hold her, she sank into another chair. How had all of this happened? The enormity of the situation hit her.

"You all right, Jasmine?" Nash asked, crouching in front of her.

Was she? Fingers shaking, she pushed back a length of her

hair that had fallen to her hips. "I am. Thank you, Mr. Bond. I don't know what happened."

He looked grim. "I'm sorry it did. You know I don't put up with men grabbing the women in here."

"I know you don't."

They both watched Lucas with some misgiving as he moaned and attempted to sit up.

Mr. Bond frowned. "I have to admit I'm surprised by this. Has he pawed you like that before?"

"No." She waited, half expecting Mr. Bond to give her walking papers. Everyone knew that anything untoward happening to a woman was her own fault. Men didn't attack nice girls, because they didn't put themselves in their paths.

Mr. Bond glared at the prostrate cowboy again before gripping Jasmine's elbow and guiding her toward the back door. "I'll speak to Lucas, Jasmine. And don't worry. He won't be coming back."

She blinked. Tears welled up in her eyes.

His gaze softening as if he spied the tears, Mr. Bond said gently, "Why don't you go take a break for a bit? Get yourself some tea or something. That fool cowboy's going to need some assistance vacating the premises."

She couldn't help but ask. "My job? Do I still have it?"

"You've still got your job, Jasmine. I know this wasn't your doing."

Relief made the tears stop fighting to get out and go ahead and fall. "Thank you."

"Go on, now."

"Yes, sir." Then, because she couldn't help it, Jasmine gazed toward Quentin. During the whole time, he'd never moved. Never got up.

And as their eyes met, all he did was blow out a puff of smoke.

Ducking her own head, Jasmine walked quickly toward the

kitchen, wishing all the while she could keep walking. She didn't need tea; she needed privacy.

For a split second, she wished she could just leave the building and Cedar Springs. Wished she could go somewhere private, where she didn't have to walk down the street and pass Mrs. Midge before entering her room. Was there nowhere she could cry without half the town knowing about it?

"Jasmine? How about some tea?" Misty asked, stepping forward. At her surprised expression, Misty chuckled. "I admit it, I was eavesdropping. But, it don't matter. Honey, I saw what Lucas did. He stepped out of line, pure and simple." Misty motioned to her wrist, now bruised and slightly swollen.

"Let's get you a seat."

With quick movements that brooked no arguments, Misty guided Jasmine to a chair then turned to the kettle, which was already whistling.

Misty whistled a little, herself. "That Mr. Bond still has it, don't he? It's been some time since I saw him get all riled up."

Mr. Bond still did "have it." He'd come to her rescue like a knight in shining armor, ready to transform her already shaky reputation into one of almost respectability.

Madeleine Bond had to be horrified.

As Misty scurried around the large cast iron stove, Jasmine rested her head against the ladder-back chair. A whole lot of mixed-up emotions raged in her. Dismay that Lucas had all of a sudden turned on her. Gratitude that Nash Bond had leapt to her aid. Embarrassment that she had caused so much commotion.

Sadness and hurt and who knew what else that Quentin Smith, the most able-bodied man she'd ever known, hadn't lifted a hand.

"Here you go, honey. One cup of hot tea."

Jasmine immediately curved her hands around the thick mug. "Thank you."

Misty nodded. "I tell you, I don't know what got into that Lucas. Why, just last year I was sure he was just about the quietest man you'd ever meet. Then that good-for-nothing wife of his—Oh, well, hi there, Captain."

Jasmine jerked her head up and met Quentin's gaze once again. She opened her mouth to talk, but closed it just as quickly. After all, what could she say?

There didn't seem to be a bit of conversation between them.

Almost hesitantly, he sat across from her, his eyes taking in everything in seconds. The tea, her shaken expression, her rumpled dress. Gosh, she must look a sight.

"You okay?"

"I'm fine."

He swallowed hard. "Nash took care of the cowboy. It's just foolishness, what he did. Whiskey can turn the most amiable man into trouble."

"I'm sure after Lucas sleeps it off, he'll feel badly. He's never done anything like that before."

A grim smile curved his lips. "I feel pretty certain he won't again, least not in here."

Concern entered his eyes. "You're injured." With deliberate movements, he brushed two fingers along the purple marks on the inside of her wrist. His touch was a stark contrast to Lucas's hard grip. "How about I walk you on back to your room?"

"No, thank you. I've got work."

"You should take off the rest of the evening."

"I can't."

His gaze turned flinty. "Now's not the time to be thinking about your reputation. I'll be happy to walk you home."

She disagreed. "I think now is definitely the time to think about it, sir. For some reason, Lucas decided he could ask me to take him upstairs and give him a ten-minute wake-up call. That's never happened before."

"I've traveled all around the country. What he offered is nothing more than a dozen other men would do. He's at fault, not you, Jasmine."

No, she wasn't at fault. However, she also knew that no man would accost Caroline Harlow in such a way. Jasmine needed to work, keep to herself, and preserve her reputation. "Thank you, but I'll be fine."

"Thank you?" Quentin looked as if he was about to add more, but his gaze flicked to Misty, who was diligently drying a pair of pots like nobody's business. With a shake of his head, he strode out.

Hands shaking, Jasmine held onto that mug for dear life as the back door clipped shut.

Misty clanked a pot as she set it on a far shelf. "Oh, that Quentin Smith. He's such a fine specimen of a man."

Yes. Yes, he was.

"Don't you just wonder what it'd be like, to be wrapped in his arms from noon to midnight?"

"Noon to midnight, Misty?" she teased. "The broad daylight?"

"Oh, honey. Yes, indeedy. No way would I want to miss a smidgen of that man's physique."

Unbidden, memories of kissing him, of feeling his mouth pressed against hers, feeling the rush of desire pool within her— and hoping that it would pass just as quickly—left her dry-mouthed and restless. There was really only one thing to do. Go back to work.

"Thanks for the tea, Misty."

"Any time. Everything's going to be all right, dear. I promise."

But the thing of it was, Jasmine knew she'd be all right if things never did change. And wasn't that a crying shame?

Chapter 8

He'd had to leave. Quentin hadn't been able to stay one more minute in Jasmine's company before shaking her to pieces or wrapping his arms around her and calling her ten times the fool.

Why hadn't she listened to him? Why wasn't she heading on home? How come she was pretending her wrist wasn't bruised? Did she really think if he walked her home every person in the little Podunk town was going to think he had designs on her? The girl needed some sense knocked into her. She needed to get her priorities straight.

No. That wasn't right. She needed someone to care about her. To be tender. To let her know that all men weren't skunks. She needed a woman's touch.

For the first time in ages, he thought of Becky and wished she was near for completely unselfish reasons. Not so he could ease his body with her sweet kisses and gentle touch. No, so Jasmine could have gotten to know her. Becky had been tenderhearted, especially to strays. She would have braved any gossip or any number of randy cowboys to be the gal's friend. Quentin knew without a doubt that if Becky had seen Jasmine's drooped shoulders and shaking hands, she would have marched right over, taken hold of the girl, and held her tight.

She would have told her all the right things, too. Made Jasmine feel good about herself, from the inside out. Lord knows, he'd received that treatment a time or two when he'd come home from a rough couple of weeks on the road.

She'd kiss him senseless, then draw him a hot bath. And then, before he could claim her body the way he'd been aching to do, she'd make him talk.

Tell her every little secret. Tell her how he *felt.*

And, he—being a man—would do whatever she asked, especially since she would be disrobing when he was almost done. He'd feast his eyes on her soft white skin, ache to caress her breasts that would be pressing against near-transparent fabric, ache to love her—ache so much that he'd confess all, just like a sinner in church.

Finally, he'd get his reward, hours of kisses from her. Hours of feeling her gentle touch soothing his soul. Of claiming her body.

God, he missed her.

"Little late for a walk, now ain't it, Captain?"

He glanced toward George, who was sitting on the front porch of the mercantile, rolling a cigarette. Quite a feat in the cold wind. "Could say the same thing about you. What you doing out here?"

George spat on the ground, managing to look crude and dejected at the same time. "Just came from Chrissy's," he said. "We got into a bit of a fight."

"You ought to propose to the girl, George," he said, still thinking about Becky's kisses.

"Even you know about that?"

Quentin was fairly sure even the Chinaman down the way knew about George's love life. Walking over, he took a seat on George's right. "Even me."

George licked the paper, sealed the tobacco good. "My predicament is becoming a joke. Chrissy's bound to find out and wash her hands of me. And then what am I gonna do? I've got to marry her. I *want* to marry her."

George lit the cigarette with the sharp scrape of a match. After inhaling deeply, he continued. "I know it's the right thing to do. I know it in my heart. So, how come I can't seem to pop the question?"

Quentin pulled out a cigar as he thought. "I don't know. That Chrissy seems to be a fine woman."

"She is. She's real fine. There's life in her. She gives me what-for before I even know I have it coming. Hard to find a good woman who will do a thing like that." With a sideways glance, he added, "Different than Miss Harlow."

"I imagine so."

"Nash told me you were married before."

For the second time in five minutes, Becky's face swam before him. "Yes. Yes, I was."

"You enjoy it?"

"Always."

George looked surprised by his admittance. "No foolin'?"

"No fooling. My wife was a good woman. Far better than I deserved."

"I feel that way about Chrissy, too." He sighed. "Her patience is wearing away, though. And now I'm afraid everyone's going to expect a big proposal, and I just don't think I've got the words in my head for that."

Quentin almost smiled. "Then don't say them."

"She's expecting words, Captain. She's expecting it all."

"You're making it too difficult. What she's expecting is a ring. Go find one. Hand it to her. Ask her to be yours." Quentin stopped talking as his mouth went dry. Remembering his own sorry proposal.

Becky had been sitting on her parents' porch swing. He'd just come back from the war. His mind and body had been in a sorry state; both were scarred from activities he hated to recall. His mirror had showed him to be a far different man from the idealist he'd tried so hard to be.

But he'd looked at Becky and felt hope. He'd looked at her and thought that maybe, just maybe, things were going to be all right. Without even thinking about it, he'd dropped to his knee like a lovesick calf. "Becky, I love you," he'd said, not even trying to be dignified or manly. "Every moment of every hour I think of you. Every day I hope you'll be mine. Please do me the great honor of becoming my wife. Say you will. Make me the happiest man on earth."

Oh, he'd had no pride. 'Course, he hadn't needed any.

And that Becky, all five feet of her, had placed her hands on his shoulders and leaned forward. Her blue eyes wide with love. With understanding that he was just a man. And without a word, she'd nodded.

Kissed his brow.

Then giggled as he'd practically knocked her off the swing when he stood up and twirled her in a circle.

They'd spent the rest of their given fifteen minutes kissing. She'd let him place his hand on her breast.

He'd felt like the luckiest man in Texas.

He'd been so proud when she'd dragged him into her parlor and told her parents. They'd smiled. Hugged him.

Said they were happy. Said they knew he could make her happy.

And he had.

Two years later, she'd died, the recipient of a bullet meant for him.

"I'm thinking I'm going to do it, soon," George said. "I'm not getting any younger."

Quentin blinked. "No, you're not."

"And we do have some rings in my store. Shoot, I've had one put aside for nigh on eight months." George glanced at Quentin, sideways. "That's a long time."

"Most folks marry, bed, and expect their first baby in that amount of time."

George's eyes twinkled at the notion, then turned wide and frightened. "Shit. I hadn't even thought about that."

Quentin did his best to keep his expression even. Not looking at George helped. But the other man's demeanor and constant worry did remind him of the younger men in his service. The boys who'd needed a father figure even if Quentin wasn't very good at it. Seeing that look made him venture a question that was none of his business. "You worried about the bedding or the baby?"

"Both." His eyes crinkled. "Never thought I'd admit that aloud. You're sure something, Captain. How about that for honesty?"

Quentin was impressed. Once again visions filled his mind. Of Becky, nervous and eager. Of him, not much better. The way her hands had gripped the sides of her nightgown. The way he'd forgotten to breathe when he saw her naked for the first time.

Her mouth had turned to a sweet O when he'd caressed her body. He'd nearly cried when she'd climaxed.

Had anything else in his life ever been so sweet? Perfect?

"Captain? Have I lost you again?"

"Sorry. Long night."

As if to prove the point, raucous laughter filtered out of the Dark Horse, as well as another saloon down the way. "Not for everyone," George commented. He slapped his hands on his britches. "Thanks for the advice. I'm gonna go ask her soon. That's right. Get it over with and cross my fingers that she says yes." George glanced at him sideways. "I'll let you know how it goes."

"Chrissy will say yes."

Hope and humor—and doubt—entered George's eyes.

"That's what I'm half afraid of, Captain." And with that, he shuffled off.

An off-key banjo twanged in the distance, followed by gunshots, whoops and hollers, and another burst of laughter. Across the way, Sheriff Clemmons pulled open the jail's door and laboriously started down to the action. He spied Quentin sitting on the stoop. "See anything, Smith?"

"Nope."

Gunshots filled the night again. John Clemmons groaned, then methodically pulled out his six-shooter and checked for bullets. Every movement showed his reluctance to wander down the way. Quentin knew the feeling well. Bar fights were nothing if not unpredictable. Most sheriffs would rather have a clear-thinking criminal than a swarm of drunk cowboys doing stupid things. "Don't suppose you're hankering for some action?" Clemmons asked, his voice hopeful.

The humor in the man's voice, combined with Quentin's own restless memories, proved tempting. As much as he was in no hurry to get a bottle smashed over his head, he couldn't deny that a part of him would welcome the familiar territory. He'd broken up more fights than he could count.

He also liked the quiet, heavy-set Clemmons. The man had a pretty-as-a-picture wife and a passel of children, all girls. Many a day one of them could be seen riding his shoulders or sucking a lemon drop by his side.

From previous conversations, Quentin also was aware that Clemmons knew his stuff. He'd asked pertinent questions about the Carmichael Gang, and Quentin was pretty sure he'd sent out a couple of wires to check his own story as well.

Standing up, he said, "I wouldn't mind breaking up a fight or two."

"Or three or four," Clemmons said with a groan. "Those damn cowboys come off the trail with every bit of sense situated in their midsection. They eat, spend all their money on rotgut and women, then settle down to shooting anything that moves." He waggled his eyebrows. "And that's after they bathe for the cathouses."

The same predicament played itself out in hundreds of towns. Quentin thought it more than a little amusing that each randy group thought they were tougher, louder, and more boisterous than the next. "Cowboys aren't known for their good sense."

Clemmons laughed as he joined Quentin. "No. No, they're not. And, hell, at least the whores keep 'em clean. Otherwise they'd smell up my jail something awful."

The sharp crash of breaking glass sounded through the air, followed by a rush of obscenities.

"That would be Mason Pepper. He's the proprietor of this establishment," Clemmons said as they neared the Shack. "And by the sound of it, I think he's had just about enough. Guess we better go on in."

The Shack's walls shook as another crash sounded. The mournful wail of an off-tune harmonica joined in, followed by a woman's squeal. "Probably."

Quentin told himself he was just helping out a fellow officer of the law. That a man couldn't just sit there and let Clemmons deal with a dozen drunken cowboys with little or no brainpower left to them.

But as they reached the front of the building, some fool coot flew out the saloon doors and landed at their feet.

Clemmons tilted his head to one side to get a better look at the man, now unconscious. "That would be Waylen Hope. Watch your step."

Quentin fought back a laugh. Yep, he could tell himself that he was only there to lend a hand, but he knew better. He was happy to be there. Excitement was coursing through him, waking him up. Making him feel as if he could tackle anything.

There was nothing like a good fight to wake up a man.

Nothing like a good bar fight to make him forget about women, problems, and broken dreams.

Yet another cowhand came barreling out, landing only a foot away from them. Clemmons scowled. "Dammit, Slim, you almost landed on my foot. Now get up and go on home or you'll be sleeping at my place."

With a hurt expression, Slim pushed himself up, wiping a bloody chin with the end of his cotton shirt. "I'm going, Sheriff."

"Go quicker. Get on with you," Clemmons ordered.

Slim muttered under his breath but walked away.

"Damned cowboy," Clemmons said again. "Let's go. I'll take the crew by the bar."

"Right."

With the end of his pistol, Clemmons pushed open the door.

The scene that met his eyes almost made Quentin smile. By the looks of things, both the fight and the betting were in good form. Chairs were broken, women were laughing, and Pepper was standing to one side, giving everyone and his brother what-for.

As the two lawmen entered, the proprietor called out. " 'Bout time you showed up, Sheriff."

Clemmons's somewhat round face hardened. "I don't get paid enough for this, Pepper. Why the hell can't you control these boys?"

"Not my fault they want to spend all their money on booze and women," the other man replied peevishly.

Clemmons rocked back on his heels. "I'm much obliged to you for accompanying me, Captain."

"Happy to help out."

Clemmons drew his gun, smiled warmly, then carefully stood next to the crowd goin' crazy. "Here's what we're gonna do," he called out loud enough for all action to stop. "Y'all are either going to settle down and go on home, or more than a few of you are going to get up close and personal with the sole of my boot. Anyone want to take a pick?"

Silence, then a mutter of grumbling tore through the bar as each man chose his response. Quentin shook his head as more than a couple of cowboys begged to be shown that Clemmons was serious. Some things never changed.

Grumbling, Clemmons picked up two pups by their back collars and practically tossed them toward the swinging door, with a fair number of curses.

Quentin took the easier route, simply pointing his gun at a man about to use a chair as a weapon and said, "Do you like your knee?"

Almost miraculously, the chair met the floor with nary a scratch, and the man scampered out of the way.

Yet still a few men needed extra encouragement. Amazing what a belly full of rotgut can do to a hard-working cowpuncher.

He and Clemmons had their hands full for a few minutes, checking tempers and returning order. Clemmons drew a pair of handcuffs out of nowhere and neatly subdued a foul-mouthed brawler.

Then, as if someone had snapped his fingers, the commotion stopped. One by one the cowboys found their hats and moseyed on out of the Shack. A girl halfheartedly pushed a broom around, pushing the broken glass into a pile near the piano.

Pepper slapped Clemmons on the back, then stood at attention while the lawman read him the riot act. More entertained than he'd been in days, Quentin took a seat at one of the few wooden chairs that looked as if it could hold his weight.

Amazing how different this saloon was from the Dark Horse. Whereas the Dark Horse was all red brocade and fancy paper, the Shack was scarred wooden walls and beat-up furniture. Tantalizing smells wafted through the Dark Horse. Though

Nash didn't advertise it, Misty served more than a few customers meals on occasion. The sweet smell of a good cigar usually hung in the air as well.

All that could be smelled in the Shack was the scent of unclean men, stale beer, and age-old grime.

"Want a beer, darlin'?" one of the gals asked, her lips curving in appreciation. There was no doubt that she'd seen it all. Her breasts were almost completely visible; what bare skin the low cut blouse didn't show, the transparent fabric did. A faint bruise marred her neck. Her eyes were hard, calculating. A far cry from Jasmine.

Seeing that Clemmons was going to be a while, Quentin nodded. "Sure. Beer's fine."

After she sauntered off, he received another visitor. A man, thin, pale, with too-sharp eyes and washed-out lips approached. "Mind if I join you?"

Quentin knew better than ever to let someone like that get away. Obviously, he'd approached for a reason. "Want a beer?"

"Sure."

Just as the bar girl was coming his way, Quentin held up another finger. She pivoted and went back to the bar.

Glancing more closely at the man, Quentin said. "Quentin Smith."

"I know who you are."

"Who are you?"

"Don't matter. You need to hear what I have to say."

The man's belligerent tone reminded Quentin of his first days on patrol, back before his reputation began to precede him. Back then, it had taken every skill he possessed to ferret out clues or to gain information. He almost welcomed the opportunity to try his hand again. "All right."

The man waited until their glasses were sitting in front of them. Each sipped. Quentin's was warm, hardly worth the effort. He fought off a knowing smile as his guest guzzled his like a baby at a bottle.

So maybe that was where the man's motivation came from. A free drink or two.

Fair enough.

Quentin glanced at Clemmons. He was done talking to Pepper, but they shared a look. Very slowly Clemmons sat down at the bar, one leg swinging gently as he waited for Quentin to give him a sign.

It was time. "Well?"

"I know why you're really here," the man opposite said. "Why you came to Cedar Springs."

"I came here to recuperate, not that it's any of your business."

"It might be." The man sipped from his glass again, finishing it off, letting it land on the table with a thunk. He glanced at Quentin expectantly.

No harm in playing along. Quentin nodded at the bar girl and held up one finger. "So . . ."

"I've been hearing talk about you. *I know*, Captain." He stopped as his second beer arrived.

Quentin's patience dissipated along with the man's drink. He'd had enough intrigue for one day. "*What* do you know?"

"I know you're hunting for someone."

"Who told you that?"

His informant played coy. "Couldn't tell you."

"Then what do you want . . . besides liquor?"

"I'm just trying to be law-abiding."

"I appreciate that. But you're going to need to talk more if you want to keep that beer you're drinking."

Clutching his glass protectively, the man said, "Last week, there was talk in the mining camp about a train robbery. The men were well-financed. Organized. Different than most."

"You know a lot about that kind of work?"

"I'm no saint, Sheriff, but I do honest work now."

Quentin seriously doubted that.

"There's some people in this town who are hoping to make some more money, to get in on the action. But they're worried about you."

"What are they saying?"

"That you're watching too much. They're getting nervous."

"I am watching the happenings around here, but it doesn't matter. I'm only here to recuperate."

"I wouldn't buy that line with a plug nickel." Leaning forward, he whispered, "I'd watch your back, Smith. There's a pretty important man in town who's backing the gang, and he don't want none of his personal business coming to light."

"I'll take that into consideration."

The man seemed to weigh that for a good two minutes. Long enough to finish another beer. Long enough to act as if he was just waiting to dole out another tiny tidbit. Quentin was tired of playing his game. Wearily, he glanced toward Clemmons. The sheriff nodded and sauntered over.

"Hear you've been lucky at the tables, Emmitt."

Quentin was caught off guard. He'd heard the name around town before. In conjunction with . . . Jasmine?

Emmitt groaned. "Aw, shit. Why you here?"

"Know anything about who started this fight? It got me out of my bed."

"It was no big deal."

Quentin knew that there was little chance Emmitt was going to say any more without some powerful persuading. And frankly, he was too tired to sit with him for another two hours to get just a little more information. There'd be time tomorrow, now that Quentin knew who he was. "Think I'll be heading on back," he said.

"Thanks for your help," Clemmons said.

"Happy to oblige." Motioning to the cuffed cowboy, he asked, "Need any help?"

"Nah. I'm going to let him cool his heels here."

"I'll find you soon, Emmitt," Quentin promised, realizing he was going to need some time to investigate Emmitt, the "important man in town," and Emmitt's connection with Jasmine before he went any further.

Feeling more tired than he had in a month of Sundays, he moseyed on back to the Dark Horse. Jeremy was still playing, and the jaunty tune "Camptown Races" rang through the air. Jasmine was still working. Nash was nowhere to be found. No doubt he'd gone up to bed before his wife went looking for him again. Smart man.

He hesitated for a moment, wondering if he should ask Jasmine how she was doing; if she'd recovered from Lucas's advances. Maybe even go ahead and ask what her relationship with Emmitt was.

Was she working with him? Could her friendship be an act, just a device to get more answers?

But as she met his gaze, hers was decidedly vacant. The stare gave him pause, and left him feeling more than a little disappointed.

He finally went upstairs and fell into bed, haunted by thoughts of Lucas and Emmitt, Clemmons and Jasmine and Caroline.

George, Chrissy, and Becky. Always Becky.

Yet, for once, he wasn't haunted by stained sheets and the twisted-up knowledge of guilt deep within him. Instead, he felt acceptance. Regret . . . yet a tingling of hope.

The feeling felt as strange on him as a new Stetson.

Yep, there was something about Cedar Springs that had got into his bones and jarred him clear through. For some unknown reason, he was thinking about futures and happiness. Strange.

CHAPTER 9

"Let me help you with your things, Chrissy," George offered, ready to run around the counter and set things to rights.

Anything to stop her from being so mean.

But all she did was turn up that little nose he was so fond of a little bit more. "Thank you, no."

Oh, he hated this. "Chrissy, don't be mad at me. You know I can't take it."

"I'm not mad. I'm hurt. Oh, George, what do you want from me?"

Everything. He wanted everything from her. That was the problem. She'd captured his heart with her curls and her dimples and the way she tilted her head when she laughed just a little too loud.

He liked the way she walked and talked and the way her eyes sparkled when she was up to mischief. And he liked the way she made him feel when no one else was around.

He liked her.

Shoot. He loved her.

He wanted to capture that feeling and hold it close and not let another man even think about getting near her. Why, just the other night he'd dreamed of Chrissy and that pale expanse of skin he'd uncovered the last time their kisses had gotten near out of control, and he'd woken up with all kinds of thoughts running riot in his brain.

He wanted to possess her. Possess her! Now what kind of

man was he to go insert that little piddling word into his already too-full brain?

But that's all he had thought of. Yesterday, when Slim Atkins had helped Chrissy when she'd accidentally tripped, George had been feeling more than ready to bash his head in.

Which was saying a whole lot of something else, on account of him not being a violent man by nature. So, it wasn't really his fault, really, when he'd plumb ignored his best girl and zeroed in on the lanky cowboy.

Slim had gotten his just desserts, right about the time Chrissy had gotten up out of the dust all by herself. She'd skinned her elbow—and who knew what else? She wouldn't let him see— and left in an all-fired huff.

Now things didn't look to be much better.

Which was really too bad, because George had just been telling himself that morning that it looked like the perfect day to go out and propose.

"Would you like some coffee?" he asked, doing his best to make the offer like a real gentleman. "I can brew a pot right up in the back of the store."

She sniffed, not showing even a hint of his favorite dimple. "No, thank you."

"I got new ribbons. A real nice bolt of blue calico."

Chrissy's eyes widened, then she turned away. "I don't think so."

"You sure?" he coaxed, not feeling a smidgen of guilt that he was bribing his future bride with hair adornments. "The blue would match your eyes just fine. 'Course, everything would look fine on you."

"Oh, George."

"Please don't be mad with me. I can't take it."

"I'm not mad. Not too much, anyway."

"So, you'll come with me? You'll come sit a spell?" He held

out his arm so she could take it.

He hit pay dirt, because she took his arm and held on tight. Just to add another point, he whispered, "I'm sure sorry about that little episode with Slim. I just see red when you're with another man."

"Oh, George," she repeated, but this time all soft and breathless, the same way she sounded when he kissed her good and long late at night.

He used that tone to cuddle a little closer, close enough to smell her sweet fragrance of lemons and sunshine. "Tell me you're not hurt, sweetheart. I worried about you all evening."

"Did you? Did you really?"

"Of course, sugar. I'd never lie to you."

To his pleasure, Chrissy moved a little bit closer, making his pulse leap and his senses come alive. He slid his arm from her elbow to her waist, enjoying how trim her waist was, how he could almost span it with one hand. "You know I love you."

She kissed him then, right there on the front steps of his store.

George sighed as he followed her inside. One day soon, he was going to really have to propose.

Jasmine's thumb was bleedin' something awful. As she watched another drop of blood bead up on the tip, she wondered if any of the other women in the room would notice if she popped it into her mouth. Probably. She settled for pressing an especially ugly piece of calico scrap on it instead.

Of course, Mrs. Bond had to notice. "You all right, Jasmine?"

"Oh. Yes, ma'am. Just got a pinprick, that's all."

Mrs. Bond's expression softened. "Isn't it funny how something so tiny can hurt so much?"

Real funny. "It's really nothing. I'm fine," she muttered, realizing that she'd captured the attention of all seven women.

Five of them smiled then went back to the stitching. Mrs. Harlow, who had paused in her embroidery, harrumphed.

Caroline Harlow lifted up one finger to show a well-used thimble. "You need to get one of these, Jasmine."

She'd get right on that. "It sure would come in handy right about now."

Chrissy laughed. "Don't mind her, Jasmine. Everyone knows Caroline needs about ten thimbles." Turning to the blond, Chrissy chided. "You never could sew very well."

"I know. At least I can play the piano."

"You play very well, dear," her mother said with more than a touch of pride. "You ought to play for Mr. Smith when he stops by. Again."

Jasmine was glad she had stopped sewing because if she hadn't, she was sure her fingers would have been bleedin' again. Wasn't it just like Mrs. Harlow to be crowing about her daughter's suitor? Wasn't it just like her to care?

She smoothed the fabric across her lap once more, only to wad it up as the conversation continued.

Mrs. Bond took the bait. "A caller? Why, do tell, Caroline."

"Captain Smith is coming over again this evening to go walking."

Chrissy pointed toward the door. "It's near on freezing out."

"I know. I guess real, live Texas Rangers don't mind the cold."

Another woman clucked. "Most women do, though."

"You'd think he'd be thinking about your welfare," Mrs. Harlow said. "You're going to catch cold, mark my words."

"I don't mind," Caroline said, her eyes glowing. "No one's ever taken me out strolling in the winter before."

Jasmine once again spread her quilt out on her lap as she reflected on the hidden meaning in Caroline's words. *But many a gentleman had come calling and done other things.*

Jasmine's old friend, jealousy, came rolling in, catching her by the waist and holding tight. Almost as tight as Lucas had just the night before. It felt every bit as constraining and treacherous.

"I think it's kind of sweet. When my Nash came calling, we always did the same thing," Madeleine said with a trace of amusement. "He'd sit on my mother's settee, talk with my parents for a good fifteen minutes, then take me out on our porch swing the rest of the time."

"Even in the winter?" Caroline asked.

"Nope, in the winter, he'd scoot next to me on the sofa," she replied with a twinkle in her eye. "We'd kiss and hold hands and I'd pretend to listen to him." Fanning herself, she added, "He'd spend hours telling me why he wasn't good enough for me. How no lady should live above a saloon."

In spite of herself, Jasmine sighed. Madeleine and Nash Bond were most certainly a love match from the get-go.

No one was even trying to pretend they were working now. Caroline leaned forward, her eyes shining with romance. "And what did you say?"

"Why, nothing, of course. Not one cotton-picking word," Madeleine said with smile. "I just let him talk."

"He was right, you know," Mrs. Harlow interjected. "Saloons are poor homes for young ladies."

"Maybe, but I don't care. I'm one of the few women who can safely say I know exactly what my husband does when he frequents a saloon!"

They all laughed. Jasmine held up her quilt to check her seams. She knew, probably better than any of the other ladies, just how little Madeleine Bond had to worry about her husband. Nash was as good a man as a woman could hope to claim. Honest. Hardworking. He never spared a look for any of the bar girls.

Shoot, Jasmine even recalled the time a woman came in for a

job and practically stripped right there in front of him. Mr. Bond's eyes had gone cold and he'd sent her on her way.

"I think George is going to propose this week," Chrissy blurted out.

All the women gasped. Madeleine reached out and gave her a hug.

Jasmine couldn't resist replying to that comment. "You really think so?"

Chrissy nodded. "I think it's really, finally going to happen! He told me to wear my meadow-green dress on Wednesday night."

Caroline sighed. "Why that one?"

"It's George's favorite. Two nights ago he told me it matched my eyes."

Even Mrs. Harlow looked amused. "That's saying a lot for George."

Jasmine figured it was pretty darned amazing. She'd never known George to have any compliments in his vocabulary.

Caroline clapped her hands. "What are you going to say?"

Chrissy held her left hand out in front of her. "Why, yes, of course."

The women laughed.

"You're not going to play coy?" Madeleine chided.

"Not even for a minute," Chrissy replied. "If I play coy I might have to wait a whole 'nother month before he asks again."

"Or a year," muttered Jasmine.

Chrissy playfully swatted her. "I heard that."

"I'm sorry. But, that George is as slow as molasses."

"And stubborn as a mule," Chrissy finished. "Well, I'm hoping for a summer wedding."

"You might want to switch to Christmas," Madeleine said with a nod. "I wouldn't give him time to back out."

Mrs. Harlow chuckled. "You might even want to ask Pastor

Fletcher about next week."

"I'd sure love a summer wedding, too," Caroline said with a dreamy sigh.

Jasmine felt as if she'd just been punched in the gut. With shaking hands, she smoothed out the fabric once again.

Mrs. Harlow nodded. "That would give me plenty of time to make your dress, dear."

"I've already got one picked out. Thirty-three buttons."

"Lord have mercy," Chrissy said with a sigh.

"I know! But I can just imagine Quentin unbuttoning me by candlelight," Caroline said, her voice dreamy and soft.

"Caroline!"

"Oh, Mother. I'm being good. You know I will be a lady when Mr. Smith comes courting. I promise! But a girl can dream." She sneaked a peek at Madeleine. "Right, Mrs. Bond?"

Mrs. Bond laughed. "Of course, dear. I spent many a night thinking about Nash, I'll tell you that."

"I think about George all the time," Chrissy interjected. "*George*. Does that strike anyone as strange?"

"My momma told me there was someone for everyone," one of the ladies in the back said.

"I felt that way about Nash," Madeleine said. "From the moment I saw him, I knew he was the right man for me."

Caroline fluffed her skirts. "Well, Quentin's for me. I just know it."

Jasmine bit her lip as she thought about that. Did it make things easier if she thought Caroline's words were true?

No. All she could think about was how safe and secure she'd felt in his arms. How perfect his kiss had been. How she'd liked it too much.

The women chuckled at Caroline's exuberance, their laughter echoing through the near-empty building.

Then, very faintly, a click of a closing door filtered back

toward them. The reminder of who was living right above their heads made Jasmine's fingers slip again. She winced as once more her needle struck blood.

Caroline's eyes widened. "Who's up there?"

"Nash . . . and Mr. Smith," Madeleine said with a smile.

"Do you think they heard us? Heard me?"

"Oh, no, dear. Nash is most likely in his office, and Mr. Smith usually sleeps in. He's recuperating, you know."

"Oh, I know. He's so brave and wonderful."

Mrs. Harlow chuckled.

Jasmine pricked her finger again, and started wishing real hard for a thimble. Wishing real hard for the ceiling to cave in. A tornado.

Anything to remove her from this spot. Could any other situation be as painful as being forced to sit and pretend she had no feelings for a man she knew she shouldn't even think about?

But she did. She had many feelings for him. Feelings and thoughts that were carnal in nature and would no doubt bring a look of dismay to Pastor Fletcher's face.

And, even more discomfiting, feelings for Quentin that had to do with sweet emotions and love and romance.

The distant chime of the stage clock gave her as good an excuse as any to leave the slow torture of imagining Caroline's wedding day.

"I'm sorry, but I need to get on my way," Jasmine announced. Quickly, she stood up and hastily folded the fabric as well as she could with sore fingers. "I'll be back here working in just a few short hours, and I've got washing to do beforehand." Resolutely, she did her best to keep her face impassive as she backed away. But, Lord have mercy, her excuse sounded mighty flimsy, even to her own ears.

"I thought Mr. Chin did your laundry," Chrissy said.

"Not all of it."

"But—"

"I'll see you later, then, Jasmine," Mrs. Bond said sweetly, cutting off Chrissy's confusion with ease. "Thank you for coming in so early. These quilts are turning out very nice. They're going to be so lovely."

Jasmine nodded, only hearing part of Mrs. Harlow's talk about getting up at dawn. As the door closed behind her, the ever-present dust whirled around and flew into her face, reminding her once again that her life was in turmoil.

CHAPTER 10

It wasn't good that Quentin Smith walked right into her as Jasmine rushed out of the Dark Horse. Not good at all. She was still dealing with the unsettling images she'd created in her mind while Caroline had talked of wedding gowns.

Images of Quentin, naked and passionate, capturing her mouth with his, making her yearn for things she shouldn't be thinking of. Ever.

But she did.

"Whoa," he said, grasping her shoulders to steady her. "Where's the fire?"

Jasmine swallowed hard. Where *wasn't* she burning? Jealousy—and dare she say it? desire—billowed up like a puff of smoke in a silo as she stood much too close to him and contemplated how good it felt to be in his grip. And did he have to smell so good, too? Fresh mint and bay rum tickled her senses and warred with all of her best intentions to keep their alliance proper and distant. "Captain Smith. Hello."

He dared to look amused. "I thought we'd graduated to first names some time back."

"We had. I just forgot. Quentin." Jasmine wrinkled her nose as she heard her words, each one sputtering out in a torrent. The way she was talking, you'd think she was a crank-up monkey from a traveling salesman, her words were coming out so choppy.

He was inclined to talk. "So? You all right?"

103

"Fine. Dandy. You?"

"I've been better." His eyes sparkled with a hint of humor. "Hear about last night?"

She had. As his hands dropped and he stepped back, Jasmine breathed a little more deeply. "I heard you were visiting a different bar. The Shack."

An eyebrow rose. "Jealous?"

Clearly he was referring to professional jealousy. Clearly her heart was thinking about anything but. "I'm not jealous in the slightest. I don't care how a man finds his alcohol," she retorted as they began to walk down the street.

Quentin stayed by her side. His proximity gave her comfort and made her nervous, all at the same time.

"I should have stayed at the Dark Horse. The Shack had a mess of complicated characters, each sorrier than the next." Darting her a glance, he grinned. "I got into it with a trash-talking cowboy. Luckily, Clemmons was there to cover my back."

"Luckily, since you're recuperating and all."

Quentin rubbed his leg as if he'd needed the reminder. "That's right. That Clemmons was a big help. He's a mite stronger than he looks."

"He's a good sheriff." The lawman had saved her skin on more than one occasion. Once, he even jailed her father for a whole week when she was sick with the influenza and her pa was ripping into her good for not working at the laundry. "He's a good man, too."

A flurry of wind packed with red dust flew up, stinging her eyes and making her feel grimy. "I was just on my way home." Briefly she recalled her excuse for leaving the sewing circle and decided to stick to it. "Laundry."

Quentin nodded. "You working later?"

"I am."

"How was your women's group? You still in charge?"

"I don't rightly know, come to think of it. Mrs. Bond seems to be feeling better. I just do what she wants me to."

"I bet you're a real help."

It was nice to hear he thought so. As they walked along, heads down against the wind, Jasmine racked her mind for another bit of conversation. Anything to keep him near her.

Was that bad?

As she recalled his interest in George and Chrissy, she said, "Chrissy thinks George is gonna propose sometime soon."

Quentin laughed, the deep, throaty sound reverberating in the air and making her skin tingle. Oh, he sounded so good to her ears.

"Chrissy and George are meant to be together," she added. "I hope he really does ask her."

"He'd be a fool not to," Quentin agreed. Treating her to a sideways look, he added, "The right woman doesn't come along very often."

Her steps slowed as they neared the boarding house. Looking up, Jasmine caught something new in his expression. Was it a reflection of her own feelings? Or maybe more like melancholy—thinking about things he'd had and lost.

Even though it was none of her business, she asked, "You thinking 'bout your wife?"

He looked surprised for a moment. "I suppose," he finally said. "Becky was a fine woman."

"I'm sure she was."

"Why do you say that? You never knew her." Wiping his eyes with a faded bandana, he shook his head. "Damned wind. My eyes are going to be full of silt before things calm down."

His statement, so harshly spoken, brought her up short. "Pardon?"

"Why would you say you're sure she was?"

His tone scared her. It was pensive, almost angry . . . and

worrisome, as if he was beggin' for reassurance but didn't know how to get it. "I don't know," she said slowly. "I guess because she was married to you." When he still looked angry, she stumbled over herself again. "I mean, you . . . you're a fine man, Quentin. You're a captain. A Texas Ranger."

"Former."

"Oh, my goodness. No one who knows you would ever dream of referring to you by anything other than Captain. It's how it is."

Those mercurial eyes closed, erasing all hope of her being able to read his mind easily.

His discomfort transferred to her, making Jasmine feel even more worried and fretful. The thing of it was . . . well, Quentin Smith was a good man. A very good one. He deserved the best in life. At the very least, an honorable woman. More's the pity that his wife died.

Still more was the pity that she couldn't be the woman he needed.

"What was Becky like?" she asked, eager to ease his mind. "Tell me something special about her."

"Well, let's see. Here's something. She could sleep easier than anyone I've ever met," he said with a hint of a smile. "When we were moving north of Fort Worth and living in the back of a Conestoga, she'd kiss me good night, roll over, and sleep like the dead. I'd never seen anything like it. Still haven't, if you want to know the truth."

"That's 'cause you were used to soldiers and rangers sleeping on the ground."

He laughed. "Maybe so. The first time I slept beside her, I checked her every fifteen minutes, sure she wasn't going to wake up."

As the wind gave them a moment's reprieve, Quentin slowly folded his bandana and slid it into his denims' back pocket.

"When I asked her about it, asked her how come she didn't toss and turn or wake up and worry, she said she didn't need to do such things. Because—"

"Because she had you," Jasmine finished impulsively.

Surprise filled his gaze. "Yeah. She did."

Fresh pain for his loss and her future rushed over her once again. Why was life so hard?

Remembering her vow to be only his friend, since he'd never mentioned wanting anything more, she whispered, "I hear you're going courtin' tonight."

"How'd you hear about that?"

"Quilting. We don't just talk about George and Chrissy, you know."

"No, I didn't." Looking disturbed, Quentin added, "I didn't think Caroline was the type to say so much."

He obviously didn't know Caroline or Mrs. Harlow. Both women were eager to procure a husband for Caroline and not afraid to stake their claim. Quentin's attentions were going to be duly noted and crowed about.

"She didn't speak of you in any disrespectful way. You're just news, that's all. And . . . she's real excited." That was true. "She's a nice girl."

"*Girl.*" He nodded. For a split second, his gaze settled on her lips. "What do you know about Emmitt McKade?"

The question caught her off guard. "Not much."

"He was at the Shack the other night. Seemed to know a lot about me. About you."

"Emmitt's been coming into town about once a week for a year or so."

"Is he sweet on you?"

"If he is, I don't know it." She shrugged. "He's been no different than just about every other cowboy I know."

In short, he was nothing like Quentin.

"Ah."

They stopped in front of her boarding house. Jasmine felt confused and nervous. She wondered why Quentin had asked about Emmitt. Did he know something she didn't?

As she looked at the boarding house, she could see Mrs. Midge fussing with the windows in one of the front rooms. "Well, I've got to do my laundry."

The corner of his mouth turned up. "So you said."

"Mr. Chin, he needs a break every now and then," she added, rushing on. "I do my own and anyone else's for an hour or two a week."

"It's good of you to think of him."

"It's little enough. He's old and, well, I worked for him when I was little."

"Doing what?"

"I delivered and picked up." Dared she say he was kind? "So then, I've got to work. You know, some people have to make a living."

"I'm well aware of that. Good luck to you."

"Good afternoon, Captain."

"Quentin." Tipping his hat, he paid her the barest hint of a courtly bow. "Good day to you, Miss Fairchild."

Walking out with Caroline Harlow had to be one of the most asinine ideas he'd ever had. It was right up there with when he'd decided to deal with the Baxter Gang with only Jim Evans by his side. He'd ended up riding through the plains of west Texas in the summer heat with the next-to-dumbest corporal he'd ever had the misfortune to command.

Both this evening and all those years ago, he felt frazzled and put upon. More than a little irritated. Both the Baxters and Caroline Harlow seemed to have something up their sleeves.

As she gripped his arm and prattled, day in Cedar Springs

turned to night. Before their eyes, the sun set in all its glory. In its place Venus and the moon rose. Along the foothills, blue spruces swayed in the breeze, and in the distance, the longing cry of a coyote shattered the quiet.

The streets changed hands as well. Storekeepers closed up their shops, while the Dark Horse and its neighbors seemed to shine like candles in a window. Miners and a few cowboys, one on a very fine-looking pony, rolled in.

No one paid him and Caroline much mind.

That was good, since she was talking a mile a minute and seemed to be oblivious of anything but her own viewpoint.

He couldn't help but contrast her chatter with his walk with Jasmine. He'd felt at peace with Jasmine . . . and proprietary. He hadn't been able to stop thinking about her lips, the way they'd felt on his. The way her blouse pulled tight over her breasts. The quiet way she'd taken his arm when he'd escorted her down a row of steps.

"So, I told Mama that I would be pleased to help sew blankets for the needy. After all, the poor are all our problem, right?"

He'd spent years worrying only about his own problems . . . and clearing west Texas of renegade Indians and vaqueros. "More or less."

"You might think I'm just a sheltered young woman, but I mean to tell you, I've *seen* things, Quentin."

Her pretty face glowed with earnestness, her chin jutting upward at a saucy angle. He was charmed in spite of himself, and more than a little curious about what was running through her head. "I can imagine," he murmured. Though, if truth were told, Quentin really couldn't. What did a sheltered girl like Caroline "see" in a quaint town in the mountains?

"Oh, no, I don't think you can." She batted her eyes in a most appealing—and practiced—way. "Most people just look at me and think, 'Why, that Caroline Harlow doesn't have a care in the world.' But I do! I do have a care! And I think about things, too."

He bit his lip to keep from smiling. "Is that right?"

"Oh, yes. Last year, when I was attending Miss Peabody's Finishing School for Young Ladies in Denver, I saw quite a large number of people down on their luck."

"And—?"

"And, I didn't treat them with disrespect, no sir."

"Commendable."

"Our class held a bake sale to help the poor. I made two pies." Tilting her head up slyly, she said, "I bet that might come as a surprise to most people—that I know how to cook and all."

She certainly wasn't shy about declaring her attributes.

"You'll serve many a fine meal during your lifetime, I reckon."

Caroline nodded. "And I care about these quilts. I'm almost a good seamstress. Oh, nothing like Mrs. Bond, but close." She prattled on. "I know it gets chilly out here in the winter. Why, take tonight . . ." She shivered becomingly, batted her lashes with an ingénue's practiced grace, and paused.

Quentin was enough of a gentleman to know that he'd just been neatly led to the next step in their courtin', like a horse to water. And, being rather smart himself, he placed a comforting, warm arm across the girl's shoulders.

Caroline smiled in satisfaction. As she cuddled closer, the faint scent of gardenias floated upward. Quentin tried hard to pretend that the feminine fragrance did nothing to him. But, truth to tell, he did miss the allure of a clean woman and all of her feminine attributes.

Those things were hard to find on the hard trails of west Texas, and even more difficult in the mountains of Colorado.

"Yes, our sewing circle is going to have quite a collection of quilts to pass out."

He struggled to think of something to say to that. "Who's in your group?"

"Myself and Mother. Mrs. Nash and Chrissy. Mrs. Armstrong and Bellows. Oh, and Jasmine Fairchild, too."

And Jasmine Fairchild.

Even her name made Quentin think things he shouldn't. Generous breasts. Hips that could cradle a man in comfort. A backside he'd dreamed about. All covering a girl who hadn't quite realized she was a desirable woman. "Jasmine."

"Yes." Caroline's lips pursed. "I'm not one to make anyone feel bad, but I personally thought it was rude for Jasmine to push her way into our company."

"She pushed, did she?" Quentin struggled to keep his voice even and neutral. He hated to hear Caroline disparage Jasmine. Especially since his feelings for that bar girl were erupting at an alarming speed.

Emotions that he hadn't felt since he was courting Becky.

He cared for Jasmine. Very much.

"Close enough. One day she just appeared out of the blue, sewing like a demon."

"I reckon that's good—for the poor and all."

"Oh, yes." Caroline's voice drifted off. "It's just . . . well, she once was one of those people."

"The needy?"

"Indeed. I'm not exactly sure if it's proper that she should be working on this project."

"Who better? I mean, we're all supposed to help ourselves, or so I've been led to believe."

"But charity . . ." She shook her head. "Oh, never mind. I certainly don't want to spend my valuable time with you talking about another woman!"

He was in full agreement. "There are far better topics of conversation. What's new with your family?"

Caroline's mouth formed a sweet O, then, agreeable as ever, she launched into her family's past twenty-four hours in minute detail. Quentin stifled a yawn.

Somehow, the meeting with the Baxter Gang with only a widow-maker didn't seem like it had been all that bad, after all. "I better take you on home. Your mama is gonna worry about you."

She wrapped her hands securely around his forearm. "Oh, you silly. She won't worry. Mother knows I'm with you. Nothing can happen when you're around."

For a moment, Quentin wondered exactly how Caroline thought of him. As a father figure? A mere friend? Lord knew, he'd done things to Becky in mere minutes that would make any mother stand up and take notice.

Not that he had any thoughts about Caroline in that way. "In any case, it isn't seemly to have you out so late."

In the distance, Quentin could hear Jeremy on the piano, as well as raucous laughter in the Dark Horse. The doors opened and shut, and two cowboys wandered out.

Quentin pulled Caroline back into the shadows, deeply regretting their path. All he needed was one of the men to spy her blond hair, neatly curled into a cascade of ringlets and tied up in blue ribbons, and decide to get better acquainted. "Let's turn here, Miss Harlow. Like I said, you shouldn't be around here at night."

She craned her neck. "What does go on in all these saloons at night, anyway?"

"Drinking. Poker."

"My mother says such things are unseemly."

"Your mother is right."

"Hmph." Leaning closer, she whispered, "My pa has gone to the Dark Horse a time or two."

Or three or forty-five. "That's your father's business, not mine."

"I heard Mama yelling at him for losing too much money. But Daddy said he had to do it. That he has no choice. That doesn't make much sense, Captain, now, does it?"

"I couldn't say."

They walked back, and Quentin could honestly say his leg was hurting him like the devil. Maybe it was the exercise. Maybe it was the damp wind that seeped through the fabric of his trousers, making him wish for warmer climates.

Or maybe it was the company. There was only so much prattle a man could take, even if the prattler was beautiful.

CHAPTER 11

"He's late again."

Jasmine looked up from the table she was wiping. Constance stood before her, frowning, and looking madder than her pa after he'd lost all his paycheck. Treading carefully, she said, "Who are you talking about?"

"Sam Greene," she said, giving her auburn hair a small shake. Constance really did have beautiful hair. Falling to mid-back, it seemed to have a life all its own as she stepped in between the tables. More than one customer had praised her looks, although Constance didn't seem to care.

For almost a year, she'd only had eyes for one lanky cowboy, although Jasmine privately thought that Sam had plenty of eyes for everyone else.

"He told me he'd stop by around nine or ten," Constance continued. "It's almost eleven o'clock."

"I don't know what you see in him." Sam wasn't much of a prize, in Jasmine's opinion. Though he did own a small ranch, there were rumors that he'd headed west instead of fighting in the war, and that he wasn't above cheating his workers. Neither trait appealed to Jasmine. In her opinion, people needed to pick something to believe in and stick with it.

"He's handsome as sin! What more would I want?"

What more, indeed? Sam, for all his faults, was indeed handsome. "That's true. It's also a fact that he's married."

"I know." Constance sighed. "I don't know why I like him so

much." Winking, she added, "Though, lately we've had a lot to talk about, Sam, Emmitt McKade, and me."

Jasmine struggled to keep a telltale red stain from crawling across her features. Contrary to what she'd admitted to Quentin, for months, Emmitt had been flirting with her. She hadn't been doing much flirting back; there was something about him that seemed more than a little shifty. Like he was hiding a good joke.

She'd told Emmitt that she didn't have time for him, or any man.

Of course, now Jasmine knew that wasn't true. From dawn till dusk, her every thought seemed to center on Captain Quentin Smith.

Constance continued. "Yes sirree, Emmitt seems to be completely curious about Captain Smith."

Completely curious? Jasmine hadn't thought Constance had such a good vocabulary. "I wonder why."

"I don't know, but Sam sure doesn't care for him much. About a month ago, he came into the saloon all scuffed up, and tense and nervous. He got real crazy-like when the captain showed up, too. Now, he's playing hard at the tables, talks trash, and just glares at the man."

"Sam's going to get you into trouble. Maybe you ought to stay away from him."

"I would, 'cept when he's not all mean, he's mighty sweet to me."

"What about your reputation?"

"Reputation? Jasmine, honey, I don't know what you think you do, but I work in a saloon, darlin'. My reputation went and left me about six years ago," she confided with a wink.

What Constance said was true. No matter who she tried to be, she was never going to escape what she was: a gal born to the wrong people in the wrong place—if a person was trying to better herself.

Saloons didn't count for much in the way of respectability.

Jasmine wished Constance wanted more for herself than an affair with a married man. Though, why in the world Jasmine cared was truly a mystery. She'd seen enough of the world to know that sometimes things like marriage and fidelity meant nothing.

Life was hard enough without having to conform to the rules of a society that had never especially welcomed her.

"Well, I'll let you know if Sam comes in," Jasmine said before they both squeezed their way through another throng of cowboys on their way to the bar. Yep, Nash had to be pleased as punch. The Dark Horse was filled to capacity.

Several cowboys whooped it up as a particularly boisterous gent won big. "Looky here, Jasmine!" the winner called out as she approached.

Jasmine winked as she passed.

Constance frowned in his direction. "That Kurt. If he'd ever settle down, he'd make a real fine husband."

"Kurt comes in here every payday and plays the cards deep," Jasmine proclaimed. "He'd make a horrible husband!"

"Yeah, but he'd be awful pretty to look at while he was treating me bad."

Jasmine couldn't help but giggle at the outrageous remark. Kurt's antics, and Constance's eager eyes, gave her plenty to think about during the next two hours. Near two in the morning, Nash announced last call. One by one the cowboys filtered out.

"I wonder why Sam didn't show," Constance said after they finished wiping down the last of the tables and brought the final round of glasses to the kitchen to be washed.

"No telling."

"I suppose." With a sigh, she gave Jasmine a little wave. "Well, see you," she said before slipping out the back door.

Constance lived with her mother in a tiny house near the edge of town. Though it was far from a shanty, it was modest by anyone's account. As Jasmine heard Constance's laughter echo through the thin walls of the building, she wondered if Sam had finally arrived.

If he had, she wouldn't be going home at all.

"You're going to rub a hole in my copper bar top," Nash murmured.

"Mr. Bond. Sorry." Shaking her head, she said, "I guess my mind went wandering."

"Everything all right?"

"Oh, sure."

A dimple appeared in his cheek. "We had a good crowd in here, didn't we? Wish business was this good every night."

The tables had been full, and the men had been in a giving mood. Jasmine couldn't be sure, but she thought she probably had almost four dollars in tips in the pouch tied to her waist. "It was a good night, though I don't know if my feet could take it every evening. Those cowboys about wore me out."

"They tipping?"

She smiled. "Yep. It was worth it." Thinking of how that money would come in handy in her savings, she rubbed the bar some more.

"Put that rag down and get on home, Jasmine. If you stay much longer, Madeleine's going to give me grief for making you work so hard."

Jasmine glanced at her boss in surprise. "You think she's still awake?"

He chuckled. "Lord, no. Madeleine sleeps like the dead, especially now that she's in the family way." Leaning forward, he plucked the rag out of her right hand. " 'Course, don't get me started on how she wakes up."

"Not so good?"

"Not even a little bit. When she's not green, she's frowning at me something terrible."

"Oh, my."

Nash reached over to the peg by the door and retrieved her wool shawl. "I don't mind, though. I figure it's got to be hard work, growing a baby."

"Yes, sir."

"You'll be all right walking home?"

He asked that every night. With some humor, Jasmine thought that one day she was going to shake her head no, just to see what he would do. "I'll be fine. Good night."

" 'Night. Watch out for that godforsaken wind."

As if on cue, the wind picked up and rattled the side of the saloon. "Lord have mercy," she said, wrapping her shawl around her more tightly. "Makes you almost wish for those hot, still days we were having."

Mr. Bond winked. "Almost. 'Night, Jasmine."

And with that, the door closed behind her and she stepped out into the dark streets.

The boarding house was only five hundred steps away. She'd counted one evening when she was bored. Every so often, Jasmine would count them again, just to see if things had changed.

They never did.

With her head down, she kept to the right side, away from the few men still lingering outside. Although no one had ever given her trouble, she was wise enough to know there was always a first time.

"I don't understand why no one ever walks you home."

Her feet stilled. She'd know that voice anywhere. And that limp. And that scent of cigars and bay rum. "Captain Smith.

You're sure walking a lot for someone who's supposed to be convalescing."

"Quentin. And that's a fact."

"You don't need to walk me. I'll be fine."

"Humor me and let me escort you the rest of the way. I'll sleep better, knowing you're safe inside."

Why was everyone talking about sleep habits all the sudden? Was she the only person left in Cedar Springs who still woke up hourly? "It's only five hundred steps. More like three hundred, now."

"You've counted?"

Embarrassed, she tucked her head down. "I've walked this way a lot," she mumbled.

Quentin curved a hand around her elbow and stepped in closer, bringing with him all kinds of thoughts that she shouldn't be thinking. "I guess so."

"Where were you tonight?" she asked on impulse. Secretly, Jasmine had been keeping an eye out for him in just the way Constance had been searching for Sam.

"Miss me?"

Her pulse quickened as she dared to lie. "No."

He raised an eyebrow. "I paid a call on Miss Harlow, as you know, then I spent some time over at the Red Hen."

The Red Hen was the worst saloon in Cedar Springs. "You don't care for the Dark Horse no more?"

"Here we go again. Nash really needs to pay you more. You're the most faithful employee I've ever met."

"I'm not faithful, just curious." As the words floated to him, Jasmine wished she could take back those words. Not faithful?

Lord.

Quentin released her elbow for a brief moment while he lit a cigar. Then he pulled her closer once again. Jasmine tried to pretend she found comfort from the wind in his grip, but she knew that was yet another lie.

"I like Bond's place fine," he murmured, his voice gravelly and warm near her ear. "I've just got some business to attend to."

He spoke so deliberately, Jasmine knew something was up. All thoughts of romance dissipated like fog on a sunny day. "Business? Captain, are you here in Cedar Springs for more than your leg?"

He took his time in replying. "Maybe, though I'd deny it to anyone but you."

"I heard something tonight. I'd be happy to share it with you if you ever—you know—decide to be here for any reason besides your health."

In an instant, his easy demeanor was replaced by cold calculation. "What did you hear?"

"Sam Greene has been watching you." Briefly she described him. "Constance said he came back here, all beat up and bruised," she added. "She said he was worried, too. Ever since you started staying here, he comes to the Dark Horse every night. I'm afraid he's just using Constance."

"Jasmine, I'm going to need you to find out all you can."

His urgency caught her off guard. "Are you in danger?"

"I'll be fine. But you need to be careful. There might be some things going on at the Dark Horse that are fixing to spiral out of control."

She clung to his comment. "Would you care if something happened to me?" she asked softly, before she could stop herself. Goodness, what was she doing?

But he took her question to be honest-to-goodness concern. "You know I would," he replied, his gaze flicking at her mouth, making her want to lick her lips in answer. "I care for you."

"I care for you, too." Oh! Why had she said that?

But just as she tried to take those words back, the sensation of his lips on hers came rushing back with the force of a runaway locomotive. And just like that, there was nothing she could do to stop the unbidden feelings of desire. Feeling altogether too warm, she loosened the shawl and let it slip down to the edge of her shoulders. The fresh breeze skimming her collarbone should have been a welcome relief, but all it did was stir her up.

All of a sudden, Jasmine didn't care why Quentin Smith came to Cedar Springs. Why he visited the Red Hen. Why he'd gone walking with Caroline Harlow mere hours before.

All she cared about was that he was with her.

He tossed his cigar on the ground, ran a finger along the worn fabric of her sleeve. His touch along the inside of her elbow felt as silky as his voice. "If things were different, I'd ask you to come to my room one night."

Jasmine struggled to keep her voice light and crisp. But it was hard, because her insides were melting. "Your room?"

"My room. I want to be alone with you. Someplace where our every move isn't observed by a dozen people." He continued to brush his fingertips along her arm. "I know you're not the kind of woman who would do that. I'm trying not to be the kind of man who would ask you to. I just . . . wanted you to know."

Yes! Her mind called out. *I want to be that way with you, too!*

But she didn't dare voice the words. He was currently walking out with Caroline.

And it was painfully obvious that Quentin wasn't thinking about love or marriage. He wasn't talking about a relationship with orange blossoms. No, he was thinking more along the lines of a sexual relationship.

And so far—at least not yet—she wasn't that kind of woman. Well, at least her head wasn't. The rest of her body was already preparing itself for his kisses. His touch.

Valiantly, she tried to be the kind of woman she wished she

was. "I'm not like Constance."

Very carefully, his thumb slid down her forearm. Skimmed her wrist. Brushed the inside of her palm. Ripples of desire skipped through her bones as if lightning had struck.

"Right now I wouldn't care if you were."

"I would," she said, only halfway telling the truth. "I've always wanted more for myself." Respectability was too hard won to be given up easily.

Something akin to pity flashed in his eyes. "Jasmine, I've been all around this country. Seen a lot of people. Fought next to planters' sons and farmers' fathers. There are some people who are never going to see things except the way they want to see them. Those things can't be changed."

Lowering his voice, he added, "Some people are never going to think you're respectable, because when they first knew you, they didn't think you were."

"Just like you'll always be a ranger to the people who read about you in dime novels?"

He shrugged. "I suppose."

"I may not be Quentin Smith, but even I care how people think of me."

The corners of his mouth tilted up, almost in triumph. "Maybe we ought to investigate what is between us. See how things do go."

No, that wasn't what she was thinking. Not by a long shot. In fact, that wasn't what she had meant at all. "But—"

He cut her off. "All friendships don't have to be more than we want them to be. Ours can be private and close."

Close? Huh? What was he talking about?

And then, it didn't matter, because just like that, Quentin pulled her into an alleyway and tucked her firmly against him, like a new blanket.

And just as she was about to protest his actions . . . all the while trying to deposit in her memory every single wonderful sensation about being next to his body in such a way . . . he went ahead and kissed her.

In the shadows of the bank.

Right there on her lips. The feel of his lips was perfection. Firm, dry, tender . . . skilled. It seemed only natural to raise her arms and hold his neck a little closer.

It seemed only right to rub her hips against his when he caressed her back, when his thumbs curved around the underside of her breasts. She melted close to him, felt as if everything was right in the world all of a sudden.

And then, just as quickly . . .

It wasn't.

Quentin pulled away, leaving an emotional gap between them as big as Texas. "We shouldn't be doing this here," he whispered. "Someone could see us. Someone would think . . ." His voice drifted off as he swallowed his next few words. Pulling her back into the street, he added, "We'll talk more about things tomorrow."

What would they say? Communication didn't seem to be their strong point. Didn't seem to make a lick of difference.

But still, his promise sounded like an offer. Of what, she didn't know. But it was enough of a tease to make her do more things she knew she'd regret in the middle of the night when the stars came out to keep her worries company. All she knew was that something had been exchanged between them that was more meaningful than slow caresses or deep kisses.

And she wanted to have a chance to figure out what it was. So, like the witless girl so many people thought she was, Jasmine nodded. "Tomorrow," she said, then tore off down the street into the welcoming light of the boarding house, where—until very recently—everything she held dear had been located.

CHAPTER 12

The next day brought more changes to the weather. The sky grew darker, the wind kept a constant vigil, and into the air crept the tingly scent of impending snow.

The approaching weather had everyone in Cedar Springs energized. People smiled more, children grew restless, and so many people came to town to load up on supplies that the rickety clank of wagons parading down Main Street became commonplace.

In the midst of it all, over at the Dark Horse, Constance prattled on and on to Jasmine about Sam Greene.

Jasmine would have been supportive of Constance's new love except for the fact that she didn't like him.

She'd just been about to take a break for a late dinner, when Sam had pulled her over for a private conversation. "Heard you're special friends with the captain," he said, his voice low and laced with innuendo.

The muscles in her stomach tightened. What had he seen? Had he spied on her and Quentin in the alley, doing more than they should? But then, just as she was about to get all fidgety, good sense kicked in.

As did her protective instincts. Something wasn't right about Sam. His gaze was a little too squirrelly. The man was a first-class weasel and she had no desire to be his prey.

Thinking back to Quentin's words about there being more to his being in Cedar Springs than recuperation, Jasmine decided to do a little investigating. "I know him," she stated, making sure her tone sounded as if there was a whole lot she was keeping to herself.

"How well?"

"As well as some, better than others."

"Well enough to know why, exactly, he's in Cedar Springs?"

Jasmine was really proud of how easily she could lie to protect those she loved. The realization caught her up short. *Loved?* "He's recuperating."

Sam drummed his fingers on the table. "I don't believe that for a second. I think he's here on business."

"Business?"

"I have a feeling he's here because of the—"

"Sam! You're here!" Constance cried out, neatly cutting off his words while her wiles kicked in. Draping an arm around Sam's shoulder, she moved in, right onto his lap.

"You're interruptin'. Jasmine and I were having a real fine conversation about Smith."

Constance darted a suspicious glance toward Jasmine but said nothing.

"Now, like I was saying—" Sam's fingers brushed Constance's arm, but his eyes never strayed from Jasmine's. "I'm doing some work for someone in town. Someone important. He cares a lot about why the captain is here. Do me a favor and find out why Smith is really in Cedar Springs."

Jasmine had no desire to either spy on Quentin or to report to Sam. "I don't know why you'd think—"

"I've seen the way he looks at you. He wants you bad, if he hasn't had you already."

Was her face as red as it felt? "I . . . we've never—"

"Come on, sugar. Other people might pretend they don't know where you came from, but I grew up next to you in the shanties," Sam said with a knowing grin. "I know what women did for money." He held up a hand when she tried to protest. "And I know what the girls do when they're not serving drinks." He leered at Constance, whose smile turned brittle.

Jasmine's heart went out to Constance. Though they'd never claimed a close friendship, Jasmine knew that beneath Constance's rouge and hard ways, she was looking for love and companionship—for a future—just as much as Caroline Harlow was.

Sam's total disregard for her feelings must have hurt deep.

Thinking back to what Quentin had said the night before, both about his business, and about people's minds, Jasmine knew she had no choice but to pretend to agree with Sam's assumptions. "I'll do what I can."

Sam smiled. "Good girl. Come find me when you know something."

With a nod, Jasmine turned away. Now she knew she was gonna have to see Quentin alone again. She just hoped she'd be able to keep her hands off of him long enough to concentrate on what she was going to say.

Snow came and went, bringing with it a white coating that disappeared almost as quickly as it came. During all that time, Jasmine was still fretting about what to do about Captain Smith and Sam and the way she couldn't help but daydream about Quentin when she spied George sitting on the steps of the stage—almost the same exact spot where they'd perched a lifetime ago when the ranger had come to town.

Happily, she joined him. It was so nice to be with her one true friend. She needed to be around someone who wasn't asking her to sew or looking down on her because she worked in a saloon.

Actually, she was just real happy to be with someone who she wasn't thinking about kissing every moment.

The faint glow of waning sunlight warmed her skirts. Though Colorado got its fair share of sunlight all year long, she knew her days of sitting in the twilight without a scarf and mittens were numbered. Winter was well on its way.

George was whittling as usual. "I do love snow," he said by way of greeting, almost like he read her mind.

"We haven't had a real snow yet."

"Oh, we will. Butch said they had a good three feet of it in Montana Territory." He waggled his eyebrows. "And you know what they say about that."

"What? That weather hundreds of miles from here is on the way?"

A sliver of wood flew in her direction. "Maybe," he said with a smile.

Jasmine brushed off her skirts. "I'm sure glad we don't live in Montana. That much snow would be too much, too soon, for me."

"I don't know. Things look right pretty caked in white powder."

His words, spoken so poetically, made Jasmine glance at him in surprise. "How's everything with Chrissy?"

His knife's glide down the soft wood slowed. "Not so good."

"Why is that? Last I heard, you two had almost a future planned together."

George frowned. "Can you keep a secret?"

This seemed to be her week for them. "Of course." When George still looked doubtful, Jasmine crossed her heart.

"I bought a ring."

"That's a real good thing."

"And I practiced what I was gonna say. But then . . . oh, I don't know." He bent to his stick and gave it a few good swipes. The soft wood curled like a potato skin, then flew onto the worn floorboards.

Jasmine wasn't sure what the problem was. "Are you worried about what Chrissy is gonna say? 'Cause you know she's going to say yes."

"What if she does?"

George had said the words so quickly, Jasmine was sure she'd heard him wrong. "Say again?"

He sighed. "What if Chrissy *does* say yes?"

She didn't understand. "George, I may be none too smart, but even I can figure out that if she says yes, you'll be the happiest man in the world." When he didn't break into a smile, she prodded. "Right?"

"I don't know. Suddenly, I'm wondering what's going to happen if my girl regrets marrying me."

Jasmine had known George a long time, and she remembered the time when he was fourteen and asked Mary Ellen Neely to the church social. She said yes, and they'd had a terrible time. All Mary Ellen had wanted to talk about was her pet goat.

"Like if you're married, and all of a sudden Chrissy decides you aren't the one for her?"

"Like that."

"I don't know." Jasmine watched another curl form under George's knife while she pondered his predicament. Time and again, life had held surprises for her. Her job at the Dark Horse had proven that. She'd been born afraid, but she was even more afraid of her current situation. If she hadn't learned to dream, Jasmine was sure that her life would never have got so good.

"You know my mama died when I was little," she said.

"I do."

"My daddy never did want me around."

"Jaz, I wouldn't say—"

"We know it's true. He was never one to hide his feelings, George."

"Ethan Fairchild was never what you'd call a doting father."

She laughed at the description. No, Ethan Fairchild hadn't doted on anything unless it was forty proof. "George, I guess I'm thinkin' that even though my circumstances weren't the best, something good came out of it. I was lucky enough to be born in this town, and to have you as a friend. Maybe that's enough."

George screwed up his face as he twisted his stick this way and that, finally setting it down between them. "Jasmine. Was there a point to your prattling?"

"Just that I think you ought to propose to Chrissy and be quick about it. You never know what the future will hold."

"That's mighty serious."

She laughed. "No. Just truthful."

"Hmph."

The sun sank lower, removing all vestiges of warmth. The cool wind seemed eager to take advantage of the fading sunlight and blew a little harder. Jasmine tucked her legs underneath her skirt and thought about getting up.

"Working tonight?" George asked.

"Of course."

"You know, sitting here, thinking about Chrissy and all, makes me think that you don't have nobody special."

Did it count that she already had a special man in mind . . . only that he didn't think the same way about her?

Except in ways that had nothing to do with marriage?

Trying not to let on just how much George's comment affected her, Jasmine attempted to tease. "I appreciate the reminder."

"Listen. There's lots of men in Cedar Springs."

And she'd served just about every one of them. "You're right about that."

Leaning forward, he whispered, "Perhaps you ought to take a second look at some of them."

"Don't go playing matchmaker."

"Everybody needs somebody."

That was the problem. Quentin Smith made her need things and hope for a future that she knew she should have no business contemplatin'. His kisses the other night had made her want to give herself to him, right there in the alleyway, regardless of what the future held for either of them.

Which was a far cry from George's predicament. Here he was, with a bright future, and still he worried. She had nothing, and had come from even less, and she still had to force herself to remember that every choice she made came with a price. She couldn't afford to forget that.

Or to reveal so much, even to her best friend.

Once again, she tried to lighten the conversation. "Just because you're going to go get hitched don't mean it's time for me to do that, too."

"You've been single a long time."

Forever. "I've always been single, silly."

"I've heard more than one man say you carry a fine figure."

As the heat cascaded along her cheeks, Jasmine tucked her head near her chin. If George was too deep in his Chrissy-world to look at the facts, Jasmine was reluctant to set him straight. Men might look at her figure. They might talk about it. They might even try to get up close and personal with it.

But never had she known a man to think of her—or her figure—as marriage material.

Not even Quentin Smith, and he was the most honorable man she knew.

"Emmitt's always fancied you, you know that."

"I do know that. It's just that for some reason I don't think we'd suit."

"Sometimes that don't matter."

"That's easy for you to say. You have Chrissy, and she fits you like a glove."

His eyes got all dreamy, which would have been something to see if a call hadn't reverberated through the air like a screech from a barn owl.

"George!"

Jasmine started. Chrissy's voice when she was on a tear was earsplitting.

George stood up faster than a prairie dog in mating season. "Over here, Chrissy!" Panicked, he turned to Jasmine.

"Do it now, while no one's around. Go pull her into an alley or a thicket of trees and propose."

"An alley? Don't you suppose that's kind of bad? I was thinking of kneeling in front of her in front of her couch, like I heard about real gentlemen doing."

Chrissy was fast approaching, looking none too happy. Actually, there was something in her eyes that looked a little put out and off-kilter.

"You better do it now, George," Jasmine said in a rush. "Chrissy looks likes she's tired of waiting."

George stepped down two steps, neatly sheathing his whittling knife as he did so. "Chrissy, honey, were your ears ringing?"

Her steps faltered. "Why?"

"Jasmine and I were just sitting here talking about you, that's all."

Jasmine felt like sinking into a hole. Even she knew no woman liked to be told she was the topic of conversation with another woman! "Shh," she whispered. "Don't say anything about all that. She's not going to want to know."

But, of course, Chrissy heard that. "Know what? What's the secret?"

"There's no secret."

Her eyes narrowed. "Jasmine Fairchild, don't you think you're around enough men already at the Dark Horse? Can't you leave mine alone?"

George stepped to his right, effectively shielding Jasmine from Chrissy's words. But it was too late. Jasmine felt as if once again she'd gone two steps backward. "Chrissy, you know that George and I are merely good friends."

"For well on ten years," George pointed out.

"Maybe too good." Setting her hands on her hips, Chrissy said, "I want to know what you two were talking about."

George pulled himself up to his full six feet and sent her a stare that brooked no discussion. "I don't believe I care for your tone, Chrissy."

"Jasmine?"

Jasmine knew she had to be the peacemaker; there was no way George could afford for things to go south now. "Umm. Well . . ."

George, blast his darn mouth, spoke again. "It's confidential."

Chrissy narrowed her eyes. "George, so help me, if you don't—"

"Don't what? What will you do?"

Jasmine stepped to the right and interrupted quickly. "Chrissy, all we were talking about was—"

"Don't say another word, Jasmine." Walking down the last step, George stood in front of Chrissy, her nose level with his chin. "I was talking to Jasmine about how to propose to you, if you want to know the truth. I had thought that it was time I made an honest woman out of you."

Honest woman? Jasmine winced. It was really time to knock him upside the head—anything to bang some sense into him. Men just didn't say things like that to the women they wanted to marry.

Digging deep, she opened her mouth to tell George that, but

closed it once again as she got a good, long look at Chrissy.

Spit and fire turned to wonder as the blond stared right back at him. "George?"

"But now I'm having second thoughts," he said, completely oblivious to the fact that Chrissy had tears of happiness shining in her eyes.

Jasmine grunted a warning.

George didn't pay her no mind. "Come to think of it, I don't think I'm ready to be chained down to a woman who is so eager to presume the worst of me. And my friends. What has Jasmine ever done to you, anyway?"

Chrissy turned to Jasmine, her cheeks ghostly pale. "Nothing. I'm sorry. You know I have a temper. I didn't mean a thing."

The real George seemed to have left, because the new one was currently unrecognizable. "That's one piss-poor apology, Chrissy."

Jasmine groaned.

Chrissy looked worse off than a turkey on Thanksgiving. "So you're not going to ask me now?"

"Nope."

Oh, God almighty! With a purposeful stride, Jasmine sidled past the two of them. "I think I'd best be going."

"I'll walk you back," George murmured.

Jasmine glanced down the street. Chrissy's commotion was causing a big enough scene to attract more than one eager bystander. Heavens to Betsy. Now the whole town would blame her for George and Chrissy's separation.

Obviously, just when she dared to think that things couldn't get any worse, they did. "Please don't. I'll be fine."

"But I can't just let you walk away," George protested.

"I am sorry, Jasmine," Chrissy said. "You know I've always liked you. I . . . I just don't know what has gotten into me."

Jasmine was pretty sure jealousy had gotten into Chrissy, and gotten her good. And Jasmine couldn't even really blame her too much. She'd felt so riled up, just thinking about Quentin touching Caroline Harlow's hand, that she'd wanted to do both of them a good bit of harm.

Without another word, Jasmine stepped off the platform and walked past them. She was tired. Too tired to argue, too tired for company.

And for the first time since she could remember, too tired to work. Completely aware of the curious glances darting her way, Jasmine strode to the Dark Horse and searched for Mr. Bond.

"Jasmine, you feeling all right?" he asked after she found him in his office sitting across from Quentin Smith.

Doing her best to ignore the ranger's piercing gaze, she spoke. "Mr. Bond, I'm real sorry, but I'm going to need the night off tonight. May I take it off, please?"

He stood up, concerned. "Of course you can."

His concerned expression was just about her undoing. "I know it's late notice."

"You've worked for me for two years. This is the first time you couldn't come in. I don't mind."

Then Nash Bond did about the worst thing that Jasmine could imagine. He stepped right forward and took her hand. "You all right? Do you need a doctor or something?"

His tender question made the tears fall.

"I'll be fine. It's just—" She thought quickly. "A headache or some such nonsense. Thank you Mr. Bond."

Quentin stood up, as well. "It's dark. I'll walk you back."

Why in the world did every man in town suddenly want to walk her places?

And why did her insides turn to mush every time she was even near Quentin Smith? Already, her mouth had gone dry in anticipation of another kiss.

Oh, it didn't matter if he was only offering friendship. She wanted so much more from him . . . and she was afraid she'd take every bit he offered. "I'll be fine."

Clearing her throat, she whispered, "I'll be in tomorrow extra early, Mr. Bond."

Though her boss looked like he had plenty to say, he merely nodded.

And the moment Jasmine unlocked the door to her room and flung herself on the bed, she knew for a fact that she'd been completely, utterly right when she'd told George that there was no telling what the future had in store.

Take this evening, for instance. Just when she thought things could only get better, they took a miserable, stinking turn for the worse.

CHAPTER 13

Chrissy looked at herself one way in the mirror, turned smartly, then examined her reflection over the other shoulder.

What she saw was no surprise.

Same blond hair that was too curly peeked back at her. Same blue eyes, still a shade too light for her tastes. Twenty-three freckles still sprinkled her nose.

Yep, she looked the same as she always did on the outside.

So why in the world did she feel so confused inside? A mess of emotions—anger, jealousy, doubt, fear—all had settled deep inside her and were doing their best to cause her pain.

Just as she knew what ailed her, Chrissy knew what remedy would cure her as well. A proposal.

Yep, George needed to get off his high horse and finally propose.

Most folks wouldn't think that an imminent marriage proposal could bring so much stress to a girl. But, it did. It was making her go crazy. And say mean things.

And shame her, too.

Like what she'd said to Jasmine today. Jasmine, who'd never asked for anything and who'd been George's best friend forever, and had only ever tried her best to make George see how Cedar Springs' new schoolteacher would make a very fine wife.

Chrissy checked her matching blue ribbons in her hair, then turned to finish cleaning up her little home. The school board had provided the place as part of her salary. Chrissy had been greatly pleased not to have had to room in one of her children's homes, like so many teachers in the territory were having to do.

Finding nothing else to occupy her hands, Chrissy slumped against the hard wood of her kitchen chair and fretted some more. Oh, there had to be some way she could make everything up to Jasmine. Some way to make her see that Chrissy was real pleased to have her as a friend.

Some way to get George to propose soon.

The dream had come again. Quentin sat up in bed and breathed deeply, doing his best to ignore the rush of anxiety coursing through him, the ringing in his ears.

With each slow and steady breath, the room came further into focus, and with it, his reality. He was in his room at the Dark Horse, not in his bed in Texas. It was late fall, not the middle of summer.

He was alone.

Becky wasn't bleeding by his side. He glanced at the sheets again, just to make sure, recalling how stained they'd been.

How reluctant to burn them he'd been.

Knowing sleep was no longer an option, he climbed out of bed, cursing his stiff joints and muscles. Though it did him no good to think on things he couldn't undo, Quentin couldn't help but contrast the multiple maladies he had today with his former self.

There'd been many a night during the war when he'd slept on the hard ground; several nights spent in trees. Once he'd fallen asleep on the banks of a creek and had woken up with a snake curled next to him like a kitten.

Funny, but he seemed to recall that he'd moved just fine back then.

Out of habit, he strode to the window and looked out, checking his timepiece next to the bed as he did. Three a.m. Below him, the Dark Horse was still and silent, a direct contrast to how it had been four hours earlier, filled with randy cowboys and more than a few businessmen eager to lose their money.

Quentin had done his best merely to sit by the bar and observe, but more than a few men had approached him, wanting stories about his days as a lawman.

He hadn't obliged. His mind had been on a certain brown-eyed woman who'd looked put out and despondent. Even Nash had commented on it.

"It's not that I mind the gal taking the night off, it's just that I don't understand the reason for it."

Remembering the cause of Becky's infrequent headaches, Quentin shrugged. "It's probably just one of those female things."

Nash glanced toward the stairs to his own room. "Maybe, though I don't know. It just doesn't seem to fit."

Also conspicuously missing was George, who came to visit with Nash like clockwork 'most every night around nine. "It doesn't make sense that George decided to stay home, either," Nash commented. With a scowl, he added, "This sounds pitiful, but I like my life more predictable than this."

Quentin had heard the gossip about what had happened at the stage house. "Maybe he's finally courting Chrissy right tonight."

"Maybe." With a look of relief, Nash slapped his thigh. "That's probably it. Shoot, Lord knows he's waited long enough."

"Probably."

"Now, if Jasmine was here, things would be just fine."

Even to Quentin's untrained eye, he could tell that things weren't the same without her. Jasmine's efficiency and easy smiles were sorely missed as Constance and some other gal kept messing up orders and disappearing with cowboys. Nash grumbled about good help while working the bar at lightning speed.

Even Jeremy seemed a little off, playing a rag-tag assortment of songs from Wild West shows.

When it was obvious that no one was going to be playing deep or confiding in him any more, Quentin took his leave and went up to his room, sure he was destined to spend the evening pacing floorboards. To his surprise, he'd fallen asleep within minutes, only to be bombarded with thoughts of guns, bullets, blood, and grief.

Would things ever change?

Breathing deeply, Quentin laid his head against the window. The cool pane, and the empty street below him, calmed his nerves. George's mercantile was dark. The Red Hen down the way lay quiet.

The houses lining the other end of the street stood silent and still.

Just how things should be.

The thought caught him off guard. When had he become such a part of this town, so much a part of it that he knew with a quick glance just how things should be? Since when did he know piano players' names and the romantic nature of complete strangers? It didn't make sense.

He'd do better to keep his mind on why he was in Cedar Springs in the first place. Not to make friends, not to worry about their love lives. He was there to apprehend the Carmichael Gang's backer. Bring whoever was responsible for the seven murders outside of Nebraska to justice. To do a job for the Kansas Pacific. To—

A movement on the street below caught his eye. Shadows transformed into solid images, disturbing by their stealth. As two men on horseback came into view, their clothing dark and their faces nearly covered, Quentin knew it had to mean one thing. The bank was about to be robbed.

And he, being the only person in the whole damned town who was awake, was going to have to deal with it.

After slipping on his shirt and denims, he fastened the buttons then pulled out his holster, automatically checking for ammunition as he did so.

He spied the two men through the pane again, the full moon aiding his vision. For a brief moment, he'd hoped they might be part of the Carmichael Gang, riding in to make his life easy.

But as they tied their horses and whispered to each other a little too loudly, Quentin knew they were a far cry from professional criminals. By the looks of them so far, these boys were too anxious and too young.

After much arguing, the blond, lanky one picked up a rock and broke the door's glass pane, the shatter reverberating through the dark night and settling any reservations Quentin had about getting involved.

Well, shit.

Quentin slipped on his boots and hustled downstairs.

CHAPTER 14

There seemed no point in dilly-dallying. With concise movements, Quentin fastened his holster then strode down the stairs as quickly as he dared without causing enough of a racket to wake up the dead . . . or Mrs. Bond.

In two minutes, he was out of the saloon and making his way over the ruts in the street, his heart slowing as he approached the bank.

It was almost a relief to be facing armed robbers, and amateur ones at that. This he knew how to deal with. This was far easier to control than his wayward emotions or his raging dreams.

As he'd done a thousand times before, Quentin pulled out his Colt, cocked it, and approached the pair who were currently scrambling through the shattered glass.

Honestly, could he have found a stupider pair? Didn't they know that the safe was likely to be fashioned with thick walls of steel, practically impenetrable without a healthy supply of dynamite?

Eager to get things over with, Quentin made sure he stepped firmly on the spray of broken glass, the noise crackling under his boots. The crunch broke the night's silence like a bull gone wild. "Evenin'," he drawled.

Both men stilled and turned around. One, the pale blond, even made a motion to reach for his gun. Quentin fired off a shot, taking care to narrowly miss the kid's fingers.

As expected, the gun dropped.

Experience had taught Quentin to speak plainly and get right to the point. "You boys picked the wrong town to do this in. Put your weapons down."

Panicked, the other man—the dark-haired one—started shaking. Well, that was worrisome. In Quentin's experience, the more shook up the criminal, the more likely he was to do something stupid, like shoot him.

"You don't want to raise your gun to me," Quentin said evenly.

"Why's that?" The younger kid had practically spat out his question, his teeth were chattering so much.

"Because if you pull the trigger I'll be forced to kill you."

The dark one's hand trembled like the back end of a rattler. "Who are you?"

For the first time in a long while, Quentin had no problem capitalizing on his name. "I'm Quentin Smith."

The boy's hand went lax, causing the gun to fall. Quentin held his breath as he watched it drop. There was no telling how it would land.

Yet, the blond only twisted, making a move to pull out another weapon from the small of his back.

Having no desire to kill any tenderfoot, Quentin tried again. "I only shoot to kill. Surely you have someone to cry over your grave? Now, I want you to listen to me. Remove that other weapon from your body and place it nice and slow on the ground."

Maybe it was his plain speaking. Maybe it was the sight of Quentin's own gun—finely oiled and well used—that did it. No matter what convinced him, the blond followed his directions to the letter just as Clemmons joined the fray.

"What's going on?" Clemmons asked, visibly annoyed.

Quentin shrugged, his patience at its end. "These two decided to get rich quick."

As Clemmons took in the pair, he pulled out a worn pair of handcuffs and shackled each one with little flair. "Well now, boys, it looks like we're going to get to spend a little time together over at the jailhouse. I don't mind telling you that before long you're going to wish you were anywhere else. Mrs. Clemmons is not going to be real happy that I'm gonna be away so much, seeing as how we have three daughters at home, all under the age of four."

He paused as he jerked them to the door. "Do you know what that means?"

One dared to shake his head.

"It means that on a good night I get no sleep. Dammit to hell." Clemmons paused in front of the shattered pane before exiting. "Smith, is saying thank you enough?"

Quentin nodded.

"Thank you." Clearing his throat, Clemmons added, "Harlow's light was on when I scrambled down here. You're fixin' to get some more company."

"That's fine." Seeing as how more than a dozen people were standing around the bank building, gawking in their nightwear, Quentin took a seat. He wasn't about to leave just yet.

As if on cue, Harlow entered just as Clemmons and the boys were crossing the street. After a few words to the sheriff, Harlow stomped in, barely giving the crowd more than a fierce glance.

"Clemmons tells me you saved the bank," he said to Quentin.

That was putting it kind of strong. "It's more like I stopped a pair of piss-poor robbers from getting very far."

"I'm much obliged."

The man's voice held a mixture of doubt and awe. Was there a touch of anxiety, too? Was he worried about Quentin getting too close? Finding out things he shouldn't? "It wasn't no big deal," Quentin replied. "I just happened to be up and looking out the window."

"I know of more than one man who would say the robbery was none of his business and turn away. Not want to get involved."

"I'm not that kind of man."

Watery eyes blinked twice as a thin band of sweat formed on the banker's brow. "No. No, you're not." Harlow pulled out a hand. "I owe you my thanks. You did this town and me a great service. I guess your reputation is justified."

Again, Quentin sensed a double meaning. Harlow's tone was at odds with his words of praise. The combination was peculiar and disturbing.

People were generally too open to care what a stranger saw . . . as long as he was willing to lend a hand. Harlow's guarded manner made Quentin wonder once again if he was the Carmichaels' backer.

But there was nothing to do at the moment. It was late, and Quentin had no desire to be the town's hero. Favoring his leg, he struggled to his feet. "Like I said, I was just looking out the window. I'll be going now."

"Wait." Nervously Harlow looked around, as if he was afraid people were spying on them. "It's been no secret that things have been tough lately. I . . . don't know what's been getting into me. Maybe the devil or something. In any case, I'll be the first to say that I've been against you paying attention to my Caroline. Didn't think it right that my lovely girl would want to be attached to an old man like you. And, once a man knows how to kill, I just don't think he can forget about that very easily. Do you?"

Quentin knew if he had a daughter he'd feel the same way. He also knew that Harlow's words did have meaning. It *was* too easy to kill. He wasn't proud that life had taught him the best area to place a bullet, or the easiest way to break a neck.

He could have ended those boys' lives tonight and justified it to everyone. No one would have blamed him, and Harlow would've probably called him a hero. Worst of all, Quentin had a feeling that he might have still been able to sleep, at least until the early hours in the morning when life seemed to catch up with him.

"I *am* old."

Harlow laughed. "Me, too."

"I'm just getting to know Caroline," Quentin explained, once more tempting fate to judge him and his actions. What kind of man would use an innocent young woman to aid him in finding criminals?

Not the kind of man he wanted to be. "I think both Caroline and I have decided that we have no future together."

"I thought that myself, but from what her mother tells me, she likes you real fine. Real fine."

Now Quentin's conscience reminded him of the truth. While it was a fact that he didn't enjoy killing, and that he had saved the bank's cash, he was playing fast and loose with a young girl's affections in a way that his mother would say was positively rakish.

Harlow cleared his throat. "Care to join us for dinner tomorrow?"

No, no Quentin wouldn't. But duty called. There was only one true reason he was in Cedar Springs. To prevent another train robbery, to prevent more killing. That had to remain foremost in his mind.

So, there was only one good answer. He would have to go, and then he was going to need to break things off with the girl.

There had to be another way to get the information he needed. Caroline Harlow was too sweet to be used as bait, especially since it was getting to be obvious that she was woefully ignorant of her father's business or social life. "I'd be much obliged."

"Good. Caroline makes a very good dried peach pie. Afterward, we can smoke a cigar. I'd be pleased to get to know you better."

Quentin nodded. "I'll see you then."

Slowly, Quentin walked back across the street, taking time to flex his stiff muscles. At that very moment he felt as old as dirt and considerably less clean.

What if things had been different? Would he have ever courted Caroline? Was she the type of woman for him?

Yes.

Well, he'd always thought so. Caroline was a little too proper, a little too missish for his tastes, but he did appreciate her innocence and her chatter.

A man would never have to try too hard to be around her. Quentin had the feeling that he could simply nod and grunt and she'd be pleased with him.

So different from Becky's energy and laughter.

So different from Madeleine Bond's scatterbrained antics and jokes.

So different from Jasmine Fairchild's silence.

Now, marriage to Jasmine would be a far different thing. She'd expect things from him. Words, actions.

Love.

Plus, she would need him. She'd need him to help her smile.

As Quentin climbed into bed, feeling every minute of his thirty-five years, he wondered why that mattered to him so much.

CHAPTER 15

The walk with Caroline wasn't going real well. Maybe it was because all Quentin could think about was Jasmine. The last time he'd walked her home, they'd ended up kissing in the alley. She'd felt incredible in his arms. Giving and warm. Plentiful and womanly.

He wanted her in a way he was never going to want Caroline Harlow.

The dinner he'd shared with the Harlows had been awkward, as well. Details from the previous night's attempted robbery had been on all of their minds. Anna Harlow peppered her husband with questions. He fired back a confusing hodgepodge of answers. The sixth sense that had served Quentin well in the fields of Virginia kicked in with a vengeance.

Quentin was now almost certain Al Harlow was the backer of the Carmichael Gang, although he had little hard evidence. There were too many questions about his gambling. Too many secrets he was hiding from his wife.

It should have been a relief to step out into the chilly evening with Caroline, except for the fact that he felt like an old man around her.

And curiously unfaithful to Jasmine.

Yep, he had finally admitted it to himself. He might miss Becky, he might wish he'd been a better man for her, but right now he ached for Jasmine. He longed to be with her. He wanted to kiss her again, undress her in haste, and bury himself in her body. He'd felt that desire so often, he'd been walking around in a half-aroused state, which made him even more uncomfortable in Caroline's presence.

He really was too old for all of this.

Caroline, for her part, was doing her best to pretend that all was right in the world. "Why, I'm sure the snow's going to fall again any day now."

"Um-hum."

"I have a red walking dress that's going to be just the thing to wear on the first snowfall," she said, a little desperately. "It's made out of wool, and has the most becoming trim."

"Hmm." Feeling her hurt glance, Quentin rubbed a hand over his mouth. "Caroline, we need to talk."

"I guess we do. Did you want to discuss our relationship?"

Could anything be anymore painful? "Yes. I . . . Well, you see—"

"You don't feel anything for me, do you?"

The way her eyebrow arched, in that way all women seemed to do with ease, made Quentin think that maybe he'd misjudged her youthful artlessness. Suddenly their age difference didn't feel quite so pronounced. "It's not that. It's . . . I'm not the man for you, Caroline."

"Just days ago it seemed you were going to let me decide that."

Just days ago he'd been denying the truth. Now Quentin knew he was going to have no choice but to pursue Jasmine, just as soon as it was safe to.

"So. Is it Jasmine Fairchild?"

He couldn't say no. "Why do you ask?"

"People have talked." Her cheeks colored. "Someone saw the two of you walking the other night. You two were seen sparking."

She reported her knowledge as if it was a dark secret. Maybe it was? "We were."

"Do you love her?"

"I don't know." Clearing his throat, he said, "I only know that I mustn't lead you on."

Her step faltered, right before she jutted her chin up. "I was just going to tell you the same thing. I aim to be the wife of a *gentleman*, not a lawman. I went to finishing school, you know."

"I know. I think you would be a very fine wife to a man of high caliber." He wasn't lying. Caroline was the type of wife men of means longed for.

She looked as if she wanted to say more, but instead just gripped his elbow a little bit tighter. "Perhaps you should take me home, Captain. It is terribly cold out here."

"I think I should."

As they headed back to her house, Caroline said, "It's strange, isn't it? How things are turning out."

"What do you mean?"

"Here, I thought I wanted a famous ranger, when in truth, I know I need someone far different."

"You just sound smart, Caroline."

She chuckled. "I don't know about that. But," she said with a sigh, "I do know that sometimes peoples' tastes change. I mean, you could have most any woman, and you want Jasmine Fairchild." Before he could interrupt, she added, "And here, I thought my father was the happiest man in Cedar Springs, and all he does is act as if this town that he helped build is just about the worst place in the world."

"That is . . . strange."

"Even more peculiar is Emmitt McKade. He stopped by our home yesterday! My mother hardly knew what to say to such a man. And worse, he seemed to be threatening Daddy!"

"What about?"

"Money. Saying that he wanted more to keep his secrets.

Daddy said it just wasn't possible."

"Did he mention anything else?"

"Not really, only that things would be better soon, when some visitors came riding into town."

"Did he mention any names?"

Caroline met his gaze with wide eyes. "No . . ."

He hastily tried to reassure her. "I'm sorry I snapped at you. It's just that these things sound important."

"I guess they do, though just months ago, my daddy would have said the first snowfall was important, too. Nothing's how it used to be."

They were almost at her house. Panic unfolded inside of him as Quentin realized just how desperate all involved parties had become. "Caroline, you need to be careful. Don't say a word of this conversation to another person. If something happens, stay close to your mother."

Real fear entered her voice. "My mother?"

"She's not going to change, Caroline. I promise. You can count on her." Stopping outside her front door, he tipped his hat. "Go on in now, honey. Stay close to home."

"Good night, Quentin Smith," she said, her voice full of pride, and suddenly, a whole lot more wiser. "And . . . good-bye."

He knew what she meant. "Good-bye, Caroline."

"I went visiting the mining town with Nash yesterday and wrote down a list of names of all the children," Madeleine told Jasmine several evenings later.

Jasmine tried not to feel the pang of embarrassment and concern that ebbed through her at the news. In some ways, living in the shantytown seemed like a lifetime ago, and in other ways, it seemed like just yesterday. "Did you get many names?"

Madeleine looked pleased. "I did. Twenty-eight."

That seemed about right. There were probably a good ten more kids in the camp who would never admit to needing a thing. Pride—as she knew well—could leave a person cold in the dark loneliness of a winter night. "We might need a couple more, for good measure."

"Let's plan for thirty-five, then."

Jasmine liked how Mrs. Bond always took her thoughts seriously. "Thirty-five sounds good. Well, I'd say we've got our work cut out for us."

Mrs. Bond laughed. "No pun intended?"

Jasmine smiled in reply. "No pun intended."

With little fanfare, Madeleine took a seat at the bar and motioned Jasmine to do the same. Out of habit, Jasmine glanced around the bar area first, but it was early and no cowboys had made their way inside during the last ten minutes.

"I've been meaning to ask you, is this project making you uncomfortable?" Madeleine held up her hand before continuing. "And don't say 'No' right away just to make me feel better. Nash says I have a terrible habit of making plans before thinking them through. I didn't want you to be a victim of that."

"I'm no victim. And, ma'am, I've appreciated the opportunity to be a part of the Ladies' Auxiliary Quilt Guild. It's been nice."

In truth, it had been more than that, Jasmine reflected. It had been so nice to finally bridge the gap between herself and the other women in the town.

No, she was never going to be looked upon as were Madeleine or Mrs. Midge, and certainly not like Caroline Harlow. But, maybe one day soon, she would be treated like a respected woman.

The idea of a man tipping his hat to her without a leer in his eye was as tantalizing as a new blanket would have been ten years earlier.

With a sigh of relief, Madeleine smiled. "I'm glad you feel

that way." She fiddled with her skirt before meeting Jasmine's gaze once again. "Do you remember the day you came here, asking for a job?"

Jasmine knew her cheeks were turning four kinds of pink. "I could never forget it. I was scared to death."

"You looked it," Madeleine said with a laugh. "You were shaking like a leaf and just about gripped the sides of your gown to death. I thought you might even faint when Nash asked why in the world he should hire a gal from the mining town."

"I didn't know what to say. I hadn't thought that far ahead." She shook her head, recalling just how green she'd been about life outside of the mining village. The Dark Horse had been her equivalent to a mansion.

And Mrs. Bond had seemed like a princess, all starched and regal. Madeleine had had on a periwinkle blue gown that matched her eyes exactly. Mr. Bond had held her elbow and guided her by gently caressing the small of her back.

Jasmine had been enthralled to see a man treat a woman so well. "All I knew was that I needed to be someplace different, someplace where I could have a future." Her voice trailed off. "I'm sure that sounds strange to you . . . you being raised a lady and all."

"No. Not one bit. I remember how smart you seemed, just how your eyes looked, like they saw more than anyone ever realized. I told Nash that's just what we needed in here. Not just another pretty face—though yours is—we needed someone who was alert. The last thing I wanted was to have a girl getting taken advantage of on our property."

"So you hired me and gave me some dresses. Once I moved to the boarding house, I promised myself I'd never go back to the mining shanties."

For some reason, that gave Madeleine cause for concern. "Really? Do you never go back to visit?"

Not if she could help it. "I see some of the boys I grew up around. I've seen men who knew my father." She shrugged. "Cedar Springs isn't very big. We're all neighbors in one way or another. But as far as going back to visit to the place I slept at night, no. No, I don't."

"No reason to?"

"Too painful. Mrs. Bond, I see the need for the quilts. Lord knows I could have used something clean and pretty and warm in my life growing up. But there were many other things I needed, too."

"You went hungry, didn't you?"

"I did. But I was also starved for understanding. Patience." She swallowed hard. "Love." With a groan, Jasmine closed her eyes. Goodness, could she ever manage to sound less desperate? "Things weren't so bad," she said, trying to make herself sound as least somewhat decent. "I just really needed a job. A future. You don't know how much I've enjoyed working here."

"You've done a fine job. Nash's told me so."

"Thank you."

"And, Jasmine, maybe one day you'll find love."

"Maybe." Against her will, Jasmine thought of Quentin Smith and their kisses. Of how she'd melted in his arms and how he'd made her feel special. Nice.

"Ah," Madeleine said, a knowing gleam in her eye. "I think you already have found someone. Who?"

"No one."

"You sure? Do I know him?" She tapped her fingers on the card table. "Emmitt? Is it Emmitt? I tell you, Nash says he follows you with his eyes like you were the only person in the saloon."

She was well aware of that. "Not Emmitt. I don't care for him."

"Oh. Well. Let's see. Is it—"

"It's no one, Mrs. Bond."

Crestfallen, the other lady slumped against the back of her chair. "Oh," she said again.

Jasmine felt so guilty for lying, it was on the tip of her tongue to tell Madeleine everything. To tell her how she could talk to Quentin. To tell her how she knew he cared about her, too. How he didn't look down on her. How he'd been hurt, as well. But there was no point.

For good or bad, she'd pushed Caroline in his direction, and he'd grabbed that line and held on tight. No matter how he'd insinuated that he had feelings for her, or that he cared about her in a special way. All that really mattered were his actions. It was common knowledge he'd gone out walking with her yet again.

Now, it didn't matter if Jasmine loved him, or even if she just yearned for his kisses. A future, a *real* future, between them was the stuff of dreams. Even in dreams, love and romance had to have two participants.

"Any chance I could get a drink sometime today, Jasmine?"

"Huh?" The question pulled her hard out of her reverie and brought back the reality of her surroundings and her occupation.

Moving to get up, Jasmine was about to reply when Madeleine turned around and glared across the room at the cowboy. "Speak of the devil," she murmured, much to Jasmine's shock.

Emmitt stared over at the two of them, a challenge in his eyes. Then, like the ticking of a clock, his expression changed. He became almost handsome again.

Jasmine tried to feel enthusiasm for Emmitt, but all she could think was that he could never measure up to the kind of man Quentin was.

"Any time you want to do your job, I'd be obliged," he

pressed. "It's been a hell of a week, and my mouth is powerful dry."

Madeleine looked shocked at his language. "Emmitt, watch your mouth."

Jasmine stilled her boss's wife with a hand. "There's a reason I work here and you don't, Mrs. Bond," Jasmine murmured with a laugh. "You better get on your way before someone propositions you."

The idea seemed to please her. "Oh! Do you think Nash would care?"

"Maybe just a little bit," Jasmine said, in a masterpiece of understatement. Nash would throw a man out on his ear if he so much as even looked at her sideways.

Turning toward Emmitt, she called, "What will you have?"

"Whatever you're offering."

Jasmine couldn't help but smile. "You're awful. Whiskey?"

"Bring the bottle."

"You got it." She turned around and practically ran into Quentin Smith. "Captain."

"Quentin." With precise movements, he ran his hands along her shoulders and held her close. "Where's the fire?" he murmured, just as he had the other day when she'd almost run into him.

His touch spurred her pulse and caused her breath to go ragged. "No fire. I just . . . wasn't paying any attention to where I was going."

"It's good I was watching you, then. You need a keeper, miss."

"I need a lot of things," she quipped, right before she heard her words. "I can't believe I just said that."

"I'm glad you did," he murmured, his gaze caressing hers, as if he knew exactly what she looked like without a stitch of clothing on. His head moved closer, close enough that if Jasmine stood on her tiptoes and leaned forward, their lips could touch.

"I need a lot of things, too." Barely brushing her cheek with his lips, he whispered, "I need you."

Her breasts peaked, heat pooled below her belly, her lips parted to receive his touch. For the first time ever, she didn't curse her too generous curves, or the way that her dresses fit her so snugly. His gaze warmed her and made her feel good. Wanted. Desired.

At the moment, it was enough.

"I'm still waiting, Jasmine," Emmitt called out.

She stepped away, turned toward the bar. Quentin, undeterred, followed. Well aware of Emmitt's fierce gaze, she murmured, "Did you need anything?"

"I did. I do."

Jasmine stepped behind the bar, hoping the barrier would help keep her senses in order.

But the look Quentin gave her had nothing to do with libations, and everything to do with back-alley kisses. Her heart raced once again. "What do you need?"

For a brief moment, his eyes lit up with a heated promise. She was drawn to him and to the way he made her feel inside, like she was desirable, and worth his full attention. "I'd like to talk to you in private." With a dark glance toward Emmitt, he added, "I'll wait until you have a moment."

The glass she was holding slipped from her hand. As it crashed, Emmitt cursed and Quentin raised a brow.

Nash stepped out of his office. "You okay, Jasmine?"

No. No, she wasn't. "I'm fine. Just fine." Turning to Quentin, she murmured, "I'll be free in two hours."

His lips curved upward. "I'll be waiting at the livery."

CHAPTER 16

Almost two hours to the minute later, the door to the livery opened, and Jasmine appeared in the dim light. "Quentin?"

She had come. "Over here." He motioned her to a corner of the tack room, where two ancient chairs stood guard over a wide array of bridles, harnesses, and saddles. "I got tired of meeting in the cold, and I don't think my leg can take another long walk. I hope you don't mind meeting here."

"I don't mind." Her voice was breathless, husky. Her expression cautious, almost wary.

Quentin breathed deeply as her scent drifted toward him, bringing to mind her lips against his and the feel of her slender form molding to him in all the right places.

Knowing that if he held her hand, he'd pull her to him, and then do his best to get her naked, he gestured to the chair he hadn't taken. Forced his mind on the reason he was in Cedar Springs.

His job. Finding the backer. Obtaining a future.

It was the only way he was going to get a decent amount of money to offer Jasmine more than his body.

"I know I hinted a few days back that I've been in Cedar Springs for reasons other than my health."

"Why are you here?"

Her stark question calmed his nerves and made his explanations easier.

As concisely as possible, he told Jasmine about the railroad,

157

their offer, and his acceptance. He told her about meeting with Nash and the reason he'd squired Caroline about so much.

To his ears, Quentin thought it all sounded too pat. Too glib. Nothing that had been going on had been that way.

"The thing of it is, Jasmine, I came here to do a job and leave. I hadn't planned on becoming such a part of this town. I hadn't planned on helping out Clemmons or caring about who I hurt or settling in." At last, he forced himself to admit the whole truth. "Jasmine, I hadn't planned on becoming so attached to you."

There. It was out in the open.

Jasmine stared at him, her eyes looking almost golden the dim light. "I've become attached, too."

Quentin couldn't help it; he grinned. "I'm glad."

Jasmine flashed a smile in return, but said nothing.

Quentin couldn't blame her. So far in their relationship, he'd been secretive and evasive, at once distant and effusive. Hoping to set her mind at ease, he added, "Right now, I feel as if nothing else in this job went right, I'd still be okay."

Jasmine's shoulders relaxed, but still she looked worried. "Quentin, what did you want me to do? What do you need help with?"

"I'd like to put our relationship out in the open."

She wrinkled her nose. "What relationship? Our friendship?"

"I've heard from several people that they know I'm here because of the Carmichaels. They're watching me. They want to know what my plans are—if I've heard anything. Not only if I know who the backer is, but also what I'm going to do to him when I dig him out."

Resting his elbows on his knees, Quentin leaned forward. "I need you to let people know that you have my ear. That we're intimate. That anything you know—or hear—is going to come back to me. I thought I could do this alone, Jasmine, but I can't." After taking a deep breath, he continued. "I received a telegram two days ago from the railroad. They want answers. A name. People have seen the Carmichaels in action." He shook his head, desperately trying to get the stories of the murders out of his mind.

Jasmine tried desperately for a right way to describe their situation. "You think if people thought that we'd—that we were close, they'd be more likely to tell me things?"

"As I see it, I've got forty-eight hours to make somebody talk. I've tried to be patient. It's time for something more."

Jasmine didn't know whether to laugh or cry. In the space of a few minutes, the man she loved told her he cared about her, but that he also wanted to make use of her for a job.

"Someone has already asked me to watch you and report back to him what I saw," she admitted, thinking of Sam, Constance's boyfriend.

"What have you said?"

"Nothing." Helplessly she gazed at Quentin. "I guess people might already think there's something between us."

"You know I genuinely do care about you, Jasmine."

"I know." She knew, but she couldn't help feeling disappointed. Jasmine had been around long enough to know that he'd chosen his words with care. Caring wasn't love. A relationship wasn't marriage.

If she said yes, she could have him in the way she'd been dreaming of. She could possibly help catch a notorious gang. Maybe even save lives.

But she'd also lose her reputation. She also might lose him after he caught his criminal and claimed his money. He could ride off with her heart, and she'd be left in Cedar Springs with nothing left inside of herself. No pride. No respect.

No heart.

"I need some time to think this over."

"How long?"

While she wanted to tell him that she needed as long as it took, it was more than obvious that neither of them had that kind of time. "Tomorrow morning?"

"I'll wait for your answer." Crossing to her, he pulled her into his arms. His comfort brought instant relief, and the feel of his body next to hers spurred her own response. "I'm sorry, Jasmine," he whispered. "I hate the idea of putting you in danger. I hate the idea of you being in danger because of me."

She splayed her hands across his back, gently rubbing his tense muscles. "You aren't putting me in danger. God gave me a good mind, and a way to use it." She pressed her fingers to his mouth when he tried to protest. "Don't worry." Reluctantly, she pulled away and walked to the door. "See you in the morning," she said softly.

As she left the livery, Jasmine couldn't help but notice that the rest of Cedar Springs was going about its business. All of the saloons seemed to be doing brisk business; more than a couple of young gents wandered the streets, calling out to each other.

Jasmine was glad to be going home. Work had been brisk, and the conversation with Quentin exhausting.

Perhaps it was because she was warring with herself as much as with Quentin. Jasmine knew she would do whatever it took to help him. He was a brave man, and had put his body on the line time and again for justice.

How could she not admire a man like that?

The fact that he cared for her only made her feel more inclined to do whatever she could for him . . . even going so far as to compromise her reputation.

Her footsteps slowed when she spied Chrissy on the front steps of Mrs. Midge's boarding house. "Chrissy? Is everything all right?" Thinking quickly, she said, "Is Mrs. Bond okay?"

"She's fine. I was just waiting for you."

"Oh?"

Chrissy gestured down the street. "Couple of people saw you go into the livery. I peeked in a back window and spied you speaking with Captain Smith." She smiled broadly. "I'm real happy for you, Jasmine."

Obviously the only secret in Cedar Springs was who was the train robbers' backer. "We . . . well, we . . . ."

"Don't worry about explaining yourself. It's none of my business." With a wink, she added, "Though, I must say you have good taste."

Chrissy's smile warmed her heart. "Would you like to come in? It's a lot warmer in my room than out here."

"You wouldn't mind chatting with me? I know we ended on a bad note the other day."

"It's over. Besides, you already apologized."

"Well then, thank you. I'd be real pleased to come on in."

After greeting Mrs. Midge and two other borders who were sipping tea in the front parlor, Jasmine led Chrissy upstairs. Almost as soon as they entered her room, her friend began to talk.

"George and I made up last night."

"That's nice."

"He walked me home, then we snuggled on my front porch under my quilt."

Jasmine couldn't help but smile. "Do you mean the quilt you made for the children?"

"Kind of."

"Chrissy! I don't think that was allowed. Don't let Mrs. Bond know."

Chrissy laughed. "I won't. But it sure was nice. We talked and kissed and shared secrets."

That sparked her interest. "What kind of secrets?"

"Oh, the usual romantic kind. George is that kind of man, you know."

"I don't, thank goodness."

Sitting up straighter, Chrissy said, "That brings up what I wanted to chat with you about. Secrets."

"Do you have one, too?"

"Too? Who else does?"

"Quentin."

Chrissy rolled her eyes. "What's his big secret? That he likes you and not Caroline Harlow?"

"How did you know?"

"I have eyes. Captain Smith watches you like you're his next big meal. With longing . . . and a touch of hunger."

Jasmine recalled what he'd wanted her to do, and already knew what she was going to tell him in the morning. "We've become close."

"How close?"

"Close enough to know that Caroline isn't a threat."

"Well, darn. That's what I was coming over here to do. To try and convince you to give Quentin Smith a chance. But here you went and stole my thunder."

Chrissy's openness made Jasmine want to confide all her fears. "Chrissy, do you think that Quentin and I stand a chance? You don't think the two of us together is wrong?"

"Why would you think that?"

"I know who I am, Chrissy. I . . . don't believe Quentin is going to wait for any wedding day to make me his." Jasmine was amazed that she could state the facts so plainly.

"You're a nice woman who's had her share of pain in life, and done well in spite of it all. Jasmine, you told me once that you've spent a lifetime trying to earn everyone else's respect."

"I remember telling you that."

"Well, don't you think it's time to live for yourself?"

Jasmine felt tears threaten to fall. It felt so good to have a friend like her for who she was and not who she could be. "Consider your errand accomplished," she whispered. "I'm glad you stopped by. You've helped ease my mind immensely."

With a dramatic sigh, Chrissy fell back on Jasmine's bed. "Now all I have to do is find yet another time for George to propose!"

Jasmine giggled. "Chrissy, your work is never done."

CHAPTER 17

"You look as if you could use some company," Nash said as he brought a bottle and two glasses to Quentin's back table. "You've been sitting here, scowling at Constance for the last hour."

Quentin couldn't deny that he'd been in a foul mood. "I don't know if it's company I need, but I will take a drink." Doing his best to shake off his mood, he gestured to the chair beside him. "Thanks for this."

Nash grinned. "It's my job." As he sat down and lit a cigar, he murmured, "Things that bad?"

"Yep." Quentin wasn't sure how they could get much worse. He felt like ten times a louse, asking Jasmine to play a part in his investigation. His actions were shameful. If his father were still alive, he'd tell him that he needed a kick in the ass instead of a drink.

Surely he could have asked for Jasmine's help in a different way. Any way besides having her pose as his lover. What the hell did it matter that he wanted her beneath him as soon as possible? His father had taught him to respect women, not blackmail them into bed.

Certainly not put them in danger so he could track down a gang of murderers and thieves.

With little fanfare, Nash filled each glass high, then raised his own in a ceremonial salute. "To women."

"Women?"

"Obviously you're having female trouble. My guess it has to do with a certain bar girl named Jasmine."

"Everything to do with her." Admitting the truth, Quentin said, "I have feelings for her."

Nash tossed back his drink. "Oh, hell. I know that."

"Yeah?"

"Yeah. It's been obvious you've had feelings for her for some time. You watch her like a hawk."

"I watch everyone."

Nash shook his head in disgust. "For being so famous, you sure are dimwitted. You wear a proprietary look around that woman whenever she's near. Have you told her how you feel?"

He'd kissed her, several times. He'd said he cared for her. "More or less."

Slowly, Nash exhaled a batch of smoke, right in Quentin's face. "Exactly how much more and how much less?"

Waving a hand in front of him, Quentin admitted, "I told Jasmine I cared for her, then asked her to make everyone think we were sleeping together."

Whiskey spewed from Nash's mouth.

The saloon's constant din silenced.

"Boss, you okay?" Constance called out from behind the bar.

"Fine." Nash waved her off with a hand. "Quentin Smith. You're not just dimwitted, you're a dad-gum idiot! Why'd you go and do a thing like that?"

"Pick a reason. I want her in my bed. I received a telegram this morning from the good folks at Kansas Pacific wondering why in the hell I haven't identified everyone in Cedar Springs who's involved with the train robberies." He waved a hand. "The Carmichaels are coming." Morosely, he added, "The pressure's gotten to me, I guess."

"The pressure in your pants," Nash muttered sarcastically. "Any chance you want to marry her?"

"It doesn't matter what I want. I can't offer marriage. Who knows how all this with the Carmichaels is going to end? I could get killed, I could never find the backer, and then never get the money to start over again. Nash, all my life I've either been a soldier or a ranger. Neither paid well."

Trying to explain himself further, he said, "When Becky died, I left my homestead, lost what few belongings I'd scraped together. I don't want to offer Jasmine a future that I'm not sure I can provide."

Quentin frowned. Even to his own ears, his priorities seemed twisted. Had he ever put love and commitment first in his life?

If only he could stop thinking about their kisses. Stop thinking about the way she'd responded to him, the way he'd forgotten about the rest of the world when they were together.

"You could plan on living around here. Get a job in town. That would solve some of your financial difficulties." Nash brightened. "I know! Help Clemmons out. He needs a deputy in a big way."

The idea did have merit, though Quentin was afraid to plan that far in advance. First, he had to do what he was contracted to do. "I've been so desperate to conclude this, I came up with a crappy plan. I was hoping if word got out that Jasmine and I were 'special' friends, people might be apt to tell her something." He took another sip, scowling. "But the worst part of it, Sam Greene already has asked her about me. And all I can think about is if she says yes, I'll have a good chance of having her in my bed."

"What did Jasmine say?"

"That she has to think about it."

Nash had the gall to smile. "Sounds like that girl's in charge."

"Yep. I've completely lost control of the situation, and I never lose control."

"Never say never. Hmm. I know! Maybe you could . . ."

Nash's voice trailed off as he glanced around the room. "Well now. Isn't this a fair sight?"

Quentin turned to look at the pair of cowboys who just came in.

"That there is Calvin Rich and John Henry," Nash said.

At first glance, Rich and Henry looked like every other pair of cowboys in the place. Then Quentin noticed that each man was armed, and that they were eyeing him with intent. With a steady hand, he pulled out his pistol. "What's their story?"

"They work some land down south. Don't come into town very often."

The hairs in the back of Quentin's neck rose, signaling that trouble was near. "Know them well?"

"Not too well. Nobody seems to know them well at all."

Quentin watched them approach the bar, lay down two bits, then eagerly claim their drinks. "I'll bite. Why?"

"There's something about them that I've always found strange. Like they're acting in a play or some such. Word is they've got ties out east and are just biding their time."

"They picked a hell of a place to do that."

"I'd agree." Nash pursed his lips as Rich tossed back two shots in quick succession before asking for another. After Rich put more money on the counter, Nash said, "I think I better head on over there and see what's up. If they've got money to spend, I'm curious as to why."

Quentin moved to a dark alcove and watched as the two men spoke to Nash. Instantly, their posture changed, making Quentin finally understand what Nash had meant by posing. The pair for some reason looked more rough and ready as their conversation deepened.

When Nash gestured for Quentin to join them, he holstered his Colt, and wandered over, making sure his limp was pronounced.

"Captain, this here is Calvin Rich and John Henry."

Quentin nodded in greeting. "Captain Quentin Smith."

Nash was all smiles. "Smith, here, was a Texas Ranger."

"You look just like the fella on the cover of a book I seen." Rich grinned. "I'll be plumb happy to tell my family back home that I met you, though I doubt they'll believe me."

Rich's accent was in direct contrast with his looks. Citified and almost effeminate, it drew Quentin's attention like a moth to a flame. "Where do you hail from?"

"I'm sure you wouldn't have heard of it."

"I've been just about everywhere. Try me."

"Fayetteville."

"Arkansas? That's quite a ways away."

"Some would say the same thing about Texas."

"That's a fact," Henry said.

"A fact," Nash echoed, his expression dry. "Smith here is recuperating from a variety of injuries."

"Sorry to hear it," Rich muttered.

"Nothing to be sorry about. It's a part of the job."

Calvin Rich straightened one of his cuffs. "I would assume so. Of course, I have no experience in such matters."

Nash propped his foot on one of the rungs of a nearby chair. "You gentlemen in town to take the waters?"

Henry looked offended. "No. Merely to see some old friends. Catch up."

Nash narrowed his eyes. "Who?"

"Have you suddenly become the law, Nash?"

"Not in this lifetime."

"Well, then. Suffice to say that our business is of a personal nature."

While he was thinking those words over, Quentin noticed that Emmitt had just arrived, and was sitting at a back table. Glaring at the four of them. When Rich looked in his direction,

Emmitt pointed to his timepiece.

Quentin almost smiled. Finally he had identified all the characters in his investigation. Emmitt was the front man. Harlow was the backer.

Rich and Henry were preparing for the Carmichaels' arrival. All he needed to do was position them all to best advantage.

Maybe he wouldn't even need to use Jasmine after all. The relief he felt was all-consuming.

Knowing none of them would talk while he was in the vicinity, he directed a meaningful look at Nash. "I'm heading on up," he murmured. He'd visit with Nash Bond later and get filled in on the boys' antics.

At the moment, he desperately needed some time to think. He'd meant it when he'd told Jasmine that he cared for her. She was the type of woman he could relax with. Be himself.

And although he was wildly attracted to her, Quentin knew that it was her steady nature that drew him to her.

Now he had to figure out how he was going to make things up to Jasmine, to make her see that he didn't only think of her as a means to get a job done.

He took the stairs deliberately slowly, just in case Rich and Henry were watching for his limp.

Lord, he was tired. And, if he admitted it, his leg was bothering him some. Maybe he'd lie down for a bit, rest it some.

But when he opened his door, once again, nothing was how he expected. Jasmine was waiting for him.

Her glorious hair was down, framing her face and falling down her back in magnificent golden waves.

Her feet were bare.

And as he stood there in the doorway, staring at her in surprise, she smiled.

"I thought you'd never come upstairs," she said. "I've been waiting almost forever."

With a flick of his hand, Quentin closed the door behind him.

CHAPTER 18

Jasmine bit her lip as the door slammed shut. Casting a quick glance at his eyes, her heart sank. His eyes, which could glint like quicksilver when he was amused or like gunmetal when challenged, stared back at her, a nondescript gray.

Her heart pounded. What had she been thinking? That he would pull her into his arms and suddenly love her?

Praise her beauty? Admit his feelings?

A shudder of humiliation surged upward, heating her cheeks and filling her eyes with unshed tears.

"I didn't see you come in."

He hadn't moved from his position at the door. In fact, Jasmine noticed he was standing so close to it, he could be holding the door up.

He probably couldn't wait to leave.

This had been a very bad idea. "I went up the back stairs," she explained. "I didn't want anyone to see me."

A look of pain crossed his features. She felt it, too, along with an unspeakable, horrible embarrassment. "I think I'll just slip on my shoes and go out that way."

Sparks transformed gray to charcoal. "No. Stay." He shook his head as if to clear his thoughts. "Jasmine, I've thought a lot about our conversation in the livery. I realize now I was wrong. I was wrong to ask you to pretend to be something you're not."

Jasmine couldn't help but smile. His voice was hoarse, as if he was struggling to hold back a hundred emotions. She felt the same way. Unstable, excited, completely aware of him. "I don't think you were wrong at all. I've come to realize that I've been living my whole life trying to be something I'm not."

"I don't follow you."

No, he didn't. His posture was stiff, his hands clenched, but she'd noticed how his gaze had traced her form, settled on her bare feet. Quentin Smith still wanted her. He wanted her as much as she wanted him.

If he wasn't going to come to her, she would do the walking. Sliding off the bed, she asked, "Do you remember that time we talked, when you first got here? When you told me all about your life as a ranger?"

"I do."

"You told me so much. About your feelings, about your time in the war. How you had regrets."

Quentin wiped his palms across his denims. "I remember."

She stepped closer. "Well, I remember feeling embarrassed that I'd lived my life trying *not* to be things, instead of living it to the fullest. Our talk in the livery made all of those truths ring true."

He swallowed hard. Now only two feet separated them. "I want to tell you something," he said, his words choppy. "Downstairs, Nash and I met some men who I'm sure are with the Carmichaels. Their comments, together with some things Caroline said about her father, led me to believe that Al Harlow is the gang's backer. I'm not going to need to put you in harm's way." A bead of sweat broke out on his brow as she halted in front of him, the hem of her dress brushing against his denims.

"All right," she said.

"All right?" He scowled, then, as if he couldn't restrain himself, reached out and brushed a stray lock from her face.

She could have pointed to the exact spot where his fingers brushed her skin, each part of her was so aware of him. "I'm not here because of your work, Quentin. I'm here because I want to be with you."

Sheer panic entered his eyes, just as he traipsed his fingers down her arm and clasped her hand.

The contradiction was typical of him. He was a man who tried so hard to be everything to everyone . . . and nothing to himself.

Jasmine knew at that moment that she loved him. Knew it as truly as she knew winter would soon come, or the moon would shine brightly again. With a confidence she hadn't realized she possessed, she gave in to temptation and touched him, as well. Tracing a path across his chest. The muscles underneath her fingers contracted.

He reached for her hips, held her at a distance. Yet still his thumbs brushed across her hipbones, tenderly learning their shape, gently sending tremors of want through her. "I'm not going to lie to you. I want you badly. You're beautiful." With a wry glance, he examined his hands on her hips. "I obviously can't help but touch you. But this isn't the right time. One day, maybe, it will be."

She was in his room, in his arms. She knew she loved him. The time couldn't be more right. Taking the initiative once again, she pressed forward, this time molding her body against his. Enjoyed how his palms slid from her hips and covered her backside as her own linked around his neck. "This is right. I'm sure of it."

Heat had entered his gaze. His eyes turned smoky, the muscles in his jaw tight. "Jasmine. I'm trying to do the right thing."

"Then do it. Kiss me."

She barely got the words out before he did just that. From the moment their lips touched, Jasmine knew this was far different from any other embrace they'd shared before.

It was as if a dam had burst, sending a torrent of need and desire through him. He claimed her lips, invaded her mouth with his tongue, grabbed her to him and pressed his hips to hers.

In response, she pressed closer, delighted in his groan when her breasts flattened against his chest. Followed his lead when his head tilted and he deepened the kiss.

Jasmine knew what they were doing was right.

All her life she'd been alone. She'd spent nights dreaming of being cherished. Dreaming of having the kind of relationship with a man, the kind of romance, that so many characters in her books had had.

She'd yearned for this moment, ached for a lover's touch, but had always been too afraid.

Not any more. Quentin's kisses felt too good to be wrong, his touch too right to stop. Reaching up, she ran her fingers through his dark hair, smoothed a hand down his back, along a puckered scar she could feel under his chambray shirt.

Faint noises drifted up from the saloon below. Raucous laughter. The clink of poker chips. Curses as a hand folded.

Doors slammed open and shut. Jeremy played a new song.

And still they kissed. Feeling as if she was drugged, Jasmine stepped backward as he guided her to his bed. She even forgot to feel triumphant when he hastily unbuckled his holster, then his vest.

Her clothes followed next. Jasmine smiled at the way his eyes widened as she unbuttoned her dress, then loosened the bow on her chemise.

Careful hands nudged the garments from her shoulders, finally pushed them along her hips. She only spied dark appreciation in his eyes before he feathered kisses along her neck, circled a nipple with his tongue.

Sparks of longing shot through her as unfamiliar feelings

claimed her senses. Never before had she known such pleasure. Quentin's every touch was demanding and heartfelt, every sensation, from the way his tongue brought such pleasure to the scratchy texture of his beard along her skin, brought forth a new wave of love.

As his fingers brushed along the outside of her thighs, she shivered. Mistaking her tremors, he frowned. "You cold, honey?"

Quickly, he pulled off his denims, and before she could catch more than a quick glimpse of his desire, he'd pulled back the covers and nestled her underneath. The intimate brush of bare skin against skin made her gasp, as did the fevered kisses that followed.

Heat pooled low in her belly as his fingers touched her intimately. She gasped as waves of unfamiliar sensations rolled forward. Quickly she opened her eyes; met his gaze. "You're beautiful, Jasmine," he murmured, his gaze appreciative. "But, I guess you know that."

She never had felt beautiful. Not in the way she felt when he looked at her. Not in the way that made her feel loved and cherished. She opened her mouth to speak, but found she'd forgotten how to talk. Words couldn't seem to form in her head; all she felt was a whirl of dizzying sensations. She grasped his shoulders in surprise.

To her delight, Quentin smiled. "Let it happen, Jasmine."

And before she could ask what *it* was, he was kissing her senseless, caressing her breasts, murmuring all kinds of things about her body. About how much pleasure he got from touching her. Kissing her.

Making her reach heights she hadn't thought possible.

"Jasmine," he whispered, securing her beneath him. "This . . . this is everything I ever dreamed it would be." And with that, he joined her body.

She didn't cry out; there was no need. Quentin's fierce strokes felt like coming home, though no home she'd ever had. Within seconds, he'd changed her life.

And made her everything she'd always dreamed she could be. With a groan, he released his seed, curving his hands around her bottom once more, holding her close.

Claiming her lips again, tenderly kissing her. Making Jasmine realize that what they'd just done was everything she'd ever wanted but had never dared to dream of.

Quentin didn't know how long they lay together. He might have drifted off to sleep. Jasmine was curled next to him, her head on his chest, her beautiful, honey-blond hair falling across her back.

Below them, he heard the now-familiar sounds of Nash closing for the night. Little by little, the music stopped, the clink of glasses and cards faded, and laughter moved onto the dark streets.

He heard Nash tell the help goodnight, then quietly walk up the steps to his wife. Finally, in the dark silence of the early morning hours, he heard the depot's clock chime one.

Jasmine stirred. "Quentin?"

He brushed a kiss across her brow. "Hmm?"

"I must have fallen asleep."

He smiled slightly. "You must have."

She looked bewildered and worried. "Do you want me to leave?"

"I want you to stay. Here. With me." Very gently, he pushed her shoulder toward the mattress, effectively laying her on her back. Unable to stop himself, he raised himself over her, pressing a kiss on the hollow near her neck. "I never want to be without you."

She shifted, her bare skin brushing against his, awakening his desire. "Tonight was wonderful."

Her sweet words, so honestly spoken, humbled him. Made him wish to be a better man. "It was. It was wonderful . . . and more than that." He shifted, sat up. Gazed down at her. The sheet lay across her hips, leaving her breasts bare, presenting to him a bouquet of creamy soft skin to enjoy. Unable to help himself, he traced a finger along her ribs, along the soft lines of her waist. "This was special. I'm glad you were here."

She shifted. The sheet slid down, drawing his eye to her flat abdomen, to the graceful arch of her hipbones.

"What are we going to do about the gang?"

At the moment, he couldn't care less. "Don't worry. Nash and I are going to pay some calls tomorrow." Cradling her cheek, he kissed her lightly.

"But I want to help."

"You might be able to, but I, for one, am glad you won't be in danger. You're too special to me, honey."

She backed away from his touch. "But what about you? What am I going to do if you get hurt?"

"Look at my body," he said, knowing his was as scarred and ugly as hers was perfect and bountiful. "I've been hurt before. I'll survive being hurt again."

"But, Quentin—"

Tired of the subject, he gathered her up in his arms. "So, are you all right? Did I hurt you?"

"You know you didn't." Shyly she met his gaze. "I had no idea it could be like that."

He couldn't help but be pleased. "Good."

"Is it always like this?"

Against his will, Quentin thought of making love to Becky. She'd been adventurous and eager. Never shy. Rarely had they ever gone to bed without laughter.

Later, when he'd been with a woman on the road, he'd always taken care to be with widows, women who didn't expect relationships, only a mutually gratifying evening. Tenderness had never been needed.

"No," he said, cuddling her closer. Unable to help himself, he cupped her breast again, enjoying the sight of her pale, soft skin in contrast to his darker hands in the moonlight.

When she closed her eyes and her breath hitched, he brushed a thumb against the nipple. As it peaked, his body hardened once more. "I want you again, Jasmine. Are you too sore?"

"We can do it again?"

"We can do whatever you want."

Treating him to a tender smile, Jasmine curved toward him and met his lips.

Quentin knew no matter what happened next, Jasmine had been right. Making love to her could never be wrong.

CHAPTER 19

"It happened, Jasmine," Chrissy said happily, walking into the saloon as if on a bed of clouds.

Jasmine looked up in surprise from the table she was wiping. An hour before sunrise, Quentin had walked her back to Mrs. Midge's, helping her unlock the main door as well as her own. He'd left her with a long kiss, reminding her of just how many kisses they'd shared.

After sleeping until midday, she'd bathed, then hurried to get dressed and go to the Dark Horse, happy to see that Misty had left a plate of lunch for her.

She'd assumed no one had been the wiser about her experiences with Quentin. But maybe they'd been seen, after all. "What happened?"

"George proposed!"

Joy for Chrissy, as well as relief that her own secrets hadn't been divulged, made Jasmine's legs feel limp. "Well, my goodness, I guess the stars must have danced in the heavens last night."

Chrissy laughed. "I imagine so. George's proposal just shows that strange things can happen."

Jasmine motioned to the table she'd just cleaned. "Want to sit down and tell me all about it?"

"Of course." Artlessly falling into a chair, Chrissy turned dreamy. "Oh, Jasmine, it was so romantic. First, George knocked on my door. Then, before I could say another word besides 'hello,' he plopped down onto one knee."

Jasmine struggled to keep her composure. George, the size of a small brown bear, balancing on one knee, had surely been a sight to see. "He knelt in the doorway?"

"Absolutely. There he was, half in, half out, holding my hand."

"What did you do?"

"To be honest, I was struggling to keep my balance. I mean, I was having to use my other hand to keep the door open."

Jasmine couldn't help it; she burst out laughing.

Chrissy's eyes twinkled a fair bit, too. "Laugh all you want. But I'm telling you, it was perfect."

"So then, what did he say?"

"All kinds of sweet things. 'I admire you. I love you. I want you to be mine forever.' "

The sweet words chased all kinds of laughter from her thoughts. Sitting down next to Chrissy, Jasmine said, "Those are words to cherish."

"I think so, too. Actually, I didn't think George had a poetic bone in his body. I was pretty well stunned."

"Then what happened?"

"He kissed my hand." Chrissy waved her left hand in the air. "Right here, on my knuckle."

"Oh, my."

"So I said yes."

"Thank goodness." Jasmine hugged Chrissy tight. "Congratulations! Then what happened?"

"He stood up and kissed me." She blushed. "Actually, he did more than that. Within two seconds, I was pressed flat against him, learning his body like it was my own."

The image had Jasmine blushing, too. Chrissy's description of how it had felt had been exactly how it had felt to be in Quentin's arms. She'd reveled in the feel of his hard muscles. In the way each bit of her body had been eager to make intimate contact with his. Her mouth went dry just thinking how every bit of her had responded when his tongue was inside her mouth.

"Yep," Chrissy added, her face all aglow, "We were practically making love right there in the doorway."

"Was the door still open?"

"Not on your life. I pulled him in and let it fall shut." Eyes twinkling, she added, " 'Course, we didn't move from our spot for a good long time."

Jasmine's face heated as she recalled that she and Quentin had done that, as well. "Oh, my. People are going to talk. You know how Mrs. Armstrong is about closed doors and courtin' couples."

"Let them talk. I've been waiting on George for nigh on five years. I deserved some privacy when we finally sealed our deal."

Sealed the deal? "Oh, Chrissy. Have you two set a date?"

"We have. We're getting married next week."

"That soon?"

"Like I told you when we were quilting, I can't afford to wait." Batting her eyelashes, Chrissy shivered dramatically. "And I don't want to wait months and months, either. Oh, Jasmine. George, when he gets his clothes off and gets busy, why, he's pretty much a master of the bedroom arts."

A master? George? Too choked up to talk, Jasmine grunted.

"Why, just the way he touched me—"

This was becoming more than Jasmine wanted to know. Grabbing Chrissy's hands, she exclaimed, "I'm so happy for you. You're getting married! I can't wait to see George. I bet he'll look like he hung the moon."

"Maybe so." Chrissy batted her eyes. "There's no way he can turn back now, anyway."

"I guess not." She clasped her hand. "I'm glad everything worked out so nice."

"Nice? Oh, Jasmine, it was so much more than just nice." A

pink, fresh as a batch of ripe raspberries, flooded her cheeks. Eyes shining, Chrissy nodded. "I just can't believe how one thing just led to another. First George was kneeling, then we were kissing, then, next thing I knew, I was half naked on my bed."

Jasmine knew the feeling. Memories of Quentin's bare skin next to hers made her breath hitch. "Oh, my."

"Oh, Jasmine, George is so much more muscular than I'd ever imagined. I guess it's lifting all those bags of feed and sugar. Yep, it was just like I imagined it would be. George stayed until after midnight. Then I made him get on home. I knew a biddy or two would already have something to say about him being with me for so long."

Who knew so many people would be sneaking around Cedar Springs all night? Unable to locate the words to express her multitude of feelings, Jasmine only smiled.

Chrissy kept on talking, taking time to gesture toward the street, barely visible through a thick glass window. "Isn't it something that everything's still the same even though I feel so different? Here I am, an engaged woman, and a virgin no longer."

Jasmine looked out at the street, too.

Mr. Harlow's bank looked to have a line of people in it. Two wagons lumbered down the way. Beyond, Colorado fields lay before them, their grasses brown and short from foraging deer. "It is something."

"Well, here I've been going on and on without even asking how you are. Are you okay?"

"I'm just fine."

"And Captain Smith? Have you had a moment to spend with him?"

Were her own cheeks heating? "Actually, we did spend some time together."

"Did you talk?"

"Yes, as a matter of fact." Jasmine seemed to recall murmuring something during their lovemaking. "Yes, we did." Clearing her throat, she said, "I think we're going to be just fine, too. You were right about him."

The door to the Dark Horse opened, and in came George. The building could have been on fire, but it was obvious he only had eyes for one person. Like a coyote on the hunt, he made a direct path to their table.

Chrissy popped up from her spot before he could take more than three steps. "I better go. 'Bye, Jasmine."

" 'Bye." With a touch of regret, Jasmine watched Chrissy run to George and get twirled eagerly in his arms. Then, right before everyone's eyes, he kissed her something good.

Two cowboys whooped it up in appreciation, although Jasmine heard them yell congratulations, too. Obviously, George had been parading around like a rooster, shouting out his nuptial plans.

Jasmine stood up and did her part. "Congratulations, George!"

"Thanks," he called right back. "Tell Quentin I did it when you see him, will ya?"

"Sure," she replied before questioning why he would assume that she'd see him before he would. She was about to add more, but George pulled Chrissy out of the saloon in short order, most likely to somewhere a bit more private.

Alone again, she thought of the events of the night before. No, neither she nor Quentin had talked marriage or love.

It wasn't too surprising; both of them were too scarred from years of hardship to say words that might not be accepted readily.

But wouldn't it have been something if Quentin had pledged himself to her?

Oh, she knew that men, by nature, weren't romantic. Romance and fidelity didn't cross their minds most of the time. Shoot, most of the men she knew were pleased to hit the spittoon with their chew.

Her pa hadn't believed in baths, laundry, or endearments.

Why was she expecting so much?

Nash, Clemmons, and Quentin were paying a call on Emmitt. As they rode, none of the other men seemed interested in conversation, which was a good thing, because Quentin could only think about the night before.

Making love to Jasmine had been a soul-shattering experience. Her eagerness and sweetness had comforted his heart and soothed corners of his mind that had long been open—jagged and sore. He couldn't deny how pleased he'd been to have been her only lover. He couldn't help the burst of masculine pride he'd felt when she'd been eager to make love with him once more.

After he'd walked her home in the early morning hours, his room had felt bare.

And as he walked to the window and stared at the empty street below, he'd known that they were going to be together for a very long time. Suddenly, he had a partner. Someone to share stories with. A lover.

As he recalled the last five years, he recognized many truths. He'd never been very good at relationships.

Even his relationship with Becky hadn't been completely without flaws. They'd had a sweet love. A sweet marriage. He'd tried to be the kind of man she wanted. Hard-working, kind. Generous, like she was.

He'd become a good actor. He'd taken care to hide the parts of him she hadn't wanted to know. Hadn't needed to see. But those facets of his personality, while concealed, hadn't gone away.

How could they? Before they'd married, he'd fought in the war for two years. He'd learned to kill, and learned to be good at it.

During their marriage, he'd signed on with the Texas Rangers and been one of their exemplary officers. He'd hunted murderers and thieves with a cold-blooded vengeance. Kept his ranks in order through a fierce combination of discipline and order. He would be gone for a month at a time, and spend the day before seeing Becky again trying to become a different person.

And, although she was by no means stupid, she had never asked about his life on the road. It had been obvious she hadn't wanted to know the details. When they'd meet again, she'd be all sunshine and smiles. They'd talk about her garden. About her family. Never about what kept him up at night.

When Kit Warren had murdered Becky, he'd also killed Quentin's dream of ever becoming a different man.

Her death had stripped him bare and left him wondering who he was, and what his purpose in life was supposed to be. Jasmine's love had healed him.

"Emmitt's place is over the next hill," Clemmons said from his bay. "I hope he'll talk."

"He will," Quentin said.

"I contacted the sheriff over in Bayhill. Asked him if they'd seen anyone who fit your description."

"What did he say?"

"Not a one, but that don't surprise me much. I kind of figured Boss wouldn't be the kind to be out and about too much."

"No. He usually lies low until he needs something. If Rich and Henry were in the Dark Horse, I'd imagine Boss Carmichael will arrive shortly."

"We'll be ready," Nash said.

Clemmons fired off a string of curses that would have blistered his little girls' ears. "Of course it's snowing again. Damn. My wife's going to be wondering why I didn't chop more wood."

Quentin blinked as an especially big flake teased his eyelashes before melting. "Think she'll be all right?"

"She will. I just hate to disappoint her, you know?"

He knew that feeling well. When Clemmons rode ahead, Nash sidled up closer. "So, did you ever talk to Jasmine?"

There was a gleam in Nash's eyes that told Quentin that he already had a very good idea about what had happened the night before. He wasn't going to guess how he'd learned, nor was he going to deny the truth. "I did."

Nash frowned. "Smith. I never thought we'd be having this kind of conversation," he said. "Jasmine's a grown woman, and what she does is no one's business."

"You're right about that."

"But still, I thought you'd have more of a care for her."

"I do care for her. Deeply." With a sigh, Quentin continued, "The two of us have become friends. More than that. Mutually so."

"Friends. Have you proposed?"

"I can't. I'm not going to marry again unless I can promise that our life will be better than it is right now."

"No one can promise the future. Only how things are right now."

"Right now, Jasmine knows I'd do anything for her."

"Where I come from, that involves tender words and promises in front of a preacher. When word gets out you've bedded her, all anyone around here is going to think is that you'd do just about anything to have her."

Nash's words hit uncomfortably close to home. But, how

could he offer her more when it felt like he had even less to offer a woman than ever before? "I did want her."

"You ought to do the right thing. Jasmine is a respectable member of our community. She's not just some dance hall gal who sleeps around."

Nash's words were entirely true. "I know that. But I can't offer her a future. Not yet. People are going to die if I don't stop the Carmichaels and whoever is supporting them. If it is Harlow, and I think it is, things should be over soon."

Nash sneered. "Life and death? Is that what you used to convince her to fill your bed?"

Quentin didn't dare say that it had been Jasmine who came to him. That he'd tried to be a man of honor and wait. "What we did is none of your concern."

"I know there's something real between you." Impatiently, Nash pulled his hat down against the barrage of snowflakes. "From the time Jasmine asked for a job, I've felt like she's my own sister. It's killing me to think she's being used."

"She's not."

"You said you wanted some land. Someone to be by your side. Jasmine could be that someone."

"I do want those things. I even once had those things."

"And now?" Nash asked.

"Right now I can only afford to think about this job. If I fail, more people will die."

"You won't fail," Nash assured him. "We won't fail."

"Here it is," Clemmons announced as they came up to a cabin that looked snug and well tended. "Home sweet home."

The three dismounted and tied up their horses.

"Here goes nothing," Clemmons said as he led the way to Emmitt McKade's front door.

CHAPTER 20

Quentin pounded on Emmitt's door. "Open up!"

Emmitt opened it with a sneer. "What do you three want?"

Clemmons looked as if he was itching to do battle. "Whatever we want we're going to get, Emmitt. Why don't you act as smart as your mouth and let us in?"

Emmitt let them in, but his expression was full of derision. "Why are you here, Smith? You here to rub in your victory?"

"I don't know what you're talking about."

Accusing eyes stared back. "I saw Jasmine going up the back stairs to you."

Jesus! Did the whole population of Cedar Springs know they'd made love? "Again, I don't know what you're talking about."

"It's been obvious for some time. She stands just a little too close. You're just a little too quick to run to her defense. You've made her yours, damn you."

When Clemmons looked ready to slap him, Quentin stayed his hand. "I'd watch your mouth. I've killed men for saying less."

Emmitt's eyes flashed. "So have I."

Swallowing hard, Quentin tried to pretend he had a clear idea about how to work things to his advantage. If Emmitt McKade thought he was only using Jasmine, perhaps he'd be more inclined to talk. "No man is perfect. Sometimes temptation can get the best of him."

With a spark of understanding, Emmitt shrugged. "I suppose. I imagine she was carried away by your reputation. I've been trying to get between her legs for years." With a sly grin, he asked, "Was it worth it?"

Quentin's hand went to his Colt before his mind took control. He couldn't worry about Jasmine's feelings or his own at the moment. He could only worry about finishing his job. If he hesitated, more people would die, and he'd still lose Jasmine.

And now he knew he couldn't live without her. Not now. Not ever.

Ruthlessly, he tamped down his personal feelings and did his best to goad Emmitt McKade into talking. "Of course, she was worth it. She was there."

"I had plans for her," McKade whined. "Pretty soon I was going to be able to buy my own place. I wanted to marry her."

"Still could, I suppose."

"Now? After she'd been with you?" He grunted. "Even I have standards, Smith. Now no one will have her. It was one thing when her reputation was questionable. Now it's a done deal. She'll be lucky if Nash keeps her around."

"I will," Nash said.

"Maybe."

"Enough about all of this," Clemmons said. Easily, he perched on the edge of a butcher-block table. "I want to know about all this money you've come across. I want to know about why you're working for Harlow."

For the first time, Emmitt's expression lost its cockiness and became wary.

"We all know the truth, Emmitt," Quentin pressed. "I know Harlow's paying you so he can keep his identity a secret."

"I'm not saying a word."

Clemmons grabbed his shirt. "Goddammit, you little—"

"Hold on," Quentin interrupted. "Emmitt, back when I was

a ranger, there was a code of conduct that was strictly enforced. It had its benefits. I was pleased to hold myself up to those standards."

"What of it?"

"I'm no longer a ranger. I'm working for the railroad now. I don't have to hold myself up to anyone except the people who are paying me. And they want everyone involved who's been holding up their trains. A whole lot of blood and money's been lost."

Emmitt said nothing, only stared at him as if the bottom had fallen out of his world.

"I'm getting paid to do my job, and I will do it. In any way I can. By force, if necessary. I know how to kill," he said matter-of-factly. "I know how to hurt a man just enough to make him wish I'd stop playing and go ahead and do the deed."

Emmitt swallowed hard. "Point taken. But it don't matter. No one's going to talk. Boss Carmichael would skin me alive if I did."

Clemmons cocked his Winchester. Aimed the rifle right at Emmitt's crotch. "You might."

A line of sweat streamed down Emmitt's face.

Seeing the weakness, Quentin dove in. "Answer me this. Why is Harlow backing the Carmichaels?"

After pursing his lips for a fraction of a second, Emmitt glanced at the Winchester and started talking. "Gambling debts. His wife likes to live high. His daughter wants to marry a gent. And he can't play blackjack worth a damn."

Quentin knew all about making a wife happy. Becky had liked her grandmother's china tea service, and he'd gone through hell and high water to make sure they had a pretty cupboard so that she could show it off and keep it safe.

But Harlow's actions went far beyond anything he could relate to. "Does he really know who the Carmichaels are? What they've done? What they'd do for a bet? For a dollar?" Maybe Harlow was just plain naïve. Quentin couldn't respect a man like that, but he could at least understand it.

"It don't matter if he knows who they are or not. He gets rewarded tenfold for every dime he puts in."

"So he knows about the killings?"

"Why wouldn't he? Everybody knows about them." Emmitt laughed softly. " 'Course, most folks assume that the killings are random acts and that the poor unfortunates were just at the wrong place at the wrong time. They've got no idea that Carmichael staked them out special."

"There's more to this than money, isn't there?"

"Yep. Harlow's got a vendetta against the railroad. He wanted Cedar Springs to be on the map. He plied them with bribes to run the railroad through here. It would have been good for the town. For a lot of things."

Nash interrupted. "But they didn't. It stopped down near Cripple Creek and you have to take a stage to get to Cedar Springs."

Emmitt frowned. "Goddamn prairie. It's misleading. From one angle, it looks like Cedar Springs would be a right fine place to run miles of train track." He pointed to the door. "Yet, all around us there's a heap of creeks and springs, all making it too dangerous to lay rail. Our town's gonna wither and die. We all know it."

"And Harlow was planning for that," Clemmons said, understanding dawning in his voice.

Emmitt nodded. "Hell, yeah. He figured if his bank was going to die, he'd get the money out of the Kansas Pacific anyway he could."

Quentin shared a look with Clemmons before speaking again. "Why'd he need you?"

"Because he's got a reputation to uphold. You know, a reputa-

191

tion can be a powerful thing."

Emmitt's words made Quentin uncomfortable. Made him think of his own as a lawman. Of the overblown reputation he'd tried to live up to after Becky's death.

Of Jasmine's reputation—how she spent a lifetime doing her best to build it up, just to lose it in his arms.

Of Emmitt's reputation—how his total disregard for anything honorable made him sought after on so many levels.

"Where is the money?"

Emmitt grinned. "At the Dark Horse."

"Like hell it is!" Nash exclaimed.

"It's behind the kitchen, along a back wall," Emmitt said, grinning like a gargoyle. "There's a false back. I built it myself during the nights when your place was filled to capacity. No one could hear me hammering."

Nash paled. "That's hard to believe."

"Believe it! Why do you think Harlow was there so often?"

"Why not put the money in the bank's safe?"

"Banks get robbed. Remember the two kids with the sticks of dynamite from the other night?" Emmitt folded his arms across his chest. "You can't depend on a bank to keep things safe no more."

Clemmons grunted. "Maybe not." Narrowing his eyes, he said, "Why are you involved?"

"It's been good money. Easy. All I had to do was keep my eyes open and watch for Carmichael. He's already been to the Dark Horse twice in the last year."

Nash looked as if he needed to take a chair. "I had no idea."

"Of course you didn't. They don't raise no trouble in Cedar Springs."

"All you had to do was be there and pass them the money."

"That's right. Hell of a lot easier job than chasing cattle all day long. I just had to be agreeable, win big, and keep myself occupied."

"So you flirted with Jasmine to pass the time."

"She wasn't hard on my eyes."

Quentin leaned forward. "I'm going to need you to get that money and bring it to me."

"No can do, *hombre*. Harlow's going to want it in his sights when Boss Carmichael comes in. And he's due in tonight."

"Lie. Tell him that it's in a satchel."

Emmitt tapped his chest. "Hell, no. I like my heart. I don't want to even think about Boss cutting it out while I'm there to witness it."

Quentin was afraid he had a point. The men they were dealing with had a lot to lose and every intention of bringing other people down with them if they did.

Nash was still focused on his saloon. "Why the Dark Horse? Why my place?"

"It's the most reputable place Cedar Springs has. No one would think that you would chisel people out of money."

"Or hide it in a back wall," Nash said.

Emmitt smiled. "Truth is, the Carmichaels like your saloon. They like the piano playing. They like the poker. They like Jasmine."

"Jasmine?" Quentin felt as if he'd been sucker-punched. Damn, did every man dream of her?

"Boss tried to get her to go upstairs with him. When she told him no and slapped him good, he just laughed."

"She slapped him?" Quentin struggled to keep his expression neutral, but from the heat he was feeling on his cheeks, and Emmitt's knowing grin, he was sure he was doing a poor job of it.

Kind of paradoxical that he could face gamblers, murderers, and thieves more easily than a weaselly skinny cowboy who dared to speak the truth.

Following his train of thought, Emmitt continued. "Turns out not too many people say no to Boss. And having a gal who looks like her say no to him because of her reputation . . . it drew him to her like a bee to honey." Emmitt coughed. "I have a feeling, Boss is going to be making a play for her again."

"Maybe not. He'll know I'm in town. He'll know Jasmine is mine."

Nash cleared his throat.

Emmitt raised a brow. "He'll know Jasmine's reputation is gone. Hell, everyone'll know about it, not that anyone's blaming you. You lucky son of a bitch. I was going to marry her." Seeing Quentin's glare, Emmitt shifted. "Um, actually, if you aim to get the Carmichaels and Harlow, you're going to need some help."

Clemmons shook his head. "From you?"

"From me. And Jasmine. Ask her to flirt with Boss for a little bit. That will keep him distracted."

Quentin had never wanted to strangle a man more. "You don't know what you're saying. The man is vicious."

"The man likes Jasmine. If he thinks he's got a chance, he'll be sweet as pie." Eager to be of more help, Emmitt continued, "By the time you see him, I'll be ready to pass him the funds." He snapped his fingers. "Then, while Jasmine's got him occupied, you can make your move."

"And Harlow?"

Clemmons's eyes narrowed. "I hate like hell that all this has been going on under my nose. I'll handle Harlow outside."

Quentin hated to admit it, but Emmitt had a good plan. It was as sound as he could hope for, given the volatile temperaments of almost everyone involved.

Yet he was still curious about the man's new motivation for spilling his guts. "How come you're switching sides?"

"Beyond the bonus that I won't be swinging from a nearby hickory, I'd think you'd be able to read my mind. A future." He winked. "Maybe even with Jasmine, after all."

"Even if she's 'used'?"

"It might not matter. If I help you, I'll be free of the noose. And I've already pocketed a good bit from Harlow for helping him out. I'll have Jasmine in front of the preacher in no time."

Quentin felt his heart freeze up as his future dimmed once again. There was no way he was going to let another man so much as look at her with lust in his eyes.

"Jasmine likes you fine," Nash said, giving a warning glance to Quentin as he spoke. "I'll make sure she knows your intentions are honorable."

Emmitt's chest puffed out; he was obviously pleased. "You do that. While you're talking, tell her that I know her cattin' around wasn't her fault. I can understand the attraction of a famous lawman."

"I'll see you when the Carmichaels ride in."

Emmitt echoed the gesture. "Until then."

"And Emmitt? Until then, we never had this conversation."

"Don't worry, Sheriff. I've been a great many things in my life, but never a fool."

CHAPTER 21

"Well, that was entertaining," Clemmons muttered as they rode back to Cedar Springs. "Anybody as annoyed as I am?"

"I don't know," Nash said caustically. "By any chance has half the town been using your business as a facility for train robbers? Has anyone else had their wife living upstairs above murderers and thieves?"

"All I know is that I've just been told by Emmitt McKade that he's seen the best of me and I've still been found wanting," Quentin said as he squinted through the curtain of falling snow.

His quip earned him grins from his companions.

"We're going to have a lifetime to consider how the hell any of this has been going on right under our noses," Clemmons said. "In the meantime, I reckon we need a plan."

They rode the four miles back to Cedar Springs slowly, navigating their way through the falling snow while going over possible courses of action and weighing the pros and cons of each idea.

It was decided that Clemmons would stay out of the saloon and be in charge of bringing in Harlow. Nash would stay near the back of the Dark Horse, looking after Emmitt and the stash of money.

Against his better judgment, Quentin knew he was going to have to ask Jasmine to be there, if for no other reason than to assure the Carmichaels that everything was normal. Once everyone was in position, he'd apprehend Carmichael as neatly as possible.

As the mining shanties on the outskirts of town came into view, Nash said, "I'm going to ask Madeleine to stay at Chrissy's tonight."

"That's a fine idea," Clemmons agreed. Turning to Quentin, the sheriff cocked an eyebrow. "You doing all right?"

"I don't know," he answered honestly. Quentin didn't know when he'd feel all right again. Once again, it seemed as if his work was interfering with the woman he loved. *Loved.*

The force of it hit him hard, and made him wish he'd thought to tell her just how much she meant to him when they'd made love. Guilt twisted in his gut like an old friend. "For a little while, I had hoped that I could keep Jasmine out of this, but now it looks like she's going to be in the thick of things, no matter what."

"She might want to be," Nash replied. "I know Jasmine wouldn't turn to you in the way she did unless she loved you. And, like the rest of us, she loves Cedar Springs. She'll do her part to save it. We all will. Hell, I know Madeleine would try to get involved if she wasn't in the family way."

"You're not alone any longer, Quentin," Clemmons said, slapping him on the back as they dismounted.

As Quentin passed off his horse to Toby in the livery, he reckoned that was the best piece of news he'd had in quite a while.

Nash Bond whistled low as the storm intensified, swirling the snow in thick bands. "This one's going to last a while," he muttered as they stomped into the back storage room behind the kitchen of the Dark Horse. "I better check go check on Madeleine."

"I'm going to speak privately with Jasmine, then go to your office."

"I'll be there," Nash said with a nod.

As the warmth of the building thawed out his face and hands, a slow, steady heat filled Quentin's soul as he realized his waiting had ended. He felt almost calm, now that the action was about to start.

And as serenity settled in, everything else seemed to melt away but what was important.

He had friends, and he had a woman he loved. If he played his cards right, he might even get to show her for twenty years or more how much he loved her.

He felt almost lucky.

The saloon was unusually quiet for five o'clock in the evening. Only two men sat at a table, and they weren't doing much of anything except watching the snow outside.

Jasmine and Constance were stacking glasses in back of the bar when he entered. He stilled for a moment, enjoying the sight of her.

"Quentin!" she said, coming forward, a hesitant smile playing on her lips. "I didn't see you come in."

"I just did." Taking her hand, he murmured, "We need to talk, honey."

Constance stilled. "Honey?"

Not in any mood to discuss their relationship with one more person, Quentin pulled her closer. "This might take a while. Will you come to my room?"

Jasmine saw the serious look on his face. "Of course."

Constance stood and stared as Jasmine pulled off the towel she'd wrapped around her waist and followed Quentin. The two men warming their hands near the fireplace halted their conversation as they passed. Their steps slowed as they climbed the stairs and walked down the hall. After what seemed like forever, Quentin unlocked the door and led her inside.

As soon as he closed the door, Jasmine said, "This is about

the Carmichaels, isn't it?"

"Yeah." But it was also about so much more. It was about his love for her. His regret for putting her in danger again.

The way his body was already responding, being back in his room, alone with her.

When she still stared at him, waiting for a real answer, for some explanation, he forced his muddled thoughts to slow down. "Nash, Clemmons, and I just paid a visit to Emmitt," he blurted out, then cursed himself, wishing he was as good at conveying his feelings as he was hard facts.

Her eyes widened. "You went to his house?"

He nodded, thinking about how Emmitt, with his wealth of information, had spurred his temper as few men ever had.

"What happened?"

"Too much."

She tilted her head. Pursed her lips.

Those lips. He ached for her. Ached for her touch, for a moment's reprieve in her arms.

He took hold of her hands. "Jasmine, honey, I'm going to tell you everything. In a minute. But first . . ." He finally gave up and did what he should have done from the first moment he saw her. He pulled her into his arms.

Jasmine's features softened, and as she willingly stepped into his embrace, she greeted his lips. Her taste brought all of his senses alive. Brought back memories of the first time he'd touched her, by the spring.

Tenderly, he nipped at her bottom lip, turned her head to deepen the kiss. Bit off a moan when she responded to each silent instruction with eager responses.

He forgot all about the world and the dangers that awaited him. All he could think about was pressing her closer, enjoying how luscious her breasts felt against his chest.

As before, her fingers trailed a path along his chest. Curved around his neck.

"I want you again," he admitted. Shaking his head, he tried to explain himself, but then he saw there was no need. Jasmine was already unbuttoning her dress.

He stilled her hands. He tried to be the kind of man he wanted to be. "We ought to talk. About everything."

She smiled. "Later. Quentin Smith, if things are as bad as you make them seem, then I at least want this to be right."

Her words made sense. Maybe because she was already half naked.

But whatever the reason, Quentin undressed as well, and took her to bed. As tenderly as possible, he cradled her in his arms, kissed her deeply, got to know her body all over again.

This time, in the twilight, Jasmine was less hesitant, more eager. She watched as he kissed her breasts, touched her intimately. Told her how she meant the world to him.

And finally, right as she welcomed him again, he did the thing he'd been meaning to do for so, so very long. "I love you, Jasmine," he said reverently.

Her eyes glowed with unshed tears. "I love you, too," she said. "But I think you already knew that."

With a sigh of contentment, Jasmine knew everything was going to be all right. She was finally living for herself, not for the rest of the world, and with that surge of independence came a lightheaded feeling. It was as if the weight of her mother's death and her father's disregard seemed to matter just a little less.

While she'd always mourn not having a happy childhood, Jasmine knew that everything that truly mattered was right there, in her arms.

Quentin loved her.

Kissing her softly, he cuddled her closer. Jasmine loved the feel of his body next to hers, the contrast of his chest, so hard and solid, with her own feminine curves.

"I'm sorry it took me so long to say it," Quentin said, tilting her head so he could meet her gaze

"It was worth the wait."

He looked pleased. "You were worth the wait." He shook his head.

"Most good things are."

He smiled. Pressed his lips to her shoulder as they sat up.

Jasmine knew he had a job to do. Making it easy on him, she pulled the sheet up over her breasts and moved apart from him. "Tell me what happened."

Haltingly, Quentin told her about his visit to Emmitt's with the sheriff and Nash Bond. Jasmine could hardly believe what she heard.

She'd never suspected either Mr. Harlow or Emmitt to be so dishonest. She was flabbergasted when Quentin informed her of Boss Carmichael's infatuation with her. "I don't have any idea who he is," she protested.

"When he comes in, I imagine he'll look familiar enough."

She covered her face with her hands. "What are we going to do?"

He swallowed hard. "I'd hoped I could keep you out of sight, but instead, I'm going to have to ask you to keep Boss Carmichael occupied."

Feeling her new independence and sense of worth, she nodded. "I can do that."

He grimaced. "I wish to God you didn't have to. Jasmine, I don't know what I would do if something happened to you."

"Don't you think I've wondered the same thing? Quentin, I'm in love too, you know. How could you expect me not to help you if you needed help?"

Surprise, and more than a little appreciation entered his gaze. "Then I guess it's settled. Nash is waiting in his office to discuss the details. Would you like to come?"

"I wouldn't want to be anywhere else."

With a chuckle, Quentin leaned close and kissed her hard. "I don't know whether to be grateful or very afraid."

Minutes later, they knocked on Nash's door. He let them in, motioning to two chairs.

Jasmine was shocked to see Madeleine sitting in one of them.

"I wanted to be involved too, Jasmine," she said. "Even if it's just behind the scenes."

"I tried to get her to leave, but she refused," Nash told Quentin.

Quentin winked in Madeleine's direction. "I appreciate it." With a look of determination, he continued. "All right, then. Let's make plans. From what we know, Emmitt McKade is going to be stopping by tonight. Boss Carmichael is due to meet him, as well."

"And that's where I come in," Jasmine said. "Right?"

As if it pained him, Quentin glanced at Nash. When Nash looked as if he was going to argue, Jasmine stood up. "I can do this. I'm tougher than you realize."

Nash frowned. "I know you're tough, Jasmine, but this man is pure evil."

Jasmine straightened her shoulders. "From what Quentin said, I've already distracted him before. I'll be fine."

"I'll watch from the back room, just to be safe," Madeleine said.

With a look of horror, Nash turned to her. "You will do no such thing."

Quentin held up a hand, doing his best to restore order. "We have no choice. We need Boss to be distracted. Emmitt says he's sweet on you. I'm going to need you to do whatever it takes to keep his eyes on you."

"Whatever it takes?" Jasmine asked, her voice coy.

A muscle jumped in his jaw. "Within reason." Quentin took her hand and squeezed it. "Give Boss some drinks, let him talk. Talk. Smile. Flirt a little bit."

"While you're keeping him occupied, we're going to be busy trying to round everyone else up. We think Rich and Henry and one or two other members of his gang will be there, watching Harlow and meeting with Emmitt."

"Clemmons's going to be outside, waiting for Harlow to hand Emmitt the money."

"And I'm going to be shadowing Emmitt," Nash explained. "As soon as I see the transfer and hear that Clemmons's apprehended Harlow, I'm going to give a signal." He paused. "Madeleine, honey, got any idea for a good signal?"

"How about having Jeremy play Dixie?" she said brightly. "That's the kind of song that's good and loud."

Quentin nodded. "When I hear Dixie, I'll take down Carmichael." Running a finger down Jasmine's wrist, Quentin said, "You're going to need to listen and do exactly what I say."

A tremor ran through her from his touch. Yet, it was nothing compared to the satisfaction she felt by knowing that she was going to be able to truly help the man she loved. "I will."

Madeleine shot a worried glance at all of them. "This is awful, knowing that each of you is going to be in danger and I won't be able to do a thing."

"You're going to be taking care of our baby, sugar. That's the most important thing you can do."

"And one other thing," Quentin said softly. "If something happens and someone needs medical attention, I want you to be able to get help. Everyone else in the place is going to be too stunned to think clearly."

Madeleine nodded.

Nash scowled. "I can't wait till every one of them dares to set foot in here again. They've taken advantage of me and put all of us in danger."

Not caring that Madeleine and Nash were watching, Jasmine stood up and gripped Quentin's arm tightly. "I'm sure you're used to working with other lawmen, not saloon owners and bar girls. Will you be all right?" Jasmine asked.

"I'm not used to working next to the woman I love," he corrected, then chuckled. "Believe in me."

"I do. I just don't want you hurt."

"I'll be fine." With a chuckle, he attempted to tease. "You must have thought I was a piss-poor Texas Ranger, sweetheart."

She ran a hand along his arm, over the puckered scar she'd kissed just minutes ago. "Nobody is infallible. Not even famous characters in books."

"I'll be fine."

"And if you're not?"

His eyes suddenly serious, he knelt in front of her. "Then I'll die trying."

Tears pricked her eyes. She blinked frantically, not wanting to make things worse for Quentin. Not wanting to embarrass him in front of Nash. He already had enough on his mind.

"Don't worry, sweetheart," he said quietly, pulling her into the comfort of his arms. "I've been up against far worse with far worse odds."

"I wish you didn't have to be the one to apprehend him, Quentin," Jasmine whispered.

"I have no choice. I took this on. It's what I know how to do." Standing up, he added, "The Carmichaels killed seven men on the train. Most were likely someone's husbands or fathers. Capturing them will be a great service to many people." He hesitated. "Jasmine, I'm not going to pretend I know what the outcome of this night's work will be. If you'd like to change your mind about being involved, you can say no. It's not too late."

Jasmine knew she'd never felt so proud of anyone in her life. Quentin Smith was trying desperately to stand alone, though it was obvious to everyone in the room that he didn't want to be alone anymore.

Curling her arms around him, she felt his heartbeat, his tension . . . his love for her.

She didn't want to be alone, either. "I'm afraid it is too late," she replied honestly. "I already am involved. A hundred percent."

Chapter 22

From the way everyone had talked, Jasmine thought the Carmichael Gang would ride into Cedar Springs with guns raised—whooping, hollering, and ready for bloodshed.

She'd been sure each man was going to be as powerful as a steam locomotive, covered in dirt and grime, and surrounded by swarms of locusts.

She'd assumed they'd be missing teeth and have dangerous gleams in their eyes, the kind of glimmer that would signify death and destruction were on their way.

They'd probably spit, too.

And Boss Carmichael—who even knew what he was like? Though Emmitt had told the men he was sweet on her, Jasmine didn't recall a man like that at the Dark Horse.

All she knew for sure was that he had to have the eyes of a murderer, cold and calculating. She'd been a little worried about how she was gonna go about distracting a man like that.

But when Boss did ride in, he was nothing like she'd envisioned. He wore a white shirt, which was unusual, as was its spotless condition. Dark brown slacks covered his legs. He was tall, almost as tall as Quentin. His sandy brown hair—cut short and close to his head—shone like it was freshly washed. He was clean-shaven, his eyes a nondescript brown. And his voice was low and patient and almost mesmerizing.

Jasmine remembered him immediately. During his previous visits, she'd found herself sitting with him for long periods of time. She had worried about him—he always seemed so eager for company. So lost and lonely.

To her dismay, Jasmine realized that she'd sat with him just days before the most recent train robbery. They'd shared stories about growing up poor and cold.

Jasmine recollected that she admired him . . . well, before he'd propositioned her and she'd slapped him for his trouble.

As he entered the saloon and caught her eye, she sauntered over. Jasmine was glad she'd used her time since the meeting in Nash's office to alter one of her dresses. In the effort to keep his attention on her, she'd lowered the neckline a scandalous amount. The revealing cleavage, along with a tightly cinched corset, brought all of her features into full view.

She'd never felt so exposed. "What will you have?"

He winked. "You on a platter. Sugar, do you remember me?"

"I do. We talked about the winter of sixty-eight."

"We did at that. Right before you taught me my manners."

Recalling the slap, she colored. "I don't know what got into me."

"Something good, I believe. You were right to send me on my way." Smiling gently, he said, "I'll have a couple of drinks. And your company."

"I'll be right back."

As she shimmied up to the bar to collect a glass and a bottle, Jasmine nodded in Nash's direction. He was polishing the copper top of the bar with a grim expression. "Everything all right?"

"Just fine."

Boss Carmichael made no pretense of hiding his appreciation when she returned. "You sure are a sight for sore eyes, honey," he murmured, his gaze hot on her exposed skin. "What was your name, again?"

"Jasmine."

"Jasmine," he echoed, pronouncing her name like it was

special. Jasmine couldn't help but notice that while his voice was pleasant, his eyes were as cold and vacant as death.

After scanning the room nervously, she set his bottle on his table. "I don't recall your name, either. Just your voice."

Casting his scary eyes on her, he asked, "My voice? What's so memorable about it?"

Worried that she offended him, she thought quickly. "It reminded me a lot of my brother's," she lied. "He went off to California years ago, but he used to talk like you do. Slow. Steady. You have a wonderful voice."

Boss smiled at that. "Come join me. Go tell that bartender that you'll be keeping me company."

"Will do." Jasmine reported to Nash that she'd be sitting with Boss, then joined him again. Almost imperceptibly, Nash made a gesture to Emmitt, who glanced toward the back of the room where Quentin was sitting in the shadows, watching everything.

Jasmine was sure everyone involved was breathing a sigh of relief that their plan was going well from the start.

As she poured a generous amount of whiskey into each of their glasses, she tried to think of something to say. Anything that would sound flirty but not too flirty. Well, the weather was always an option. "The snow is sure coming down."

"It is at that." Reaching over, he cupped her jaw. Jasmine did her best not to flinch, but his hands were as cold as ice. "I may just have to spend the whole evening here with you."

His quip earned a few ribald remarks and chuckles from his cohorts. They were seated at the next table over, watching Jasmine circumspectly.

Their easy interest made her nervous. As her hands started to sweat, she set them on the table before she did something silly and dropped a glass.

But her movement, accompanied by Boss Carmichael's sudden shifting, rocked the table. With a clatter, one tumbler rolled right toward Boss. Amber liquid sloshed out, coating the surface of the table. With lightning speed, Boss grabbed the glass before it fell to the ground.

His quick reflexes reminded Jasmine just how deadly he must be with a gun. She sputtered apologies. "Oh, my goodness!" she exclaimed, grabbing at the cloth tied around her waist. "Are you all right? Did your shirt get wet? I'm sorry, I don't know what happened."

Boss set the glass to rights, then placed his hands on her hips, settling her down. "Whoa, honey. You're a bunch of nerves."

Only Quentin had ever touched her so familiarly. Boss's hands, gripping her like a vise, brought forth a wave of revulsion.

He narrowed his eyes. "What's gotten you so jumpy?"

"Nothing." When his hands fell, she took a calming breath. "I . . . I guess I can't stop thinking about the time you were here before. I am happy to see you." Hastily, she sat back down.

"Yeah?" Boss screwed up his face in confusion. "Honey, you need a drink."

Oh, yes, she certainly did. "I'll do the honors." With a practiced hand, she poured two more fingers into each glass, then held up her own in a toast. "To you, mister."

"Boss."

"Excuse me?"

"My name. You asked earlier. It's Boss."

"That is unusual."

"It used to be William. That gave way to Bill, then Boss. I changed it about the time I went out on my own." He frowned, as if remembering his past brought back bad memories. "I wanted to remind myself that I'd never again follow anyone else's orders."

"I like Boss. It . . . suits you."

He laughed. "And Jasmine suits you. All exotic and special and sweet. You captured my attention from the first moment I saw you. Not too many gals can claim curves like yours and still pour a drink."

It was all she could do to not tremble. As best she could, she tried to keep her voice calm and even. Tried to imagine she was sitting with Quentin. "I'm special, I guess."

"You are, at that." Boss sighed, emptying his glass in an easy swallow. "Pour me another."

She did as he asked, daring to glance around.

A group of poker players were looking at her strangely, one with an odd mixture of revulsion and want. To her shame, Jasmine realized that they probably considered her ripe for the picking. Obviously her low-cut dress was attracting notice.

She would also be surprised if word hadn't gotten round that she'd gone up to Quentin's room in the broad daylight. Sitting with a stranger, drinking with him as if they were old friends, was sure to cause a stir, as well.

Boss seemed to sense the change in her demeanor, too, because he sat a little closer. "You're one of the reasons I keep coming back here, sugar. Tell me, what's it gonna take for you to kiss me?"

She forced herself to remain calm. Pretended she was flattered by his attentions. "More than a drink, I'm afraid."

He laughed. "I can give you more."

She played along. "Like what?" With a cautious glance toward the bar, she noticed Nash was nowhere to be seen. She couldn't feel Quentin's presence, either. What if everything was going wrong?

Boss covered her hand with his. Though his skin was softer than Quentin's, his grip was twice as hard. "I've got me, and I've got money. A lot," he added. "Probably more than you've ever seen in your lifetime."

His grip was unyielding, his words chilling. An unpleasantly cold band of perspiration formed along her spine. Feeling everyone's disapproving glares, Jasmine had never felt so alone.

She forced herself to remember Quentin's words. How he'd vowed he'd do his best to protect her if only she could help him by distracting Boss. *Look natural! Act interested!* Jasmine cautioned herself. "I've seen a lot of money pass through here," she teased. "You might not be able to impress me much."

"I would. Promise." He released her hand, but his fingers traced a line along her cheek and down her jaw, stopping at her collarbone where the edge of the fabric clung for dear life.

Boss flicked a finger along the top of her breast. His touch shamed her. "So soft," he murmured. "So lovely." He looked as if he was going to add more, but one of his men approached and whispered something in his ear.

With obvious regret, he dropped his hand. Repositioning himself, Boss appeared to be trying to decide whether to stay with her or go investigate something.

What if he got up and left? She couldn't allow that to happen.

Leaning forward on her elbows, she offered him the kind of look at her bosom that even Constance hadn't even dared to flaunt.

Boss's eyes darted to the generous expanse of skin, back to his man, then darted her way once again.

Jasmine tried to pretend she didn't notice every other man in the place trying to catch a gander, too. She felt as if her finely built reputation was lying in tatters on the floor around her. Oh, she hoped she didn't fail now!

"Are you warm, boss?" She fanned herself lightly, bringing his eye back to her breasts. "It's stifling in here."

Boss gripped his man, whispered something, watched when

he left with another two men, then picked up the bottle. "Honey, I tell you, I'm feeling stifled too, just looking at your little oasis. We need another drink."

This time Jasmine didn't even need to pretend to sip. She tossed back the fine whiskey with practiced grace, welcoming the sting as it slid down. "I feel better already," she whispered.

Boss took her hand, linked his fingers through her own. "You sure do."

In the distance, the stage clock chimed, signaling the new hour. As if on cue, the front doors to the Dark Horse opened again, this time bringing in Emmitt . . . and Quentin.

Jasmine caught Quentin's eye. Caught his surprise as he realized how she was sitting across from Boss, her breasts nearly completely exposed.

Watched his eyes narrow as he spied the whiskey.

Emmitt looked like he was ready to scamper on over and do some harm.

Boss Carmichael's whole demeanor changed once more. No longer relaxed, the muscles in his arms clenched. "McKade. Come here," Boss called out.

Emmitt trotted forward.

Jasmine peeked over her shoulder. Saw Nash standing sentry by the back doorway.

Jasmine felt almost queasy. She was surrounded by men who knew how to kill—and would do so at a moment's notice.

Glancing to her right, she saw that Quentin had a hard look about him. Cold. Calculated. At the moment, it was hard to identify the affectionate man who'd cradled her so tenderly in his bed just hours before.

"Boss, I think I'd better go ahead and leave," Jasmine said, getting up.

"Stay," Boss ordered, his voice as calm as ever, but with an added bit of steel. As if to seal her fate, he circled her wrist and held on tight.

"Jasmine," Emmitt said before sitting opposite to her. "I can't believe you're sitting her with this man like . . . this. Have you already gone upstairs with him? Like you did with Smith? I wanted to marry you."

Every bystander heard him and cast judgment. Boss chuckled. Quentin glared.

"I've heard about Quentin Smith," he murmured.

Like quicksilver, Emmitt's demeanor changed again. Becoming subservient, he said, "So, you ready, Boss?"

With his fingers still linked around Jasmine's wrist, he replied, "You tell me. Is everything ready?"

Emmitt nodded. "It is."

"Where's our man? Is Harlow here, or did he send you once again to do his dirty work?"

Emmitt looked uncomfortable. "You know Harlow likes to stay in the background. He's got a reputation."

Boss turned to Jasmine. "What do you think about men who are afraid to get their hands dirty?" As if to prove his point, he pressed his knuckle against her breastbone.

His touch burned. Fear tore through her. Afraid to look for Quentin, afraid even to glance at Emmitt, she replied shakily, "Not much."

Boss laughed. "I like your style, Jasmine. Very much." Immediately, he released her, pushing his glass her way. "Pour me another, sweetheart."

Jasmine did, just as all hell broke loose.

Jeremy started playing "Dixie."

Clemmons stormed in, Harlow cuffed at his side.

Emmitt pulled out his own pair of shotguns, and aimed each one on Carmichael's subordinates.

Quentin pulled out his six-shooter, cocked it, and pointed it at Boss's heart. "You're under arrest for the Kansas Pacific murders," he said, his voice a low growl.

Boss's chin rose an inch. "Like hell."

Jasmine tried to break free, but Boss grabbed her wrist again in a death grip. All thoughts of being brave and playing a part were now long gone. "Quentin?"

Boss's face became a thundercloud. "You're his lover?"

She didn't know what to do, whom to lie to. How to act. All Jasmine wanted to do was run home and cover herself up. "I . . . I . . ." She tried to pull away from him again.

With that motion, Boss yanked out his own Colt. Bystanders gasped and moved away. "Don't do a thing, Smith. I'll kill her. You know I will."

"You kill her, you'll be swinging two minutes from now."

"And I'm going to do the hanging," Clemmons called out from his position on the left.

Jasmine turned back to Quentin. His glare was as cold and vacant as Boss's. His hand didn't shake from nerves. He looked so solid, he could have been sculpted from granite.

Obviously, he was biding his time before he pulled the trigger.

His stance obviously rattled Carmichael. His hand began to sweat. Jasmine used it as an opportunity to try to yank herself free.

Boss glanced at her in confusion, his grip slipping when she tugged again. Seeing that he was shaken, she screamed in his ear and made herself go limp.

His hold on her slipped.

Then finally, finally, she found freedom.

Constance screamed, as well. Guns all around her cocked. Fists were thrown.

And one lone bullet discharged.

"It's over, Carmichael," Quentin said as he hogtied him with a piece of rope. "Over."

Jasmine felt funny. Worried that some of the whiskey had spilled on her dress, she wiped at it. Then felt the sharp stinging. "Quentin?" she said, just as the room began to spin.

"Nash! Jasmine's been shot!" Madeleine called out.

"Jasmine. Jasmine, can you hear me?" Quentin's voice echoed from a terrible distance. Foreign hands picked her up.

"Where's the doc? She's bleeding something awful."

"Madeleine, go find Neely," Nash said before leaning over her. "You're going to be fine. Just fine."

Jasmine tried to open her eyes. Smile.

"Be still," Quentin ordered. "Don't do a thing."

Obediently, she closed her eyes again.

Clemmons said gruffly, "Quentin, you gotta get a grip on yourself."

"Get a hold of myself? Do you *see* her? Jasmine?" Pure pain filled his voice. "Jasmine. Honey. Come on, honey . . ."

His arms tightened around her, bringing comfort, yet scaring her, too.

Jasmine sensed his worry, his doubts. Needing to reassure him, she murmured, " 'S'all right."

"No. No, dammit, it's not. Don't say a word," Quentin ordered.

Don't move.

Don't talk.

Don't do a thing.

The orders had come out like gunfire, but the thought behind them was clear as day. He cared.

"I love you, do you hear me? I love you and you're mine. *Mine.* No one is taking you from me, Jasmine. So you'd better hold on. Hold on."

He loved her!

Holding that thought close, she sank into blissful oblivion, thinking that maybe everything was going to be fine after all.

CHAPTER 23

Quentin felt his eyes burn as he blinked back a tear. Damn, but his heart felt as if it had been stomped on and shredded.

Jasmine lay silent and still before him, her creamy pink skin pale and wan.

Dark circles framed her eyes, surely from pain and stress.

He was to blame for that.

In addition, Jasmine was bruised and broken by his reckoning, and it was all his fault. As the pain in his heart grew, he moaned.

Doc Neely looked up from stitching Jasmine's wound, his expression grim. "Smith."

"How's she doing?" Just as he said the words, Quentin cursed. Only a fool would forget that she was clinging to her life only three feet away from him.

Thank God, Neely didn't mind dealing with fools. "She's gonna live, but she's going to be sore. The bullet embedded itself right under her collarbone. Amazing the bone didn't shatter. Was a bitch to dig out."

As he tied off another stitch, he leaned back. "I cleaned things out good and patched her up pretty. One day she'll barely notice her scar."

Quentin had enough scars for the both of them. He hated the fact that because of him, she was marred as well. "I'll tend to her."

It was so painfully obvious that everyone now thought of

them as a pair, he was embarrassed he hadn't seen it earlier. Shoot, if his mama were living, she'd hit him upside the head for any number of reasons. "I'll stay with her," he added.

Neely threw him an irritated glance. "In a little bit. Right now, I need you to go on out of here. I need the space. Come back in a few minutes."

Quentin didn't want to go anywhere. "You sure she's going to be all right?"

"Positive. 'Course, not right away. It's going to take some time before she is feeling right as rain."

But what if she never did? With a new sense of resolve, Quentin knew there was something he had to do that couldn't wait. "When will she wake up?"

"No telling."

"Can you give me an idea?"

"Hell, whenever she's ready." Placing a compress over his handiwork, Neely added, "She's been drifting in and out of consciousness for the last hour. Why?"

"We need to get married."

Neely groaned. "Lord, save me from lawmen with a conscience. This wasn't your fault. It was that damned Boss Carmichael."

Neely didn't know the half of it. Jasmine had been injured because he'd asked her to be in the thick of things. He'd been so sure all that mattered was his job, he'd forgotten what life was like without someone to love.

And he hadn't even proposed before, to let her know how much he loved and honored her. "I don't want to wait a moment longer to do the right thing."

"Listen, your idea may not be the right thing at the moment. Wait until she can walk down the aisle, Smith. Trust me on this."

Leaving all pride behind, Quentin said, "She might be carrying my child." Though panic laced his voice, Quentin knew he couldn't back down from his position. All he could think was that he wanted to be bound to her. Forever. "Something might happen to me. I want her married. I want her to have my name."

The irony of it wasn't lost on him. For what seemed like a lifetime, he'd run from his past, afraid to live up to his notoriety, to his good name.

He'd cursed his fame when Becky had died, and did his damnedest to become another person, but fate and his inner self never seemed to give a care. He'd once again become the person he hated.

Now, Jasmine and the two-bit town of Cedar Springs had given him a reason to be proud. He'd joined forces with other men. He'd done a good thing with the Carmichael Gang. He didn't regret killing them, didn't regret turning Harlow over to the law to pay for his mistakes.

But he'd never forget the sight of Jasmine taking a bullet right there in front of him. It was as if God was teasing him, daring him to forget about Becky and all the bad things that his life had done to her.

Now, instead of running away again, he had a chance to make up for everything. And that meant marrying the woman who'd done so much for him.

Neely just closed his medical bag. With a concerned expression, he leaned over Jasmine and brushed a strand of hair from her brow. "She's fussing again," he announced. "I'll be dosing her with laudanum shortly."

Quentin stood up. "Tell her to hold on. I'm going to go get the preacher."

"Smith."

"Just do it," he said, his tone evoking images of the battlefields in Georgia. Of his band of men in west Texas. For once, he wanted no regrets. "Please."

Neely cracked a smile. "I'll be a witness."

With determined steps, Quentin exited Neely's back room and made his way to the mercantile. "George," he called out the moment he entered. "George, where are you?"

The burly man rushed forward. "What's wrong? Is Jasmine worse?"

Quentin gripped his shoulder. "She's going to get better. She's going to be fine. Neely's sitting with her." Rushing on, he said, "But I need something from you."

"Name it."

"A ring and some lace."

His face broke into a grin. "You marrying her? Finally?"

Quentin wasn't so panicked that he didn't catch the irony of George asking him about finally proposing. "I am. Well, I am as soon as I can get the preacher there."

Without another question, George unlocked a small safe in the floor and presented Quentin with a tray of rings, most in silver, two in gold. A couple of them had fancy filigree work. Quentin's eye was drawn to the gold filigree. "I like that one. Do you think she's going to like it?"

"I do. It's expensive."

"She's worth ten of those rings. Every girl should wear a ring meant for her."

Chrissy showed up then and promptly burst into tears when she saw the rings. "You and Jasmine?"

George answered. "Yep. Finally."

"When?"

"Now."

"Oh!" she cried with a little hiccup, then ran to the corner of the counter and pulled out a handkerchief.

George looked on with a combination of pride and bemusement. "Don't mind her, she's all emotional these days."

"I'm going to need some lace," Quentin said to Chrissy. "I

thought maybe if there was something pretty . . ." He swallowed hard. "Maybe one day she'll make it into something, to remind her."

"I know a piece that would be perfect," Chrissy said, her eyes shining with joy. "You've risen in my standards, Captain."

He'd risen in his own standards, too. It felt good. "I'll take that."

Quickly, she brought over a pile of lace collars, each one more frilly than the next. "I like this one."

"Then I'll take that, too," he said, teasing.

"Here you go," George said.

Quentin fished around in his pocket, but George stayed his hand. "We'll settle up later. Go get the preacher. Chrissy and I will be right there."

Already worried about what Jasmine would say to him, Quentin attempted to still their plans. "That's not necessary—"

But this time it was. "See, we're her family. It wouldn't be right if we weren't there."

No, no it wouldn't. Quentin nodded as he rushed out toward his next stop, farther down the road—Preacher Fletcher's home.

It didn't take too much persuading to encourage the man to make an honest woman out of Jasmine. In fact, for a fee, the preacher promised to be there within fifteen minutes.

Which only left two more things to do. He knocked on Mrs. Armstrong's door.

"Yes?"

"I'm marrying Jasmine. I need some flowers," he said without preamble.

"All right," she said, directing him to her bountiful garden.

There wasn't much left. But Mrs. Armstrong, being the savvy gardener that she was, had rigged a glass shed where the light could shine in but the cold would stay away. There, in the small area, was an array of white roses.

"May I have four?"

Misty eyed, Mrs. Armstrong snipped off every last one and tied the whole dozen with a white satin bow from her gown. "I'd say this was a fine bouquet."

"I owe you, ma'am. Thank you."

She lightly kissed him on the cheek. "You owe me nothing. I heard about Harlow and Emmitt and the Carmichaels. It's you we need to thank, son."

Finally, he rushed back to the Dark Horse and made his hardest call of all—at the Bonds' apartments. He knocked lightly, and was taken aback when Madeleine opened the door to greet him. "Jasmine? Is she worse? Nash made me lie down after all the excitement."

"Doc just finished with her. She's still unconscious, but Neely said she's going to be fine." With a deep breath, he said, "I need a favor."

Her eyes narrowed and a faint smile formed. "Anything. What are you up to, Quentin?"

"I'm about to marry Jasmine. I . . . I was hoping for Nash's blessing."

A wistful expression filled her eyes. "Nash's blessing? I figured you stopped asking other men for permission about the time the war started."

"I did. I'm not used to explaining myself or asking anyone for much. But I need this. Jasmine will need it, too."

"Then you better come in."

With silent steps, she retreated, making Quentin wonder if he was doing the right thing.

"Quentin," Nash said, shaking his hand. "You all right?"

"I will be." He gestured toward the street. "The preacher is on his way to Neely's. I . . . I'm going to marry Jasmine. I'd like you to stand up with me. And, I'd like your blessing."

"Why?"

"A lot of reasons. You've been a good friend to Jasmine, gave her chances few others would have ever done. You've been a friend to me. I trust you, and there are far too few people in my life I can trust. I thought you knew that."

"I do."

Quietly, Quentin admitted, "It's going to take some time before I'll ever be able to look at Jasmine without thinking about how I put her life in jeopardy. I can only say that life shaped me into what I've become, and I'm imperfect, in every sense of the word."

Madeleine came up behind Nash and hugged him tightly. "We all are, Quentin."

"When I first arrived here, all I wanted was to find the Carmichaels' backer, arrest the gang, and take time to dream. I never imagined my dreams would have already started to come true from the first moment I spied Jasmine."

With a deep sigh, he added, "I've heard that there's people in this world who go through life knowing what they want and doing their best to get it. That wasn't me. I didn't. And I was too focused on the things I'd lost to figure out how wonderful the things I gained were. But I need Jasmine," he said, his voice cracking with emotion. "God help me, even if she doesn't feel the same way, I need her."

"You know she loves you. Her actions have proved it, time and again. As have yours."

Nash turned to his wife. "Madeleine, go get your coat, honey. We've got a wedding to attend."

"You'll stand up with me?"

"Yes. For you and Jasmine."

Madeleine Bond hugged Quentin. "Oh, I'm so glad you're here. Today will surely be one of the happiest days of our lives."

As Quentin rushed to Jasmine's side, he knew it would be for him. He just hoped Jasmine would feel the same way.

CHAPTER 24

Feeling somewhat like the Pied Piper, Quentin entered the back room of Neely's office, Madeleine and Nash only a few paces behind him.

"How is she?" he asked the doctor when he stepped out from behind the cloth partition surrounding her.

Neely laid a hand on his arm. "She's awake. In pain, but asking for you."

"Go on in," Nash said. "We'll be right here when you're ready."

Quentin was comforted by his words, overcome by doubts. What if she was angry with him? What if she never wanted to see him again, let alone get married? He'd been so intent on getting what he wanted, he'd neglected to remember that Jasmine most likely would want to have a strong say about her wedding day.

But no matter what he'd done, Quentin had never been the kind of man to back away from his insecurities. With a heavy heart, he pushed aside the curtain and stepped forward.

Jasmine blinked as he approached, then smiled. "Quentin."

"Thank God. Oh, it's so good to see you smile." Kneeling beside her bed, Quentin took her hand, then gave up all pretense of dignity. As gently as he could, he kissed her knuckles, then pressed his lips to her brow. "I was so worried about you."

"I've been worried about you, too."

"Don't." She looked pale and bruised. Peeking out from the

sheet was part of the patchwork of bandages Neely had placed on her shoulder. "Are you hurting real bad?"

"Some." She smiled. "A lot. Now I'll know how you felt, when you received all your injuries."

He'd never have wanted her to know the feel of a bullet. "This is all my fault. I should never have put you in harm's way."

"Shh," she whispered, squeezing his fingers. "This wasn't your doing. It was Boss Carmichael's."

"I should never have asked you to be there. I should never have involved you."

"I'm glad you did. I wanted to be involved. Quentin, all my life I've been wanting to be important, to do something worthwhile. This was it."

He shook his head before brushing her knuckles with his lips again. "You didn't need to get shot to be important. You're very important to me already. I love you, Jasmine."

Jasmine couldn't help but reflect how her hardest moment was also, suddenly, her most wonderful. Quentin was everything she ever dreamed of. And he loved her! She couldn't imagine a more special moment in her whole life.

"I'm glad. I love you, too . . . but you already knew that," she replied, enjoying being able to tease him a little.

The grumble of a dozen voices, accompanied by the privacy curtain being shaken, interrupted their moment. "What's going on?"

Quentin's expression went blank as he stood up. "Well. There's a whole slew of people outside, all excited about some upcoming nuptials."

Nuptials? In the doctor's office? "Whose?"

A faint stain of rose tinted Quentin's cheeks. "Ours." Taking her hand again, he said, "I went a little crazy while Neely was fixing you up. I wanted us married as soon as possible." He paused, "That is, if you'll have me."

She was trying to follow his train of thought. "You planned our wedding?"

Something flickered in the back of her eyes. Doubt? Regret? Hope? "I did," he said slowly. "Fletcher's on his way."

With a laugh, Jasmine guessed she now knew what a hot spring must feel like. A dozen emotions zinged through her, making her feel giddy and excited, jumpy and happy, all at the same time. "You want to get married now? Here? While I'm lying here in Doc Neely's back room?"

Quentin visibly winced. "Pretty much. I . . . guess it's not what you want."

Jasmine would never say that. Though the pain in her shoulder was fierce, she tried to sit up. "No. I mean . . . Oh, Quentin."

Two strong hands, so capable, so gentle, supported her shoulders as he propped a pillow behind her. Sitting on the edge of her bed, he whispered, "I love you so much. I didn't want to wait another moment . . ." His voice drifted off.

She leaned forward, needing to be in his arms no matter how her body felt. "Quentin—"

"I bought you a ring," He blurted out, just as he held her close, his body cradling her weight.

She'd been wrong earlier. This was the most amazing moment of her life. As she opened her mouth to reply, he spoke again.

"If you want, we can wait. I know this—getting married like this—isn't what a woman envisions. We can wait until you're ready. Until you're sure."

"Quentin, yes."

"Yes?"

She laughed, then moaned as the movement sent a burning pain through her. "I'm ready. If you want to have me in sickness right away, then I want to be yours," Jasmine whispered.

"You're sure?"

"Quentin Smith, I'd be honored to marry you right here, right now."

Tears stung his eyes. He was just about to say he was glad when the curtains moved again, followed by what seemed to be a push and a shove.

"Jasmine, have you said yes yet?" George called out, his voice more than a little irritated. "It's getting crowded out here, and Fletcher's got stuff to do."

Quentin rolled his eyes. "You all just hold on a minute."

Laughter greeted his request.

"Hold on?" George called out loudly. "Quentin Smith, you've got to be kidding."

"I said yes!" Jasmine called out, grinning at her fiancé of a minute.

After Quentin wrapped another sheet securely over her shoulders, she called out, "Come on in, everyone."

With much commotion, the door opened and half the town paraded in, led by the preacher and organized into respectful obedience by Chrissy.

"Oh, Quentin," Jasmine said, as person after person squeezed into the room. Men took off their hats, women held white handkerchiefs.

Somebody handed him a bouquet of white roses, which he, in turn, handed to her.

After a barrage of greetings, Neely glared at them all. Finally, every last one stood in respectful silence.

Madeleine and Nash had somehow made their way to the opposite side of her bed.

"You sure about this, Jasmine?" Nash asked.

"Very sure," Jasmine replied.

He shook his head. "This is absolutely—"

"The most wonderful wedding I've ever attended," said Mrs. Armstrong. "Get on with it, Fletcher. It's late and it's getting hot in here."

And so, Jasmine held Quentin's hand and said her vows. Right there in front of all of her friends and half the town.

It didn't matter that her dress was cut up and bloodstained.

That her husband's clothes were bloody and torn up too.

All that mattered was that she was surrounded by people she loved, and was pledging herself to the one man who had made her feel as if she was worth everything.

"Do you take this woman to be your lawfully wedded wife?" Pastor Fletcher asked. "To love, honor, and cherish, from this day forward, until death do you part?"

"I do," Quentin replied.

As Fletcher repeated the vows to Jasmine, she felt God's love, and a true sense of happiness engulf her. "I do, too," she said.

And then they were kissing. Gently. Reverently.

All the folks in the room clapped.

Wished her congratulations.

And then were shooed out.

"You feel married, Jasmine?" Neely asked.

"I do," she said, smiling at Quentin.

"Good. Drink this."

She sipped her laudanum.

"You, bridegroom, go get cleaned up. I don't trust you within ten feet of her. The girl needs rest."

Kissing her brow, feeling curiously lightheaded, Quentin stood up. "I'll come back in an hour."

Neely rolled his eyes. "Make it two. Three. Mrs. Smith needs her rest," he said again. "You can't touch her until I say so."

Jasmine winked.

"I'll be back in an hour to watch Mrs. Smith sleep," Quentin replied. After all, he knew exactly what he needed: his wife.

CHAPTER 25

A day passed. After spending a restless night in a rocking chair next to Jasmine's bed, Quentin convinced Neely to let him take her to his room in the Dark Horse. It wasn't home, but the bed was comfortable, and Quentin figured that Jasmine would rather have privacy and quiet than the constant noise behind Neely's office.

He was also sure that Jasmine would rather have Madeleine care for her needs, instead of Mrs. Midge.

As Neely predicted, after another day, Jasmine was sore, but able to walk around unassisted. Quentin poured her a bath and helped her bathe, taking special care to wash her hair.

"You don't have to do this," she murmured as he massaged her head and neck. "But I'm so glad you are."

"Me, too." Deliberately, he brushed suds from the space behind her ear and kissed it. Jasmine's back arched, making him ache for her.

As if reading his mind, she murmured, "I can't wait until we can make love again."

"I'm not touching you until Neely says it's all right."

A pretty blush stained her neck. "Ask him soon."

"I will not. He'd tan my hide for asking."

She chuckled, "I'd like to see him try."

"We're waiting."

She pouted. "I don't want to."

"I can and we will. Listen to your husband." Gently, he

moved her, so he could pour a cup of clean water through the silky strands of her hair. "I aim to take care of you."

"I'm going to take care of you, too," she promised. She didn't realize how much he loved hearing those words.

Two more days passed. Jasmine felt as if she was living in a dream world, so many of her wishes had come true. Quentin hardly left her side, and he looked extremely relieved when Doc Neely declared her almost as good as new.

Of course, that wasn't anywhere near the look he gave her when she asked Doc Neely when they could resume their relations.

"We are married, you know," she said importantly.

"I'm well aware of that." With an eye on her wound, Neely said, "One more week. Good Lord, Smith. Can't you control yourself?"

Quentin had the grace to look embarrassed, although Jasmine knew she was the one who could hardly wait.

"One more week will be just fine," Quentin replied to the doctor. "Right, Jasmine?"

She did her best to look patient.

George could hardly believe he was sitting with Nash Bond and discussin' marriage stories.

"I couldn't help it. We were in the midst of an emergency last week, Nash."

Nash put down the cigar he was puffing. "What emergency? Jasmine was injured almost two weeks ago."

"Yeah, well, it was last week when Chrissy and me couldn't stop getting to know each other real well, if you know what I mean."

Nash knew exactly what he meant. "No matter what you

might think, I don't believe you're the first couple to rush the date."

George wasn't quite sure if that was a fact. From the moment Chrissy had told him "yes" and offered her sweet lips to his, he'd been a lost cause. Like a man possessed by a spirit, he hadn't been able to keep his hands off of her. Every waking moment was a new opportunity to explore.

"Did you do that with Madeleine? Rush the date?" he asked, hoping against hope that he wasn't the only man in Cedar Springs to lose control where a future bride was concerned.

Nash looked thoroughly offended. "I did not. I held myself away from her for seven long months, until we spoke our vows in front of half the town . . . and most importantly, her parents."

George knew there was a reason he held the saloon owner in such high esteem. "Figures."

His expression softening, Nash said, "It was different with me and Madeleine. She was a wealthy, pampered little thing. Her parents expected more than a saloon owner for her, and rightly so. No way was I going to prove them right and do anything that wasn't strictly proper."

"I suppose."

"So, what did Fletcher say when you woke him?"

George winced as he recalled the scene. "A whole lot about promises and daylight. Of course, I had to explain to him that we had a potential fallen woman on our hands."

Nash's cigar just about fell out of his mouth. "Lord have mercy."

George couldn't help but smile. "It did the trick. Fletcher put his pants on quicker than a jackrabbit in fox season. We grabbed Butch—he was in town with the stage—and said our vows in short order."

"And Chrissy didn't mind?"

George recalled the way she'd smiled sweetly, said her vows

with a smile, and then raced him up to the bedroom. "No, sir, I don't believe she did."

Nash laughed. "Have a cigar."

"Don't mind if I do," George replied, lighting it with relish.

Quentin stood to one side as Clemmons handcuffed Harlow and got ready to escort him to Colorado Springs. The court system in the territory was sketchy at best, but after days of waiting, Clemmons had received the word to deliver their prisoner.

Quentin had just agreed to become his deputy, and was preparing to take care of things when Anna Harlow ran in.

"Why did you do it?" Anna Harlow cried, as Clemmons was walking her husband out the door.

Clemmons scowled. "Sure you want to do this here, Anna?"

"I couldn't let him leave and not know." Turning to her husband, she looked at him wild-eyed. "Why, Alan?"

Quentin noticed that the man's face softened and his voice gentled when he answered, although he didn't look the least bit regretful. "Because I had no choice."

Clemmons, never shy about sharing his views, grunted.

Anna looked flabbergasted. "No choice? Alan, you *ruined* our lives. You helped *murder* innocent people."

"I did no such thing. I'm no murderer."

"But the Carmichaels—"

"Paid me well to help them. We both hated the railroads. Both of us had reasons to make the Kansas Pacific pay."

"But—"

"Anna. I had no choice. Caroline wanted dresses. You—a fancy dresser."

"Don't you dare make Caroline a part of this."

"She is. I am. You are. I did what I did for our future. You can't look beyond that."

"You just chose not to. We could have done without. You're not being fair."

Al Harlow shook his head. "It wasn't fair at all. I never planned on losing every bit of money I had. With no railroad, the town's going to die. I had to do what I could or I would have lost you."

"I never would have left you."

"You would have made me regret it. Dammit woman, didn't you know how hard I was trying? It's a fair share harder for a man to hold on to his things than to get them in the first place."

His shoulders slumped as the last bit of fight went out of him. "Let's go, Clemmons. I've nothing more to say."

Clemmons nodded, for once silent. The normally loquacious man merely shook his head in sympathy for Anna and guided his charge out the door.

She turned to Quentin when they were alone. "What's going to happen to him?"

"They'll try him in Colorado Springs."

Her face pinched, she asked, "Do you think he'll have much of a chance?"

Between Harlow and the Carmichaels, almost a dozen people had been killed, and thousands of dollars stolen. Harlow wasn't likely to last a month before being tried, sentenced, and hanged. "Do you really want me to answer that?"

"No. No, I don't." Her mouth quivered, making her age a good ten years before his eyes. "I hope I'm not responsible—"

"You're not," he interrupted quickly. "Don't carry the guilt for something you had no control over. Each man makes his own way in the world. It's his right, and his responsibility."

"You sound like you know that from experience."

"For years I carried around another person's guilt. It never fit well on my shoulders, because I never truly deserved it. I blamed myself for things I couldn't undo."

"Are you talking about your first wife's death?"

Startled, he asked, "You know about that?"

"Of course." With a small smile, Anna said, "Even though Caroline didn't care about your past, I did."

"What are you going to do? Do you have family?"

"My sister and an aunt. They live in San Francisco." She sniffed. "Society, from her letters. I do believe they're about to be treated to some of the finest women Cedar Springs has to offer."

"You will be sorely missed."

"I loved my husband," she whispered softly. "I wanted to be married to him forever. But . . . I think if I didn't leave him, I would carry the guilt of a dozen men if I overlooked his part in the train robberies. Is . . . that bad?"

He didn't know. Very gently, Quentin wrapped an arm around the grieving woman and patted her on her shoulder as she cried out her sorrows. "Take care of yourself. And of Caroline."

"I don't think she was ever the person for you."

"No. Jasmine was. But I did enjoy getting to know her. She's a fine young lady. She's someone to be proud of."

Anna set a palm on his arm. "You are, too, Captain. You are, too."

CHAPTER 26

Another week had passed. Seven long days. Doctor Neely had finally pronounced Jasmine fit. Now all she had to do was convince Quentin that she was fit, as well.

Ever since the shooting, he'd taken care of her as if she was a precious china doll. Though his mouth might have tightened when he helped her change or when he told her good night, he refused even to share the same bed with her until the doctor gave him permission.

Instead, he'd set her up proper next to the Bonds' suite of rooms, saying that it would be better for them both to stay apart as much as possible.

Jasmine hadn't liked that one bit.

Aware that he was down at the jailhouse chatting with Clemmons and due back any time, Jasmine decided to surprise him by being in his room once again.

With eager footsteps, she padded down the hall.

"Doc say it was all right, Jasmine?" Madeleine asked with a wink.

Jasmine was sure she was blushing to the tips of her toes. "Yes. I . . . uh . . ."

Madeleine laughed as she patted her stomach. "I know exactly how I got in this condition, Jasmine. When I see Quentin, I'll tell him to hurry on to see you."

"Thanks," Jasmine said, though she knew Quentin would likely not need any inducement to see her. He spent time with her often, helping her get used to the idea that she no longer would be serving drinks at the Dark Horse. Instead, they'd be building their own home in the near future.

Alone again, Jasmine unlocked Quentin's room. Immediately, she was bombarded with his scent. The air, the sheets, the clothes hanging on the back of an old ladder chair, all smelled of Quentin.

Lime, bay rum, tobacco, horse.

Heaven.

So different from most men she knew; and she'd served whiskey to a fair number of them. She'd always thought Quentin's scent was not only filled with things . . . but also with a liberal mixture of independence and remorse. The aroma had attracted her to him from the very first, perhaps because she knew those things so well.

The familiar sounds of the saloon drifted upward, along with the faint echo of the chimes from the stage clock. Quentin would be back soon. To keep her hands busy, she remade his bed, tsking at the way all the covers were twisted and in disarray. Carefully, she folded back one side, smiling at its unmistakable invitation.

She was just considering unpinning her hair when his door opened.

"Jasmine? Are you all right? I saw Madeleine, and she said to come see you, but you weren't in your room . . ." His voice trailed off as he eyed the bed.

"I'm sleeping here tonight," she said by way of explanation.

"You saw Doc Neely?"

"I did."

"And he said?"

"For you to make love to me as often as possible."

Warmth heated his gaze as he gently pulled her to him. "I've never heard of such a prescription."

Jasmine laughed.

His gaze flickered to her mouth as his laughter faded.

Once again, he looked as if he was searching for control. His restraint made her melt a little bit, and feel even bolder. She longed for his touch, ached for his kisses. Was eager to be wrapped in his arms.

Opening her own arms, she crossed the room to him. "Aren't you going to kiss me hello?"

He kissed her gently, pressing his lips against hers with a reverence that made her insides pool. "Hello."

Action needed to be taken. While she appreciated his patience, she was oh-so-tired of waiting. "Quentin," she murmured, "take off that silly holster."

Ever obedient, he unbuckled the worn leather, carefully placed it on the table. "Better?"

"Almost." Carefully, she loosened the top three buttons of her calico. "I'm not made of porcelain, Quentin. I'm the same woman I was two weeks ago."

He swallowed. Looked as if he was about to argue, but said nothing, only stared at the expanse of skin now open to his gaze.

Feeling bolder, she unfastened another button, then shrugged the dress off her shoulders, taking care to step out of it as it pooled on the floor. Quentin untucked his shirt and blew out a ragged breath.

Quentin's bedroom had a crack in the window. The cool air filtered through the gap and chilled her skin. All at once, it felt as every nerve ending stood on end. She felt brave and very alive.

So ready to be in his arms again.

Remembering how it had felt when he'd caressed her, when he'd teased her with his tongue, she pulled the first bow of her chemise loose.

"Have mercy, Jasmine."

She met his gaze. "Am I doing this right?" she teased, "because you know that I don't have much experience—"

"You're doing everything right," he murmured, walking to her in a rush. In almost no time, he had her stripped bare, and was kissing her senseless.

The cool breeze, combined with the soft abrasion of his worn clothes, set her on fire. His hands, before so gentle, were now more demanding as they caressed her body, reacquainting themselves with her form. Jasmine breathed deeply as she reveled in his touch. Oh, she was so glad she had him. Even though she had quite a scar, Boss's bullet could have done much more damage.

Oh, she was glad that the fates had transpired to bring Quentin to Cedar Springs. "Make me your wife, Quentin."

He crushed her to him, kissing her deeply, kissing her with enough passion to set the town on fire.

Quickly, he shucked off his boots. Denims and shirt followed. Then, before she knew what he was about, he picked her up in his arms and carried her to their waiting bed.

"Quentin. My husband," she murmured, loving the sound of his name, not able to think of anything more profound to say.

"My wife," he replied, answering in need, kissing her again, plundering her with his lips as his fingers ran along her hips, her breasts, to the very core of her.

She gasped as he knelt over her and brought one nipple in his mouth.

She, in turn, reached for him.

Finally, when they were both panting with need, Quentin posed himself over her. "I can't wait," he said apologetically.

"Don't," she gasped. Nothing else needed to be said.

And then they were joined. Preciously. Perfectly. The way

they were meant to be together. With a cry, Jasmine found her release.

His own followed soon after. "I love you, Jasmine," he murmured. "You're mine."

"That's all I ever wanted," she admitted. "It's all I ever wanted to be. Yours."

"On account of the sorry state of our town, I'm delivering this special to you," Sheriff Clemmons said the following day. "It's your payment from the railroad."

"Thank you," Quentin said after a split second's hesitation. As the events of Boss Carmichael's capture came back to him, all he could recall with clarity was a space of three long minutes, when he had been afraid that everything had gone terribly wrong, and he was going to lose another love in his life.

He'd known that he wasn't strong enough to recover from such a blow. But as he held the paper, and caught Clemmons's understanding eye, Quentin knew that he'd just passed another milestone. He was among the living again.

"So, was it worth it?"

Quentin looked at the scrap of paper that represented his future. "More than I ever imagined."

Not only did he hold in his hand more money than he'd ever had at one time in his life, but he now had the most incredible woman to go home to.

He now had Jasmine. And, Quentin realized, a much easier, much more rewarding job than he'd ever had in his life. He now had a future.

Yes, it was all definitely worth it.

Clemmons rocked back on his heels. "There's some fine parcels of land available on the outskirts of town. Just the thing for a young couple starting out. Or, maybe you want to look at the old Harlow place. Might be nice for you to occupy a home in the city limits."

"Both sound good. I'll talk to Jasmine and see what she wants."

"She's going to want whatever you do. You married her!"

Quentin caught the teasing in the man's voice. "Is that what Mrs. Clemmons does? Do whatever you tell her to do?"

Clemmons had the grace to look shamefaced. "I have four daughters at home. Who do you think does the jumping?"

Quentin laughed. "I might be doing my fair share of jumping, too." Quentin wanted Jasmine to realize that he wanted—and needed—her to be an equal partner. He needed her desperately. It didn't matter to him who her parents were, what she'd done for a living. All that mattered was that she'd honored him by agreeing to marry him. "I lost a wife once. I want this one to know that she means the world to me."

"Marriage is supposed to be all about commitment, but sometimes people forget, now, don't they?" Clemmons said, nodding toward the jail.

Word was that Harlow was wasting away in Colorado Springs. He couldn't understand how his wife could have left him when he'd compromised everything he was to make her happy.

"Anna and Caroline hightailed it out of here quicker than a prairie dog with the trots," the sheriff added. "On one hand, I can't say I blame them . . . but something about it still don't set right with me."

"I know what you mean." As Quentin looked around the small office, now crammed with two desks, two chairs, and a large box of cigars, he felt completely at peace. "By the way, have I thanked you yet for the job?"

"Once or twice."

"I'll do my best for you."

Clemmons's mustache twitched. "You're talking awfully pretty for such a famous lawman."

"I only talk like this to people I work for."

Clemmons grinned. "We make a pretty good team, don't we?"

"We do."

Thinking back to the time they'd broken up the bar fight, Quentin laughed. "Don't let this get around, but I enjoyed myself the night we broke up the fight at the Red Hen."

"I did, too. Brought back memories of chow lines back at the war."

"I thought for a time I was just going to do this job and give it up, but I realized it wasn't going to be possible."

"Once a lawman, always a lawman," Clemmons said sagely. Tipping his hat, he pivoted on his heel. "I better get on home. Missus Clemmons has a fit if I'm not at the table on time."

"Goodnight," Quentin said, watching the sheriff trot outside and hurry down the street.

He couldn't blame the man; it was a good feeling to be wanted.

Snow came, and just kept coming. The people of Cedar Springs had taken to watching the clouds hover over the Rockies and started taking bets about when it was going to stop.

Although Jasmine enjoyed the picture-perfect scenery, she would have preferred to stay home.

"Are you sure we need to ride out in this weather?"

"Positive," Quentin said.

With a sigh, Jasmine bundled up more closely in the blankets. "Where are you taking me?"

"Surprise."

"Give me a hint."

"There's snow everywhere."

"Ha, ha. There's not a patch of brown or green for miles."

"Yes, but the sled sure glides well, doesn't it?"

It did at that. Feeling as if she was in a picture postcard, Jasmine snuggled next to Quentin as he drove their sleigh across the snowy banks of Cedar Springs.

She wasn't cold, though. She was warm in her heart, knowing she had everything she'd ever wanted. Especially since she was fairly certain that all of their catching up had produced a baby of their own.

More snow fell, tingling her cheeks and making her laugh.

Quentin looked free of spirit, as well. As they sped across the wide-open expanse of countryside, he hugged her tight with one arm and pressed sweet kisses on her cheek.

Finally they stopped.

"Where are we?"

"Home," he said, his face wearing an expression of pure contentment.

All Jasmine could see was miles and miles of winter wonderland. "Quentin Smith, it looks like four feet of snow! What do you have planned?"

"To build you a home here. I know it's a little bit out of town, but it's not so far."

She heard the hesitancy in his voice. "I can't wait."

"Until then, Chrissy's old place is fine, right?"

"Yep. I'm glad we convinced the town council to let Chrissy still teach school, even though she's married."

"You just wanted her cabin."

"I did. It's cozy, Quentin."

He rolled his eyes. "It is that. This will be better. This, Jasmine, is what I had in mind when I accepted my new job."

"Then this is what we should have," Jasmine said, though in truth, she really didn't care where they lived. As long as Quentin came home to her every night, she would be content.

He kissed her then, and one kiss led to many. Finally, chilled and relaxed, Quentin turned the sleigh back around. "Happy?"

"Of course."

As they slid along the snow, blinking in the bright sun, Jasmine attempted to explain herself. "For most of my life, nothing seemed quite right. I'd try and I'd pray. I'd hope and I'd smile. But I was never happy. Then, suddenly, like a northern breeze and the first, unexpected snow, you came to town. And when you did, everything good in the world showed itself to me."

Turning to face him, she said, "Suddenly, there was more to this world than I realized. Suddenly, I had hope and giddiness and kisses. Suddenly, I had a future."

And as they sped into town, Jasmine pressed a kiss along the jaw of the west's most famous former lawman. "Suddenly, Quentin Smith, I had you."

EPILOGUE

The day was colder than a day had any right to be. Which was pretty damned perfect, considering Jasmine Smith was in labor and her husband was the notorious Captain Smith, former Texas Ranger.

Just the thing for a struggling doctor to have to deal with on his third day in town, Christian Cook reflected as he knocked on the door of the pretty clapboard house.

Chrissy Lange opened it up. "About time you got out here. George appeared a full five minutes ago."

Christian held up his medical bag. "It took me a moment to get my things together."

"Well, don't take much longer. Jasmine needs you."

Concerned, Christian asked, "Is she in much pain?"

"She's doing her best to keep her husband calm. But that's pretty hard to do," Chrissy confided. "From what I can tell, things aren't going so well."

Christian was confused. He'd examined Jasmine himself just two days ago, and she assured him that everything in her pregnancy had been easy. "But I thought—"

"Cook? Is that you? Get the hell in here."

"Is that Captain Smith?" he asked, hoping that the gruff voice he heard belonged to someone else.

Chrissy winked. "Did I tell you that in addition to being a former ranger, Quentin is also a former cavalry officer? He has a way of bossing people around like nobody else."

She led the way into the bedroom, where Jasmine was visibly upset and Captain Smith looked ready to strangle the first innocent soul who happened along.

"See?" Chrissy whispered. "You couldn't get here soon enough."

"Thank God you're here," Jasmine said, panting. "I don't know what's wrong." Her face was flushed, and her nightgown was soaked with sweat.

Quentin Smith turned steel-colored eyes in his direction. "Do something, dammit."

Christian didn't dare comment. He was too busy steeling himself to tell the lawman to leave Jasmine's side and leave the business of delivering babies to a professional.

Him.

Smith grabbed his arm. "Cook! Do something."

"All right." Turning to Quentin, Christian matched his tone. "Be quiet."

Quentin narrowed his eyes.

Jasmine looked at him with hope.

With an understanding smile, Christian squeezed Jasmine's hand, then turned to her husband. As plainly as possible, he said, "Smith, you have two choices. You can either sit in here, behave, and do exactly what I tell you to, or you can go sit outside and make friends with your horse."

Quentin grunted. "Did you say 'horse'?"

Chrissy ran over to Jasmine. "You all right, honey? Now that Doctor Cook is here, I'm sure you'll be just fine."

"But the baby?" As another contraction seized Jasmine, she struggled against it.

Quentin glared at Christian. Hoping to diffuse the situation, Christian took Jasmine's hand and spoke softly. "Mrs. Smith, how are you?"

Quentin scowled. "How is she? Cook, she's just—"

Christian glared. Quentin didn't say another word.

Sitting by her side, he took her pulse and patted her hand. "We need you sitting up. It will help the delivery."

"Sit up? Are you sure?"

"Positive. I'm not used to giving warnings, sir."

Jasmine sat up with his help. Breathed raggedly as another pain tore through her. "Dr. Cook!" she exclaimed, panting furiously.

"Breathe through it," he said, his voice as calm and smooth as molasses. "Slow your breathing. I promise. The baby wants to see the world."

Within minutes, he had Jasmine comfortable in a fresh nightgown and visibly calmer.

"Smith, come here," he ordered.

Quentin came.

"Sit and rub your wife's back. Let her have little sips of water, nothing more."

To Chrissy, he said, "Sheets, clean towels, and some whiskey."

Chrissy's eyes widened. "For you?"

"For Smith," Christian said, gazing at him with pity. "You're going to need it."

A look of pure respect entered Quentin's eyes. "You sound like a man used to giving orders."

Christian laughed. "Captain Smith, you aren't the only man here who is a former Texas Ranger."

Jasmine groaned. "I just don't know if I can deliver a baby under these conditions. Two rangers!"

"Don't worry, honey," Quentin said, rubbing her back in smooth circles. "If there's one thing you can count on, it's a Texan. For my money, there's no better man to have around."

Christian laughed. "Let's deliver this baby now, shall we?"

An hour went by. Almost two. And then, just as the sun rose

over the Colorado Rockies, Jasmine Smith delivered a daughter. Quentin never left her side.

Christian wandered out after a hearty breakfast made by Chrissy and inhaled deeply. Things were mighty fine in Cedar Springs.

Just then the wind changed directions, scaring a sparrow into taking flight. George whistled low. "Wind's picking up. Last time that happened, Quentin Smith came to town. Wonder who'll be arriving next?"

As the cries of Rebecca Judith Smith filled the air, Christian grinned. Obviously, grand entrances ran in the family.

ABOUT THE AUTHOR

Shelley Galloway earned her bachelors degree from the University of Colorado and her masters of educational administration from the University of Phoenix. She used those degrees to teach fifth and sixth grade in several states. It was only when her husband was transferred to Ohio that she decided to finally give her hobby of writing a serious try.

Since then, she's sold twelve romances to several publishers.

Shelley loves to write positive stories about good people . . . and loves it when other people like them, too.

When not writing, she can be found either at the pool watching her daughter swim, or at a gymnasium, trying not to wince during her son's wrestling matches. She also loves to read and travel.

Shelley loves to hear from readers, and can be reached at www.shelleygalloway.com or at 10663 Loveland-Madeira Rd. #132. Loveland, OH 45140.